Firecloud ruled the land.

In a flash the stallion was down off the hill and onto the valley floor, pounding through the rain toward the column of Kainah warriors. He surged ahead, snorting now and flattening his ears.

The lead Kainah rider reined in his horse at the sight of the big stallion bearing down on him. He shouted to his followers who tried to turn their horses. It was too late....

FIRECLOUD

E. P. Murray

CHARTER BOOKS, NEW YORK

FIRECLOUD

A Charter Book / published by arrangement with
the author

PRINTING HISTORY
Charter Original / February 1985

All rights reserved.
Copyright © 1985 by Earl Murray
This book may not be reproduced in whole
or in part, by mimeograph or any other means,
without permission. For information address:
The Berkley Publishing Group, 200 Madison Avenue,
New York, New York 10016.

ISBN: 0-441-23820-3

Charter Books are published by The Berkley Publishing Group,
200 Madison Avenue, New York, New York 10016.
PRINTED IN THE UNITED STATES OF AMERICA

Prologue

HE RAN WITH THE STORM at his back, the long hair of his mane and tail flowing in white streams as the wind whipped it. The thunder rolled across the sky, and streaks of jagged lightning stabbed the hillsides. The long column of horses stretched from the rocks and yellow pine down over the valley floor, through the stream, and up into the hills on the other side, the stallion leading his herd, their blood hot from the run.

The clouds thickened in the late afternoon sky, and the flashes of lightning continued, followed by the heavy rumble that meant rain. The shower began as intermittent drops, but quickly turned to a downpour. The stallion, tossing his head and kicking his hooves, moved his herd up into a hollow among the trees and turned to look down into the valley below.

From below came a column of riders, young warriors from the Black Horse band of the Kainah Blackfeet. They had come in pursuit of the most coveted stallion in the lands that stretched from the high mountains to the buffalo-darkened plains. They had come to capture the stallion that was known to possess the speed and strength of ten of his kind. He was the Thunder Horse, the leader of all the wild herds.

He was Firecloud.

No other stallion could match his majesty as he stood

proudly on the crest of a hill, the fire-red of his coat made more brilliant by the pure white of his mane and tail and the white markings on his back.

The horse tenders in the villages knew him, for he would occasionally appear like a phantom to steal mares from their herds. Many stallions had challenged his supremacy, but none had ever matched him. Firecloud ruled the land.

Now this legend among wild horses was again the quarry as the Blackfeet warriors pursued him. The proud stallion saw this chase only as another opportunity to display his power.

Down on the valley floor, the young Kainah warriors forded the stream, whooping and hollering. They came up onto the stretch of bottomland that would take them into the hills above, where the wild stallion had hidden his mares. The rain beat steadily against the rocks and trees; the thunder echoed across the sky. With a snort and a shake of his head, the stallion lunged down the hill toward the Kainah warriors, leaving his mares safely hidden in a thick stand of trees. As always, the big stallion would attack when his adversaries least expected it; he would now become the hunter instead of the quarry.

In a flash the stallion was down off the hill and onto the valley floor, pounding through the rain toward the column of Kainah warriors. He surged ahead, snorting now and flattening his ears.

The lead Kainah rider reined in his horse at the sight of the big stallion bearing down on him. He shouted to his followers who tried to turn their horses. It was too late, for Firecloud was already among them, having sent the lead rider sprawling in the mud.

The big stallion charged each rider, rearing and bumping until the rider had fallen or run away. Though they had heard many stories of the stallion's fierce attacks, the Kainah horsemen were unable to withstand the fury that had charged out of the thunderstorm at them. Confusion and fear kept them from organizing and casting their rawhide loops at the big red stallion. His power was so great and the attack so sudden that there was no chance for them to do anything but dis-

FIRECLOUD

band and run their horses away from him in all directions, stopping when they could to pick up their fallen comrades, some injured, some only stunned. There was no power to match the fierce pride of this wild stallion.

EVEN AS A COLT, Firecloud had displayed the qualities that would one day make him a powerful leader. From his first year of life he was strong and swift enough to keep up with the rest of the herd, having energy left at the end of the runs to kick and frolic. Everything aroused his curiosity. He would leave his mother's side to explore and search out adventure. Each new river crossing and mountainside, every ravine and hidden canyon presented a fresh challenge to the rugged colt.

As he grew older and became the leader of his own herd, his power and speed increased, and he learned to fight with his hooves, his teeth, and his powerful shoulders. Before many years had passed, Firecloud had taken control of several herds, and he stood now as their unchallenged leader.

The legend of Firecloud had spread among the Indian peoples of the region, all of whom had lost mares to him. He came quickly, and herd stallions could not stop him. His size and speed had no match, and after the summer of his third year, no man could catch this stallion and tame him.

He had once been driven into a trap by a herd of Kainah horse medicine men. Had he stayed at the edge of the herd with the older and more experienced horses, he might have found the chance to escape. But he had let himself become trapped in the middle of the milling herd, with no way to spring loose.

Then, in the Kainah village, he had felt the rawhide noose tighten around his neck, strangling the air from his lungs. His legs had felt the hobbles that robbed them of movement. He had spent days in the agony of captivity, longing to run free again. One morning a careless young horse tender had given the rope just enough slack so that Firecloud's powerful legs could pull the rawhide tight and snap it. He had thundered through the camp with the young horse tender calling out after him. Now he knew that the two-legged creatures wanted to take his freedom from him and that he must stay away from them.

As the red stallion grew older, he realized these two-legged animals did not possess nearly as much strength as he did, and he knew there was no cause for fear as long as he had open space in which to maneuver. Even the best of their horses was not a close match for his speed and power, and most of their stallions feared Firecloud and grew skittish whenever he was close by.

AS SOON AS IT HAD BEGUN, the rain stopped. The dark clouds moved apart to allow the rays of the late afternoon sun to push through. Behind the storm was stillness, and the light shone gold against the jagged hills. The stallion led his herd on a run through the rocks and scrag timber that covered the slopes above the valley. Tossing his head, the proud leader took his herd ever onward over the hills and finally to the valley floor, where the horses could drink at the stream before moving into the hills on the other side of the valley.

Evening had come, and Firecloud again stood on a hill with his herd overlooking another valley, not far from the place where they had left the defeated Kainah warriors. Below was the Kainah Blackfoot village, from which the young warriors had ridden in search of the stallion known as the Thunder Horse. The camp was quiet, with the women doing evening chores and the older men sitting around fires telling stories of their youth. On the flat near the village a large herd of horses grazed, watched only by young horse tenders, too young to have gone on the wild horse hunt with the warriors. There were a great many mares in the herd, and Firecloud had come to take them for his own.

Again the big stallion hid his mares and made his way to a ridge just above the village. He snorted and raised his nose to the sky. The evening breeze carried the pungent odor of burning sage. The stallion knew the smell and was not alarmed by

FIRECLOUD

it. It was smoke from the leaves and branches of the long-leaved silver sage that grew on the bottoms and all along the valley floor. The Indians burned this sage during ceremonies, and Firecloud almost always saw an old Kainah warrior seated next to the fire when the odor came out into the hills. He had seen the old warrior many times and knew him to be trustworthy, for he always paid homage to Firecloud in chants and ritual dances. Firecloud knew that these two-legged beings considered him a magical horse, and he also knew that the old warrior somehow gained power whenever they met. These meetings gave the old warrior much pleasure, and Firecloud could sense the Indian's reverence for him.

Firecloud moved farther along the ridge and looked down into a small clearing where three Kainah men were seated around the fire of sage. They leaped to their feet in amazement, at the sight of the Thunder Horse. One of the men was the old Kainah warrior. With him were two younger warriors whose eyes were wide with amazement. The old warrior spoke and pointed to Firecloud, addressing the two younger warriors, both of whom were still standing rigid in awe and disbelief.

A row of clouds had formed behind the stallion in the sky just above the horizon. The sun had fallen to just under these clouds, bathing them in crimson. The deep red light washed over the stallion's coat as he stood above the three warriors. The Spirit Horse had come to them, and they were breathless at the sight of him.

The old warrior began to chant:

> He is the one who rules the mountains.
> He is the Red One, like sun on clouds.
> Ah, hau, he has more power than any other of his kind.
> He has come from the Thunder Lodge.
> He is the one called Firecloud.

E. P. Murray

The red stallion snorted and loped forward, holding his head and tail high. Then he hurled himself up the slope in a few easy bounds and stood at the top of the ridge. The herd stallion on the flat below was a powerful black for whom the people of this band of Kainah, the Black Horse band, had named themselves. Firecloud reared in challenge, tossing his head, his heavy mane flowing along his neck and withers.

Below, many villagers ran out to watch Firecloud challenge the black horse. The black squealed in answer and left his mares to face the red stallion. The young horse tenders of the village knew they could not stop the black from defending his herd. They also knew from stories told in the village and among other bands that the red stallion called Firecloud was invincible. They felt helpless knowing they would lose most of their herd mares.

Firecloud met the charge of the black, and both reared. The black was as strong as any antagonist Firecloud had ever faced, and he fought with a fierce determination. In the village below shouting began, and the two younger warriors followed the old one to the crest of the hill where they watched the two massive horses clash in their deadly struggle.

They continued to fight as the sun lowered itself behind the horizon and shot scarlet into the sky. Their mouths were open, showing their strong teeth, and their hooves flew at each other with speed and power. Though the black had been a proud ruler, the powerful Firecloud had begun to wear him down. The big red stallion was too strong and too wily, and the neck and back of the black soon ran red with blood.

The old warrior nodded as he watched the red stallion take measure of the faltering black, once the proud leader of the Kainah herd. Firecloud, he knew, was like no other horse born in these lands. This powerful stallion would rule these lands for many winters to come. It was indeed an honor to have seen him this day and to have shown the two young warriors that such a horse lived.

Finally, with the blazing twilight at his back, Firecloud left the black dazed and beaten, struggling to regain his feet.

FIRECLOUD

Shouts rang through the village as he rushed down the hill and began to move the herd away. The Spirit Horse then vanished into the hills with the Kainah mares to rejoin the rest of his herd, still hidden in the secluded clearing.

For a long time after the stallion was gone and the sun had disappeared, one of the two young warriors sat alone in the darkness. He could not get the big stallion out of his mind. He was the half brother of the other young warrior, and the two were longtime rivals. Though the two had just reached their twentieth winter, they were already well respected as fierce competitors in games and as mighty warriors of the Black Horse band of Kainah Blackfeet. But among warriors within the band, one must stand above the other; there could be no equals.

The young warrior knew that ownership of the magnificent stallion would bring him more honors in the band than a hundred triumphs during battle. All the maidens of the village would look at him with pleading eyes while he decided which of them would become his first and most important wife, his sits-beside-him wife. The others would then be satisfied to be taken as additional wives. They would proudly tell all the other villagers that they were wives to Nighthawk, powerful warrior and owner of the Thunder Horse, the ruler of the mountains, the one called Firecloud. As owner of the mightiest stallion in any land, his name would be sung around celebration fires, and stories would be told about his bravery.

Nighthawk would need to gain as much power as possible, for Black Owl, his half brother, had already begun to destroy his reputation. He knew that Aged One would help him as much as he could; but that would not be enough, for Black Owl knew how to lower his half brother in the eyes of the people.

But Nighthawk could only dream, for no warrior was any match for the wild and proud stallion. Still he clung to a hope. The Aged One had told him of a vision in which he had seen a mysterious rider on Firecloud's back. In the vision, Aged One had seen Nighthawk standing nearby with joy on his face and in his heart. Aged One had seen the vision more than once. Each time the rider appeared on the stallion's back, but only once had he seen Nighthawk himself on the stallion's back. What did the vision mean? Who was the mysterious rider?

For many nights thereafter Nighthawk sat in the darkness and wondered at the visions of Aged One.

1

CLARA MELTON wore her long black hair loose more often than not and was rarely seen in the company of persons who did not spend most of their time around horses.

Charles Melton, whether he cared about such things or not, had always seen that his daughter was exposed to the best that New England could offer an aristocratic family so soon after the Revolution. That dustup had earned the Melton family even more wealth than they had brought with them from England, and siding with the colonists had been a wise political choice. But for Clara, wealth and the family name were not important.

Charles had lost his wife and younger child when Clara was twelve, but he had done, in Clara's mind, a more than adequate job of providing love and understanding to a daughter who was becoming known in the highest circles as "the Melton rebel."

Clara's presence in society caused whispers and, at times, gasps. Young women simply did not carry themselves in that fashion, nor did they disregard fashion so persistently. Some well-meaning women had sought to correct her faults, and with an indulgent smile, Clara remembered the evening she had overheard her aunt talking to her father in his study.

"It's deplorable, Charles! She cares not in the least how she dresses. Nor does she care what a picture she presents to the public. She sets a shocking example for young ladies her age. She has all that lovely black hair, but she lets it fly loose in the wind in a disheveled tangle, streaming out behind her as she thunders along on that big horse. And she rides without a hat! My land, she is as brown as an Indian!" Clara's aunt paused for breath. She needed all her lung capacity to emphasize her last point. "And, Charles, for heaven's sake prevent her from riding in a manner so improper for a lady! What a scandal it will cause if the important people learn that she rides like a man!"

Knowing Clara was careful not to allow anyone to see her riding astride, Charles Melton quickly asked his sister, "Pray tell, Katherine, who told you that?"

Clara's Aunt Katherine had fumbled for words and avoided answering the question. "It just isn't proper behavior. She must be aware that her actions are a direct reflection on other members of the family, and not just the immediate family." She let a light cough escape and caught it with her handkerchief.

"My dear Katherine," her father had replied, "I see no good reason why, in no other presence than her own, Clara cannot ride in any manner that she sees fit."

"Now, Charles, there is no reason to become aggravated."

"I have never told Clara how she must act," he continued. "I have left that up to Clara's judgment, which I must say has always been excellent."

Clara's aunt was not to be outdone. "Well, Charles, I must say, you seem to have no concern for the manner in which that daughter of yours presents herself. I fail to understand why you care so little about her behavior. After all, Charles, your own reputation is at stake."

Charles Melton had made his last point very clear to his sister. From Clara's vantage point out of sight on the stairwell, she could hear her father's words clearly.

"You worry about your reputation, Katherine, and I'll worry about my daughter's and mine."

FIRECLOUD

The look on her aunt's face as she left the study stayed with Clara all her life. Like many other New Englanders, Katherine could not accept behavior that deviated from the accepted standards. Clara and her father had always been able to talk and smile their way through an awkward situation, but Clara knew that time would bring her to a direct confrontation with someone in some place. As she got older, Clara knew that confrontation was approaching.

Since her mother's death, Clara had had more important things to concern her than proper etiquette. The loss of her mother had certainly saddened Clara, but she had been more upset by the tears her father shed late at night in his study and by the small, thin lines that had crept into his face. The loss of both his wife and his only son had done him immeasurable harm. Outwardly, Charles Melton was stern and forthright. Within, as Clara well knew, he was warm and loving. Since her mother's death Clara had really come to know him and had herself become a woman.

Lately Clara had enlarged her vision of the world, had begun to look out across the New England countryside to worlds beyond. She had become active in her father's business, Melton Enterprises, and had, through hard work and business sense, become an invaluable partner. She had expanded her knowledge of the mercantile system and had learned how commodities were discovered and developed for markets. This had taken her mind from the routines of daily life and set her at a distance from other women. She had learned much about the far reaches of the world from which came many of the goods in which she and her father dealt. The business fascinated her, and it had done her mind a measure of good. Much of what Clara had learned had benefited Melton Enterprises, and she had more than proven her worth as her father's partner in the business.

And so Clara Melton could not be molded into the vaporish maiden her Aunt Katherine wished her to become. She had marched beyond the scented drawing rooms in which proper young ladies blushed and fanned themselves. Yet now, once again, Clara found herself confronted with what was expected of her in life. She could not blame her father, for he loved her deeply and had her best interests at heart. But no matter how close to him she was, Clara had discovered that he never thought quite the same way as she.

"I haven't seen you with any gentleman callers lately, Clara," he began as they started up a hill behind the stables after a brisk evening ride.

"The young gentlemen I am acquainted with," Clara answered, "don't really interest me that much, Father."

"What has become of young William? At one time you two were hitting it off quite well."

"William is tiresome, Father," Clara said with a shake of her head. "He needs to think about someone besides himself for a change."

They reached the top of a hill and sat down in the grass, looking out over the expanse of the estate. Along a road in the distance, a coach moved with four spanking white horses and a driver dressed in solid black.

"I had hoped you and William could strike something up," her father continued. "Not that I'm trying to be a matchmaker, Clara. You know me better than that. I had just assumed that, of all the suitors who have made their way here to see you, William most held your interest."

"Father, they are fops. They must dress like one another; they must be seen in the most fashionable places; they must curl their hair just so. They are more vain than the women!"

Charles cleared his throat. "I suppose so, but a woman of your age needs a husband and a family to share the joys of life with. You cannot expect me to live forever."

"I understand your concern, Father," Clara said with a sigh. "But I am not like other women. I don't care to learn French, and I dislike having men step on my feet when we dance, and I cannot put up with their hen-witted remarks. I just don't fit in."

"Oh, nonsense, Clara."

"It is true, Father. Everything about me is wrong. I haven't

FIRECLOUD

found any man I even remotely wish to marry. I know I am supposed to be happy with a husband, cater to his needs, jump to his every wish and command, and care for his children. But that is not the life for me. I could never stand next to a man and act like a child while he controlled my every movement. There has to be something very special about the man I will do that for. Perhaps you would have been better served had I been a son instead of a daughter."

"Nonsense," her father repeated. "Clara, I have never wished you were a son. You know that. You please me just the way you are, and I have never given you cause to believe otherwise."

"Oh, Father, I am sorry," Clara said, letting him take her into his arms as the tears slid down her cheeks. "I know you have never wished I was anyone but myself. And I love you for it." She squeezed him tightly.

Charles pulled his handkerchief from his sleeve. "Now, now. Dry your eyes. I had no idea our conversation would come to this."

Clara took a deep breath and looked out across the rolling hills to where the horses had buried their heads in the lush grass, enjoying themselves in the evening freshness. The trees shone deep green in the late sun, and the calm air carried a touch of something wild, something that reached deep into Clara and again made her think of faraway places that promised a different sort of life.

"I feel foolish," she told her father. "I feel trapped, though I have the best life anyone could ask for. And the best father."

Charles put his hand on his daughter's shoulder. "I understand how you feel," he said. "That same restlessness brought me over here from England many years back. And I spent a great deal of time by myself before I married your mother." He laughed a small, gentle laugh. "Yes, and she, like you, took some time to persuade."

"You certainly had enough money," Clara said, not understanding why any woman wouldn't jump at the chance to marry her father. "It couldn't have been lack of money that made her hesitate. And I'm sure it wasn't because of your looks."

He laughed again. "It seems strange to hear those words from you. Money and good looks certainly won't win every woman's heart."

At that Clara had to laugh. "It does sound silly for me, of all people, to say something like that, doesn't it?"

Then her father took in a deep breath and winced, leaning forward a bit, holding his chest.

"What is it, Father?" Clara asked quickly. "Are you sick?"

"No need to worry," he told Clara, though the pain was still evident. "I'll be fine in a moment." He let out a breath and sat back. Forcing a smile, he said, "I suppose I should be more selective in what I choose to eat at mealtime. My stomach is no longer capable of handling all those rich foods."

Clara tried to laugh with him, knowing deep inside that food had nothing to do with his pallor and the beads of sweat that had collected on his forehead.

"Father, maybe you should see a doctor."

"Nonsense, my dear. I'm fine, just fine."

Still Clara worried. She had noticed these same symptoms at a ball the previous Christmas. Her father was not one to complain, even to Clara, of any problem, trivial or serious. He had been a strong man all his life, and he could not admit that his health was failing.

"I must tell you something now," he said. "I asked you about William Bradbury because he asked me if he might call on you tomorrow. I told him I saw no reason why not. Perhaps I should have conferred with you first."

Clara shrugged. "I suppose it's all right. But keep no expectations about him and me."

"Certainly not," her father said quickly, rising to his feet. "You have a good mind of your own, and you can make it up for yourself."

As they walked together toward the mansion, Clara found herself looking out beyond the hills to where the setting sun sent a last flush of reddish light over the darkening sky. A low bank of puffy clouds above the horizon picked up the glow and absorbed it, turning red also. Clara sighed, wishing she could see some of the places the sun had passed over that very day.

Promptly at two o'clock the next afternoon, Clara received William Bradbury in the drawing room. Dressed fashionably in dark clothing that had been carefully tailored, he wore the confident smirk for which he was well known. He approached Clara, allowing the smirk to widen into a broad grin, then made a sweeping bow and bid her good day.

"Your father suggested I come this afternoon," he said, too casually. "I can assure you, I take a great deal of pleasure in this visit. It is a compliment that a young woman of your charm and beauty should bid me welcome."

"William," Clara said, with thinly disguised aggravation, "if I never saw you again in my life I would lose precious little sleep because of it. And furthermore, never say anything regarding my father that is not true!" Clara knew full well her father had not suggested that William visit her, and that small lie made her far angrier than his presumptuous attitude.

William knew he had taken the wrong approach, and was therefore prepared for her reprimand. With other ladies, he was used to taking liberties with the truth and getting away with it. Most young ladies fluttered and blushed with pleasure in his presence. Clara Melton, however, was another matter.

"Forgive me, Clara," William said, fumbling with his beaver top hat, a new hat with a most luxuriant texture. "Please accept my apology for upsetting you. I trust I haven't made you angry with me?"

Clara noticed the new hat William was holding. Perhaps, she thought, he had not given it to the butler in order to show it off a bit. "No," she finally said to him. "I am not going to lament over it for the remainder of the day."

"I shall mind my tongue, Clara," he said quickly. He saw her interest in the hat and took the opportunity to use it as a conversation piece. "The newest thing, you know," he began rather carefully. "Made from the finest beaver pelts. Take a look if you wish."

Clara accepted the stylish top hat and was impressed by its feel. It was very different, both in texture and appearance, from the common tricorne.

"It's a grand sort of hat," William went on. "Every gentleman will soon have one, that is, if they can get enough pelts to make them fast enough."

"What do you mean?" Clara asked.

"Well, there is a great demand for beaver pelts from which to make hats such as the one you are holding, as well as other items, and precious few of the furs are being supplied. I daresay the haberdashers are asking a great price for such hats nowadays."

"Tell me," Clara said, "how is it you know so much about the fur trade?"

"An interesting sort of story." William had regained some of his lost confidence. "You see, I have an uncle in St. Louis who is well acquainted with John Jacob Astor, the German gentleman who has done so well in the fur trade. Do you know the name?"

Clara nodded. "Yes, I believe I do. Is he not the gentleman who has dealt in furs just below the Great Lakes and is now planning to seek greater fortunes in the Northwest Territory?"

"He is the same," William answered. He laughed. "You know, it is quite amazing, someone like him. And those other adventurers such as the Mackenzie fellow and Manuel Lisa, gallivanting around in wild country that is fit for neither man nor beast. Fighting off savages and devising shelters out of animal skins and such. The stories they tell about those men!" He shook his head and laughed again. "It takes a different sort to live the way they do. They must be part savage themselves."

Clara still held the hat, but she was looking past William through a window to the world outside. For a moment he watched her, then asked tentatively, "Clara, is something the matter?"

FIRECLOUD

Clara blinked once, then looked at him and laughed. "No, William, everything is fine."

"You had me concerned. You didn't seem to be at all yourself."

Clara cleared her throat once. "Well, perhaps I do feel a bit weak."

William quickly helped her to the sofa. "Should I call for some assistance?"

"No, no thank you, William. That won't be necessary. All I need is a little rest. I am sorry to cut your visit short. Please forgive me."

William looked blank for a fraction of a moment, then responded, "Of course, Clara. It can't be helped."

"It was nice of you to stop by," Clara went on. "Perhaps I can make it up to you by offering you a dance at the charity ball the end of the month."

"Well," William cleared his throat. "I had hoped—"

"If I am able to attend, that is," Clara cut in.

The butler appeared in the doorway, and William bowed to Clara. "Let's hope you are able, then," he said. "I certainly would enjoy that dance." He bade her good day and marched out to his waiting coach, his stride somewhat stilted and his shoulders more rounded than they had been when he first arrived.

Clara immediately turned her mind to the relatively new fur trade business. How could she learn more about it? She would need to read the account written by the government explorers Lewis and Clark, of course. And there had been talk of another explorer sent out by the government, a gentleman named Zebulon Pike. The blood in Clara's veins quickened as she thought of the possibilities the fur trade held for Melton Enterprises and the chance it offered her to see the distant places she had dreamed about and to lead the kind of life that had been on her mind for a long time. As soon as William Bradbury had spoken, Clara realized that this was the opportunity she had so long awaited.

Clara could visualize the vast, snow-capped mountain

ranges reaching for the sky, streams that bubbled down over rocks to find deep lakes that mirrored the peaks above. She had heard so much and read volumes about this vast land to the west. Her father would certainly disapprove of her decision to go on an expedition, even if the idea made sound business sense. Still she could see herself surrounded by that vast untamed land.

Settling back, Clara put her mind to the practical matter of the business ventures that were now under way. Melton Enterprises had been flourishing, and money was available to finance a new venture.

Clara knew, however, that her father would be reluctant to embark on a venture he was not informed about. And her struggle to convince him to enter into the fur trade would become even more difficult when he learned that she herself wished to set out for the wilderness as soon as possible. As much as he loved her, Clara knew he was far too practical to grant her every wish.

Charles Melton intended to provide not only for his daughter's future financial situation but also for her social future, since she did not seem interested in marriage. Upon seeing William Bradbury's coach leaving the estate, he quickly entered the study. "I hope William left under amicable circumstances," he said, his eyes holding the question.

"Yes, he most certainly did, Father," was Clara's reply. "And, I might add, he provided me with some interesting insights into a business we might want to consider ourselves."

"And what might that business be?" her father asked.

"Fur trading."

Clara watched her father's eyebrows rise ever so slightly. After a moment, he responded, "Interesting. But we don't know the first thing about it."

"I can supply that information in little time," Clara said. "I believe a venture into the fur trade could provide us with some healthy profits." Clara noticed her father's face had taken on a concerned look.

"Clara, I don't know." He shook his head. "They say that

fur trading is very, very risky. With luck, one stands to gain a fortune, but it would be equally easy to lose everything."

"I believe," Clara said, "that if our expedition is correctly planned and the right men secured, our company could realize measurable profits, even the first year."

Her father walked around his study, his hands clasped behind his back, his head bowed in thought. Finally, he asked, "What in the world possessed you to come up with a business of such gigantic proportions?"

"There is nothing so gigantic about this endeavor," Clara argued. "Why, we have two enterprises in India that make this investment look rather small."

"The seaport in India and the other locations where we have committed ourselves are settled," her father said. "The people in those locations have been there for some time and have established some sort of civilization. The fur trade, though located on our own continent, extends far beyond even the last settlement. There is nothing out there to guarantee our investment will be safe. To the contrary, there is much out there to circumvent even the most remote possibility of success."

"You are most generally in favor of my suggestions," Clara told her father. "Why are you so adamant this time?"

"The fur trade is a terrible risk, Clara."

"There is risk in every venture, Father. India was not secure at first, if you remember. And I shall go along on this venture."

"What kind of suggestion is that?"

"I think it would be a good idea," Clara said without hesitation. "I could protect our share in the investment. Besides, I need a change."

Clara watched the furrows in her father's brow deepen. Both of them had known this day would eventually come. Clara had watched her father over these past few years as he tried to ignore the restlessness growing within his daughter. He knew Clara would someday wish to explore some different place, get away from the rigid structures within which the wealthy families of New England moved. She had gone with him to France, Germany, and Scotland. He had taken her to London, where she had discovered life among the wealthy to be much the same as it was at home. Clara could see the past in his eyes, the times he had shaken his head and said, "I suppose I have to agree, Clara. Life in a civilized society does develop a certain pattern that we cannot escape." She could see him now reliving the times he had told himself he was someday going to have to let her go off and satisfy her desire to be free. Still, Clara knew he was not going to let it happen without trying to talk her out of it.

"My darling Clara," he said, "the frontier is no place for a woman."

"It is not as if I will be gone forever," Clara said. "I will travel back here on occasion."

"My daughter, what you refer to as mere 'travel' is nothing less than a major expedition across thousands of barren miles. There are no roads, no coaches, no means of travel except horseback or boat, when possible."

"I am aware of that, Father. You well know I would rather travel on horseback than by any other means."

"But, Clara, I don't believe you really know what lies ahead of you."

"I think that is exactly the point, Father. I can only imagine what I will see and do, maybe far too readily! This journey is the very thing I have dreamed of for so long. This is my one chance to free myself."

Her father took a deep breath. "I suppose I cannot stop you, then." He kissed Clara on the cheek and stood for a moment, as if he now cherished every moment he spent with her. "I shall see you at dinner," he finally said.

Clara watched him climb into the small open carriage he used during the warm months and thought about the look she had seen in his eyes. He understood her desire to be free, and yet he was determined to try to keep her home where he thought she belonged. He did not want to lose her. His arguments against the soundness of the fur trade had been but a pretense to discourage her from leaving. Clara knew that he thought the idea very sound indeed. There was an incredible amount of money to be made if the venture was properly planned and executed. But Clara knew her father would give up all the money in the world to keep his daughter with him.

Clara watched the carriage weave its way down the winding roadway out of the estate. Just before it disappeared into the trees, her father lurched forward much as he had on the hillside the evening before. She turned from the window, and a sinking, morbid fear clutched her, making her hurry to the stables and saddle the black herself. Tears formed, and a numbness made her fingers and hands awkward as she placed the bridle on her horse, threw the saddle on his back, and fastened the cinch. The stable hands stared as she mounted and urged the horse out across the open meadow.

The wind blew the tears into her long black hair. An eternity passed before Clara came up on the coach, stopped at the edge of the road a short distance from the estate boundary. The driver was standing beside the coach, his hat in his hand, and her father was slumped over in his seat.

"I'm sorry, Miss Clara," said the driver. "It must have been his heart."

Her tears were now a steady stream as Clara climbed up into the coach next to her father. She placed his head on her shoulder and stroked his hair. "Father, dear, why did you have to leave me now?" She began to rock him gently, still stroking his hair, and with an occasional kiss on the forehead, repeated over and over, "I'm so sorry for wanting to leave you. I'm so sorry."

She stayed there with him, rocking him and talking, until the sun had sunk far down in the west. She told him things she had always wanted to say, as the driver waited silently, his own eyes unashamedly filled with tears.

2

A MONTH AFTER her father's death, Clara made her decision. She sold the estate, keeping the horses and enough land on which to build a modest house. And she decided to invest in a fur-trading expedition deep into the wilderness near the headwaters of the Missouri River. She would, of course, be a member of the expedition.

After a few short discussions, Clara formed a three-way partnership with her father's dearest friend, George Whittingham, and a friend of his named Martin Folmon. George Whittingham was an honest man who had been like an uncle to her. Martin Folmon lived in St. Louis, and Whittingham planned to move there and look into the fur trade. It seemed as if fate had called the three of them together.

Clara had learned that the headwaters of the Missouri River, the Valley of the Three Forks, was the richest beaver area in all the Rocky Mountains. The major drawback to previous trading and trapping ventures had been the Blackfoot Indians, who considered that area the southern extension of their hunting grounds. Even the successful fur trader Manuel Lisa had been forced to abandon this region because the Blackfeet had killed many of his men. Since his recent death, the mountains and northern plains had harbored no ambitious American fur traders. The time was right, Clara decided. The

British, who were already entrenched farther north, were now expanding their trade networks down through the river valleys, which would lead them right into the new territory called Louisiana. Soon they would be inciting the Indians to attack new traders. The time to move was now.

Clara also learned that the Blackfeet seemed to prefer British trade goods, no matter who offered them. In addition, the Blackfeet were known to trade amicably with certain white men who they trusted and looked up to. One such man was a John Huston, who had agreed to lead the expedition. He had worked with Manuel Lisa, and his experience would be invaluable. Huston was told to hire experienced *voyageurs* to man the expedition. They would be paid the highest price ever offered to members of an expedition of its type.

Clara and George Whittingham arrived in St. Louis the day before the expedition was set to depart. John Huston, Martin Folmon, and the *voyageurs* were already there, making last-minute preparations.

St. Louis was the departure point for most expeditions into the wilderness. It was the last city, the edge of civilization, overflowing with adventurers of every description.

Their coach took them down to the river, a wide, sweeping flow of dark brown water. One of their associates in St. Louis was a French-Canadian named Jacques LaCroix, who met them at one of the landings. He looked more than once at Clara, no doubt having heard she was to accompany the men up the Missouri. He spoke in broken English with many French words mixed in, and as he spoke to George Whittingham, Clara picked up many references to her good looks and the hardships of the wilderness. Clara knew LaCroix was a typical *voyageur*, and she also knew she would have to be firm from the very beginning with all of them.

LaCroix suggested they go down to where the men were working while they waited for Martin Folmon to arrive. Clara and Whittingham followed him past the line of warehouses and storage facilities to the water's edge. The air was filled with stale smells, and every worker on the docks was covered with mud from head to foot.

FIRECLOUD

LaCroix pointed to two large keelboats that were being loaded with provisions. "There she is, your boats," LaCroix told them. "They are good ones, are they not?" He smiled widely and nodded a number of times.

Whittingham asked him some questions about the boats and the men while Clara watched. Many of the men were without shirts and were a deep brown. A few wore cotton, but most wore heavy buckskin leggings blackened from smoke and grease.

"Where are the fur traders?" Clara asked, a bit confused. "Did they bring Indians back from the mountains to help us load the goods?"

LaCroix turned in astonishment, and Whittingham quickly said, "They rather look like Indians, don't they?"

LaCroix flashed the broad smile and began nodding again. "Ah! The Indians, they are the same color. *Oui!*" He laughed out loud.

Clara, realizing her mistake, blushed with embarrassment.

"There is Huston," LaCroix pointed. "That is the John Huston." He hurried down to the boat to get Huston, taking off the cotton handkerchief he wore as a cap and waving it to get Huston's attention.

Clara frowned and wrinkled her nose. "Do these men ever bathe?"

"Something you'll have to get used to, I'm afraid," said Whittingham.

John Huston came up from the boat to where Clara stood. His stubble of beard and his hair, which hung down to the collar of his shirt from under a wolfskin cap, was tinged heavily with gray. His blue eyes held a sparkle that spoke of confidence and years in the wilderness.

"You come to see what you paid for, I'm thinkin'," he said. He bowed slightly to Clara and extended his hand to Whittingham. "Welcome to the fur trade."

Clara saw in his eyes all those things she had known she would find there. He was wild and untamed, with a dislike for society, which he could not help but display somewhat, though he was far more courteous than most of the men on the dock. He was independent beyond measure, showing a loyalty only because he was being paid handsomely for it. In a different sort of way he was as self-assured as young William Bradbury back in New England. He certainly didn't have that kind of money, but he could control his own destiny just as well.

"Come to see what things are like where the world ends?" he said to Clara. "You should find a story or two for your friends back East, I'm thinkin'. I'll bring you back a Blackfoot scalp."

George Whittingham quickly spoke up. "No need to do that, Mr. Huston. Clara will accompany you into the wilderness. She can take her own scalps if she cares to."

Clara had to grin at that. She could not have said it better herself. But John Huston dropped his smile and looked sharply at both of them.

"This is the wrong day for a joke, I'm thinkin'."

"No joke, Mr. Huston," George told him. "I must presume by your surprise that some of our letters did not reach you and that you were not aware of Clara's intention to join the expedition."

"I ain't takin' no woman under my wing."

Clara stepped forward and said, "Mr. Huston, I can take care of myself. I have no desire to be under your wing."

LaCroix was yelling and waving with his cap. Martin Folmon had arrived.

"I'll have a quick word with them while you get acquainted with Mr. Huston," Whittingham told Clara. He turned and left the dock.

John Huston took off his fur cap and scratched his head while he studied Clara for a long moment. Unlike most of the men she had met before, John Huston was not overwhelmed by her beauty. Or, if he was, he hid it admirably. Though much older than she, he was a handsome man.

"I ain't never seen nor heard the likes of this before," he finally said.

"You had to go out into the wilderness for the first time yourself once," Clara pointed out.

FIRECLOUD

John Huston went on as if he hadn't heard her. "There ain't one woman between here and the Rockies that's got a drop of white blood in her veins. I ain't about to make you the first one."

Clara's eyes darkened. "You aren't taking me along on this mission, Mr. Huston. I am taking myself. I own part of these boats, and I am going along partly to protect my investments. You have no responsibility for my well-being. I am perfectly capable of taking care of myself."

John Huston's eyes again traveled Clara's length as if he were trying to determine what manner of woman could speak with such authority. It was clear that he had not expected to hear such a speech from Clara, nor was he accustomed to arguing with a woman about anything.

But he was not angry. Somewhere behind the hard features and deep blue eyes Clara saw a glint of humor. Possibly he wasn't used to being talked to that way by men, let alone women. Still, he shook his head. "Your talk is good, miss," he said. "You don't back down, I'll say that."

"Clara is my name. Use it when you speak to me, if you would."

"Clara it is," he clumsily tipped his fur cap. "And John is the name I go by."

"Then we understand each other?"

"Well, Clara, I ain't never seen the likes of you. I seen some Indian women, but none of them got the tongue you do. Now, have you ever seen Blackfoot sign or ate dog meat from a Ree meat pot? Not hardly you ain't! No matter what you talk, you ain't seen the likes of the hills west of here. You ain't seen men crawlin' on hands and knees, cryin' like babies, with arrows in their guts. No, and you ain't seen a man with both legs froze black and stiff, nor found what's left of a man after a white bear has got him. And that outfit you're wearin'. You expect to trade furs in that?"

"I'll agree with you there, John," Clara admitted. "I am not appropriately dressed for the journey. I have every intention of rectifying that in due time."

"Can you drink whiskey?"

"I have tasted it, but I don't see your point. I should have the choice to drink or not to, as I wish."

"You can't trade without drinkin'. There ain't a man in the hills who'll trust another that don't drink whiskey from a jug. None of your fancy glasses with stems."

"I'll learn," Clara insisted.

"Ever been on a keelboat?"

Clara shook her head.

"Land o' Christ! How in the hell you mean to stay aboard on the Missouri? I ain't no good at fishin' out drowned rats!"

Clara squared her shoulders and took a deep breath. "John Huston, I am going to be part of this expedition, like it or not. You need not worry about me. If I fall off the boat, so be it; if I don't like your whiskey, I'll drink it anyway. I will not be discouraged by your descriptions of what lies ahead. Have I made myself clear?"

John Huston stood silent for a moment.

"I assure you, Mr. Huston, I can easily find someone else to replace you if you can't live with my company."

John Huston nodded. He had thrown everything he could at her, and she had held up. She could not be browbeaten. She was more determined than any woman he had ever seen. And even a lot of men.

"I expect you to control the men," she went on, "and I will accept your judgment concerning matters with which I have had little or no experience. In short, John, you will be in full command. I shall merely act as counsel when and if you need me."

John nodded in agreement. "I can't say how the men will take to this," he said. "Like as not it won't set good at first, especially when they learn you ain't to be used by none of them. But they'll do what I tell them." He nodded slowly. "I'll take you up to the coaches."

Clara suddenly realized that John Huston had had some formal teaching. He held his arm out for her and matched her strides. He was now a far cry from the unkempt fur trader of just moments before. Though there was little talk between them on their way to the coaches, Clara could feel the mutual understanding and admiration that had developed. He would probably always feel responsible for her on the expedition, despite her words to the contrary, but she knew that he would never have consented to stay on, no matter how good the pay, if he hadn't devised in his own mind that she could withstand the rigors of the journey ahead. She would need time to adjust; of that there was no doubt. But this was something she wanted to do, and she would do it.

"What would you say if I was to help you pick out some possibles for the hills?" he said just before they reached the coaches.

"Possibles?" Clara felt herself blush. "John, forgive me, but I don't understand all your words."

John laughed. "Possibles, Clara, is your goods for tradin'. You get yourself a good knife, some lead and powder, maybe some beads and such. Then, after you're all fixed for the hills, you got your possibles." He laughed again.

"Oh, very well," Clara laughed with him. "I would be happy if you helped me obtain some possibles."

"You've got a whole passel to get used to," John told her before he went back to the river to oversee the remainder of the loading.

Clara watched the men load the keelboats and secure the provisions on board, thinking how true John Huston's words were. She had no clear idea what the men were doing. She spent some time on board, learning as much as she could about the cargo she had paid so much money for and how it would be used to trade for furs in the Rocky Mountains. Besides the food provisions—beans, salt pork, coffee, and flour—Houston and LaCroix had procured a large selection of trade articles: knives of all sizes and shapes, guns, mirrors, steel arrowheads, lances, beads, cloth, vermilion, tobacco, and other items known to be valuable to the Indians. The cargo was designed to create a wealth in furs.

A WIDE, SWIFT TORRENT OF BROWN, the Missouri was Clara Melton's gateway to a new world. The mighty river drained the wild country far to the west where she planned to establish the National Fur Company within a year's time. It would take them until the fall to reach the river villages of the Mandan, the area considered the edge of the western fur region.

When they were two weeks out of St. Louis, Clara found the change a welcome one. Overnight she had put aside the amenities of Eastern society and learned to withstand the surge of a keelboat through the current and sleep on a bed of buffalo robes. The smoky fires of a riverbank camp, the smell of roasting venison, turkey, or goose had replaced the fine imported china and the sparkling white tablecloth she'd come to expect. The roof overhead was the wide sky, and though her body had been stiff and sore at first, her spirit was refreshed. She had never been happier in her life.

Gradually she had become used to the outdoor life. The strange foods settled in her stomach, and she could feel her body growing stronger with each night she passed on the hard ground of the riverbank. She was no longer exhausted when evening came and did not fall instantly to sleep in her warm bed of buffalo robes. Now she could better appreciate the night sky, with stars that seemed bigger and brighter than any she could remember seeing. The sounds from the woods along the river—the croaking of frogs, the hoot of owls, the song of crickets—rang in her ears as she gazed into the flickering campfires. It would take her months to gain the strength she would need to survive in this land, Clara knew. And it would take even longer to gain the respect of the *voyageurs*. The men said nothing to her, but they stared whenever they were sure John Huston could not see them.

The wind had picked up, and John Huston ordered the men to raise the sails on the keelboats for greater speed. Clara smiled to herself as the wind whipped her hair. This was the best time of her life; the wilderness belonged to her. She stood next to John Huston in the bow of the lead boat, the *Rosebud*. The *River Otter* followed off port, piloted by Jacques LaCroix. With a hearty laugh, he received the order to raise sail. He, like John, had started in the fur trade years before and knew the ways of the land and the people who lived in the Northwest. He had served as an interpreter for many fur

FIRECLOUD

traders in their meetings with the Indians. On Clara's expedition he was to serve the same purpose, as well as command the *voyageurs* under John Huston.

LaCroix was known among the other fur traders as an unpredictable adventurer. According to a widespread rumor, he had killed an Indian woman who refused to grant him sexual favors. Immediately afterward, in a fit of remorse, he had cut deep gashes into his legs, rendering himself helpless for nearly two months.

Despite his volatile nature, LaCroix was considered an invaluable link between the western tribes and the newly established fur trading enterprises. His trapping and hunting skills were also highly prized. As valuable as LaCroix was to the expedition, however, Clara had come to dislike him intensely. Upon leaving St. Louis she had overheard him talking to John Huston.

"The lady interests me," LaCroix had said. "She is not like any others I have known." He had paused to laugh. "She will be my woman soon."

As evening approached and the sun fell close to the western horizon, Clara returned to the bow of the *Rosebud* and looked out across the vast river. When the wind calmed, the sails were lowered, and the boats were powered by the *voyageurs*, who sang in French while they rowed, heaving their oars in unison and pushing the long, flat keelboats through the shadows of the cottonwood trees.

"You seem to see visions out there across the river."

Clara turned to see John Huston with a thin smile on his lips. "Perhaps I do," she answered him. "It's so very beautiful."

"How does it feel to be a fur trader?" he asked her.

Clara smiled. "It hardly seems real at this moment."

"You'd best think of it as real," John said with a quick nod. "We're too far out to take you back now."

Clara gave him a quick look. "I meant that it is all so wonderful to me that I can hardly believe it's happening."

"Just the same, you'd best get ready for what lies ahead. There's country out there you never dreamed of, and it can swallow you alive."

Clara turned and looked back out across the river. She took a breath and fought the frustration building up inside her. Everyone else on the expedition still resented her presence. Only John had talked with her, and each conversation with him ended in a similar fashion. In so many words, he said that she did not belong on the expedition. She had felt the men's lack of confidence in her since the beginning, and she knew it was up to her to change things.

Clara folded her arms across the front of the doeskin dress she wore. It had been made by an Iroquois woman in St. Louis, cut to the style of the Plains tribes. John had picked it out for her, one of the many items he had advised her to purchase for the trip. She now also owned a newly made Hawken rifle, plenty of powder and ball, and a Green River knife. John had taught her how to shoot the rifle, but he had laughed when she told him she would soon be a better shot than he was. John Huston had laughed at her too often lately. She unfolded her arms and turned to him.

"Order them to head for shore," she said.

Surprised, he said, "I don't see any sense in that. There's plenty of sun left."

Clara stiffened and spoke clearly. "Do as I say, Mr. Huston."

John ordered the *voyageurs* to pole the boat through the shallows to the riverbank and waved the other craft alongside. Soon the men were talking among themselves in excited French as they disembarked. LaCroix waded over to Clara and John, who had made their way to shore.

"Mr. Huston," Clara began, "it has been several days since we've tasted venison. You have provided only turkeys and geese from along the shoreline, and I have decided to kill a deer for our supper."

John Huston threw his head back and laughed.

"Mr. Huston," Clara declared, her eyes growing narrow,

"that is the last time you are going to laugh at me. Order the men to make camp while I shoot a deer."

John blinked a few times.

LaCroix, who had been listening with a broad smile, said to John, "The lady, she tell you what she thinks. No?"

John turned quickly. "LaCroix, have the men haul the boats ashore and tie them. Then repair the hull of the *River Otter* where it struck that log this afternoon."

"That will take hours!"

"Do as you are told, LaCroix."

The smile left LaCroix's lips, and he nodded in acknowledgment, turning to shout orders to the *voyageurs*.

John turned back to Clara and saw that her eyes were still drawn into narrow slits. "I'd best get the deer and show you how it's done," he suggested.

"Those men will work faster if you stay here," Clara told him. "As for my ability to hunt, which you seem to doubt, I watched you shoot a deer once, and I saw nothing difficult about it. Besides, you've watched me practice. I can shoot."

"Those are thick woods behind you," John protested. "The Indians here may be unfriendly."

Clara held up her rifle. "This gun isn't hard to use. Let me show you something." She then raised the heavy weapon to her shoulder and fired at a small dead cottonwood thirty yards distant. The ball made a whap as it smashed into the brittle trunk. The top half of the tree swayed and then flopped over, held now by only a few splinters.

John's jaw dropped.

Clara turned and pushed her way through a stand of willows and into the brush beyond.

"Wait!" John called after her. He leaped into the *Rosebud* and rummaged among the supplies before joining her in the brush with a pair of buckskin leggings. He knelt down before her. "You'll need these," he told her. "Your legs need protection from the rose and gooseberry thorns."

Clara felt his hands slipping the stiff buckskin around her ankles, just above her moccasins, then along her calves. To make it easier for him, she sat down on a fallen log and lifted the doeskin skirt above her knees. For a moment, John stared at the trim curves of Clara's legs. Then he quickly tied rawhide thongs around her legs to hold the buckskins in place.

Clara stood up, and John turned to rejoin the *voyageurs* at the boats. "Fire three shots if you get yourself in a fix," he said over his shoulder.

3

Clara carefully checked the rifle and then turned to face the dense brush that seemed to stretch along the riverbank in an endless mass. The trees were alive with birdsong, and the brush hummed with insects that flew among the delicate blooms dotting the shrubs. Clara pushed her way through waves of color, tiny bell-shaped blossoms of gold and red and orange. Here and there massed clusters of wild roses blossomed a brilliant pink, their paper-thin petals smoother than the finest silk.

As Clara made her way through the brush, holding the rifle above her head and turning her face to avoid being scratched by the thorned branches, she was aware of the scoldings of numerous wrens and warblers, whose tiny nests swayed on the branches above her. The thorns tore at her dress and leggings, as if attempting to trap her in their clutches. She stopped frequently to measure the distance she had traveled and to regain her bearings. The rush of the river behind her helped her to determine her location, but the going was slow and she could not remember working harder at walking in her life.

Soon exasperation set it, and Clara began to thrash her way through the dense growth, making the thorns on each branch lash even deeper, stinging her skin. To add to her frustration, she knew the woods were alive with deer, but she could not get a clear shot at them. She heard them running out of their hiding places ahead of her as she fought the tangle of brush, but she caught only a glimpse of a flashing tall disappearing into the dense growth. In addition, the sun was dropping ever lower on the western horizon. She began to take deep breaths to remain calm, to still the rising panic within her. Then, as she left the brush and entered a thick stand of cottonwoods, she looked up into the branches in amazement.

Among the branches were many small logs tied together with rawhide to form platforms. On each platform, Clara knew, lay a body. An Indian burial ground of the sort she had heard stories about.

She began to walk slowly among the trees, looking upward. The trees, which seemed to stretch on forever, were filled with such scaffolds. The ground underneath was littered with pieces of cloth, pottery shards, and fragments of Indian jewelry; arrows and knives and headdress feathers had been scattered off the platform by birds scavenging the bodies. As Clara looked closer, she could see among the fallen objects a number of bleached bones. She stood motionless, as if turned to stone, her eyes riveted to a pelvis, with a leg and foot attached, which lay in a grotesque position at her feet. Suddenly there was a thud in the grass behind her, and she turned to see a skull bounce and roll sideways before coming to rest with the eye sockets facing her. From a scaffold overhead a raven cawed and flapped its wings, then vanished among the trees.

In blind panic, Clara rushed through the grove of trees, falling often, and back into the tangle of brush. With her rifle she pushed her way through the thick, thorny undergrowth, unaware of the added cuts and the stinging welts on her face and neck. Seemingly from under her running feet a flock of turkeys rose and flapped their wings wildly, scolding her in alarm before they lost themselves in the canopy of trees overhead. She turned blindly in still another direction, confusion clouding her judgment. She ran, not knowing where she was going, until she reached a small clearing. There she collapsed in exhaustion.

After regaining her breath, she noticed that she was lying in

FIRECLOUD

an area where a fire had cleared out the brush. The charred stumps of trees and brush litter were nearly covered entirely by new green shoots of grass and young shrubs. The ground was a soft carpet of new green and she lay back a moment longer to relax.

Quickly she sat up again, for nearby she could hear the gurgling of water. Within moments she found a clear pool where groundwater bubbled to the surface. She knelt down and filled her hands with the icy water, pressing it to her stinging face and neck. She knew a mirror would show her a mass of red lines along her checks and around her neck, puffy and sore from the thorns and briars.

With her fingertips, Clara could feel the zig-zag scratches, many of them. She reached into the mud at the edge of the pool, bringing handfuls up and pressing the cool, wet earth on her face. As a child she had learned to use water and clay to draw out an inflammation. The mud in this clear pool would serve the same purpose.

Taking a deep breath, Clara lay flat on her stomach and drank deeply of the cool water, letting it relax her. It was now close to sundown, and she knew she would need a clear head to find her way back through the dense underbrush to the river.

Suddenly Clara became conscious of movement nearby. She looked up to see that the clearing was alive with deer. All feeding on the new grass and shrub sprouts, they paid no attention to her. More deer were trailing in through an opening in the brush. This told her there was a trail from the river and that her journey back would be far easier than her trip in had been.

Slowly and deliberately, Clara raised herself to a sitting position, her back against a tree, and leaned forward, resting her elbow on her left knee. She chose a buck of modest size with full antlers. Taking a deep breath to control her trembling, she checked the rifle carefully and then aimed for a spot just behind the shoulder, telling herself this was no harder than target practice. She pulled the trigger and felt the jolt as the rifle thundered in the small clearing.

The buck fell immediately and lay still. The other deer quickly bounded into the security of the surrounding trees and brush while Clara sat for a moment, her heart beating wildly. She got to her feet and moved over to the buck. The shot had passed through the heart and lungs.

Taking another deep breath to again control the trembling, which seemed to have grown worse, she began to dress out the buck, using the techniques she had seen John perform with precision and skill. It was not as easy as it had looked, and she smeared blood all over her arms and the front of her doeskin dress and leggings before the last of the entrails were finally cleaned out and cut away.

Invigorated by the success of her hunt, Clara took hold of the antlers and began to drag the buck back to camp, handling the weight with ease. The deer had worn a clear path to the river, and the walk was more pleasure than work. She felt much stronger now and pulled the deer nearly to the edge of the thicket before stopping to rest on a fallen log near the trail. The sun had reached the horizon and the woods were bathed in a gold light. Among the branches, the birds sang their evening songs, preparing to roost. It was a moment of calm for Clara, and she enjoyed it to the fullest.

Clara turned quickly when she heard John Huston's voice behind her.

"Not a bad shot. You did good by checkin' to see that the rifle was charged up right."

"Where did you come from?" Clara asked. "Have you been following me?"

"You need to learn when you're bein' followed. That's part of surviving out here."

Clara's anger flared again. "Mr. Huston, I'll certainly tell you when I need your company. You can be sure of that. Until then kindly refrain from sneaking after me."

"You learned a heap of things today, I'd say." He walked past her to look at the deer, then picked it up by the hind legs with one hand and said, "I'll take this buck to camp. You can wash yourself off in the river if you have a mind to."

FIRECLOUD

"You will not follow me," Clara warned. "Is that understood?"

"You've never been out in country like this before," John explained. "I couldn't let you wander into some sort of trouble."

"Leave me alone, Mr. Huston!"

John shrugged, adjusting his fur cap. "I'll leave you go to the devil if you've a mind to." He started to turn, then looked at Clara. Without expression he said, "While you're washin' at the river, maybe you'd also think to clean that mud off your face. Them cuts are most likely closed up good by now."

Clara's hands went to her face, where the caked mud felt rough and hard. In her excitement over the deer, she had forgotten about her face.

John gave her a slight smile and added, "You've got my word, Clara. I won't ever laugh at you again."

Clara watched John turn, drape the buck over his shoulder, and make his way back to camp. She could not stay angry with him, for he was only trying to protect her from the wild land she knew so little about.

The river water was cold and refreshing, a welcome change from the humid heat of the forest. Clara sat down in the riverbed close to shore and let the current swirl around her while she rinsed out her dress and washed the mud from her face and neck. The mud had drawn the inflammation from the wounds, and the cuts would heal quickly. She had to laugh, thinking of the sight she must have presented to John, who must have had to use every ounce of his control not to break into a roar. He had been kind to her and now seemed to understand that her struggle to adjust to the land was something she wished to face by herself; a challenge she had to meet alone.

Days went by and the expedition moved ever closer to the western streams, where beaver dams covered the waters and a fortune in furs awaited. It was a different river now, more difficult to navigate, and full of sandbars and floating debris. Rowing was possible only occasionally, and the *voyageurs* took to the backbreaking task of pulling the keelboats along from the shoreline with tow ropes and pushing with long poles from the decks. Clara had never seen men work so hard. Day in and day out they pulled and pushed the heavy boats against the current, their sinewy muscles corded in their labor, sweat drenching their clothes and giving their faces a perpetual shine.

They passed an occasional village. Boone's Lick, where Daniel Boone's family had settled for a time, was a small community that John said was rapidly gaining in population. So was Franklin, its counterpart across the river.

Some distance upriver they reached an Omaha village whose entire population seemed to have gathered along the riverbank to shout and wave. The *voyageurs*, longing for a good trading session and the feel of a woman under them, argued heatedly in favor of going ashore. John shook his head and ordered them forward, explaining to Clara that they had no time to waste. There would be plenty of opportunities to trade with the tribe upriver. Wasting tradable goods on the Omahas would be foolish; they would need every item to obtain horses and information when they reached the western region.

As she watched from the deck of the *Rosebud*, Clara wondered if these Indians relied solely on river trade for their existence. To her they did not now represent the spirit of the free nomadic tribes she knew existed on the plains and in the mountains and foothills farther west. Once as proud and independent as any Indian people, the Omahas were now reduced to giving their women away for a drink of whiskey. Their dress reflected the dramatic changes trade had brought to their nation; cheap cloth and glass trinkets had replaced fine fur garments and hand-fashioned jewelry. As the Omahas ran after the boats, Clara turned to look upriver.

The days were beginning to cool, with only midday bringing strong heat. Summer was nearly gone, and their journey had brought them to the mouth of the Kansas River, where the Kansas Indians, like the Omahas, raced to the riverbank to watch the boats pass. The *voyageurs* shouted and whistled at the women, but John was adamant: They would not stop here.

FIRECLOUD

The Kansas had a reputation as expert thieves who welcomed any opportunity to add to their supply of stolen trade goods. Clara could see that John Huston deserved his reputation as a first-rate frontiersman. He knew the land and the people and could manage the unruly *voyageurs* without difficulty. Though the *voyageurs* protested his decisions to deprive them of the pleasure of going ashore, they respected him, and their complaints never became unreasonable.

As they continued on upriver, Clara could see the sparkle in John's eye grow brighter as they moved ever nearer to the mountains. He began to tell her stories of the land and of the people, legends passed down through generations. He spoke of the Indians' beliefs about their ancestry and the creation of the world. Some, it was told, had descended from the coyote, some from high-flying birds of prey, and still others from the beaver. Clara learned that the Indians had a religion all their own by which they lived and died. They lived from one day to the next, with war and famine a constant threat to their populations. Some of the things John spoke of made Clara's blood run wild with excitement. She longed for the sight of tens of thousands of shaggy buffalo migrating from spring to winter feeding grounds. She imagined herds of prong-horned prairie goats racing over open flats, their tawny white coats flashing in the sun.

John Huston had lived in the wilderness, and he knew this land as if by instinct. No book, he told Clara, could teach a person to read sign or make trade talk. John Huston knew every intricate detail of this land and its people. He knew every river and every stream, every valley and mountaintop; he knew the Indians—their religion, their customs, their character. In many ways he was like an Indian himself. The life he had chosen had forced him to learn the secrets of survival. He could live as part of the land itself, and now it was inside him; it was his very soul. Clara could see it in his eyes when he hunted or when he gazed out over the river from the deck of the *Rosebud*. Watching him, Clara began to understand what she would need to accomplish in order to succeed in her venture. It would be difficult, she knew, but in time she would learn.

At the midpoint of their journey, the Kansas made a gradual turn to the north, and they approached the Platte River, the wide, shallow waterway that flowed down from the mountains and across a wide expanse of plains that was Cheyenne country. Horse Indians, John called them. They were all horse Indians in the West now, he went on to say, ever since the Comanches and Pueblo tribes farther south had begun stealing horses from Spanish garrisons and settlements. Horses were vital in fighting and in hunting, the two things Indians lived for.

The keelboats would reach the mouth of the Platte that evening, John had said. Clara was looking up at the late evening sky when she saw something in the hills that made her breath come in a little gasp. She called to John, who came up to the bow of the boat and looked toward the hills in the distance.

"You catch sight of some buffalo?" he asked.

"No." Clara shook her head and pointed toward the hills. "Horses. They ran up on that highest knoll and looked down at us, then turned and ran down the other side."

John smiled.

"Who do you suppose they belong to?" Clara asked. "There isn't an Indian village nearby, is there?"

"I doubt if they belong to a village," John told her. "The Indians wouldn't let their horses go runnin' off in the hills. I'd say these are most likely wild. This country is full of wild horses. There's a passel of them in Sioux and Blackfoot country."

Clara shuddered with excitement. "It would be thrilling to catch one and train him. Maybe a special one."

"There's a legend about a big red stallion with a white mane and tail that no warrior or trapper has ever caught."

Again Clara shuddered, her body tingling with excitement. "Have you ever seen him?"

John nodded slowly. "Just once. In Kainah Blackfoot

FIRECLOUD

country." He pointed out over the water to the bank of clouds that had formed in the western sky where the sun was setting. "I had heard he was the color of the clouds at sundown, and when I saw him it was just before nightfall. They were right, by God. That stallion is the color of the sun on the belly of the clouds out there. Just as red as fire. They call him Firecloud."

"Firecloud." Clara whispered the name, her eyes bright in the glow of the setting sun. "Firecloud," she said again. "He must be beautiful."

"He takes a mess of mares away from the Indian villages," John said. "He's never been beaten by another stallion, though a good many have challenged him."

"Where can I find him?" Clara asked. "Where does he live?"

"Out where we're headed," John answered. "In Kainah Blackfoot country. He owns the mountains, they say, and claims them all as his territory."

Clara shook her head in amazement. "He must be of real quality stock."

"You know horses?" John asked her.

"I grew up on horseback. I left behind a big black stallion that I love dearly."

"That's good to know," John told her. "That's one thing I won't have to teach you."

Clara straightened, and her jaw came out ever so slightly. "Am I adjusting to this life too slowly?"

"No, I didn't mean that," John said quickly. "Fact is you're comin' along almost too fast to believe. But you ain't faced up to no stiff test yet, neither."

"What do you mean?"

"What we've come through this far ain't nothin' to tell no stories about," he explained. "We've lived fat and had plenty of fresh water. It's not always that way where we're headed. By the time you've been out here a spell you'll know what the feel of a hollow gut is like. And like as not the cold and snow will one time or another nip your face and fingers till they're black."

"Do you think I can endure all those things?" Clara asked him.

John laughed and nodded. "I'd bet good beaver on you, I'll say that."

"Then why are you concerned about my horsemanship?"

John folded his arms, and his face became stern. "A horse in Blackfoot country means life or death. A good horse can keep your hair off a lance or coup stick. If you stick to a good horse when he's runnin' full bore, you got at least a chance of makin' it to the next trappin' season. Otherwise you'll go under before you've got time to spit."

"I've been on horses at breakneck speed," Clara assured him. "That doesn't worry me."

"It's hard ridin' out in this country," John said. "The slopes ain't gentle and sweet like you're used to."

"How do you know what I'm used to?"

"I know the land back where you come from," John answered. "I lived there for a time myself."

Clara studied him a moment, and a grin crept over her face. "I thought so. Tell me, John, why is it that I've sensed all along that your roots are in the East? Why do I somehow feel you should be teaching geography in a marble lecture hall, not out here with me on a flatboat headed for the mountains?"

John flashed a quick smile and then grunted in disgust. "I didn't know it showed all that much. Not after all these years in the hills."

"Then you know the East better than the West?"

"Not anymore I don't," he answered quickly. "You hit it right when you said I've seen marble lecture halls. Harvard, if you want the truth. I was a student back then. But that was a long time ago, and the beaver streams have been my home now for more winters than I care to count."

"Do you have family back there?"

"None that care to claim me. Not now, not since I traded tailor-made suits and horse-drawn carriages for buckskins and a stout pony to carry me downwind from Blackfeet."

"Ever since the first day," Clara said, "the first time I

talked to you, when you escorted me back up to where George Whittingham was waiting at the carriage, I knew you had been to places other than the mountains. What made you decide to leave the East?"

John chuckled again, and even in the twilight that shone from the distant horizon, Clara could see the sparkle that came into his eyes. "You're a fine one to be askin' that question," he said. "What brought *you* out here? You didn't get pushed into this trip. You came of your own accord, and I'd bet there was next to nothin' that would have kept you from puttin' off with us."

"Yes," Clara admitted, "I was looking forward to this more than anything else in my life." She looked out into the deepening twilight. "I've always wanted to get away."

John said, "There's a big piece of the free country inside you, judgin' by the look in your eyes when you see a wild horse or hear me talk about the mountains. I told you hard times lay ahead but it ain't been that easy even up to now. Most women would be sick or dead by now, but not you. No, you enjoy all this. Only thing that would make a person think you was maybe a little bit normal is you get to lookin' at your hands at times, as if you wished they wouldn't get blistered and all calloused up."

Clara self-consciously rubbed her hands together. "I've always had to keep them looking soft and pretty," she said with a laugh. "Think what the ladies would say if I walked into a Sunday tea today."

John shook his head. "Most women ain't cut out for this sort of life. It took me time to get the soft out of me, and I worked to get it out. But no harder than you. I'd say you want this life as bad as I ever did."

Clara nodded. "For the first time in my life I feel as though I can be myself."

"Well," said John, "things are open and free out here. You come and go as you see fit. You don't have to listen to nothin' but the wind and the rumble of buffalo on the flats. No, the hills is the place for me. I couldn't go back. Not ever."

Clara watched John as he stared out into the last faint glimmer of pink in the western sky. His words still lingered in the depths of her mind—"I could never go back." That statement had come from him with a conviction and a sureness of tone that seemed to be a measure of the real John Huston. His eyes were steadfast on that last bit of light, as if he wished his arms would become wings to carry him up out of the river, out across the rolling hills and over the distant plains to the vast wilderness he talked about: beaver country, the high mountains.

They made camp in the dark just upriver from the mouth of the Platte. John told Clara that the Platte was known among fur traders and river travelers as the point of success. Many expeditions had turned back before even reaching the Platte, and most of those who did come this far made their arrival a cause for celebration. John broke out whiskey for the men, for the first time since the journey began, and ordered that all feast and have a good time.

The men built fires and immediately set to eating and drinking. John filled a cup from a tap on one of the kegs. Clara watched the thin stream of whiskey gurgle out. With a wink and a little nod, he handed her the cup.

"Don't drink it all down in one gulp," he laughed.

Clara put the tin cup to her lips and took a small swallow. It left a trail of fire all the way down into her stomach, and for an instant she stopped breathing. It was like drinking flame.

"I promised I wouldn't laugh," John teased. "Better get used to the stuff, though. Indians expect you to drink it when you trade with them."

Clara sat with John and some of the other men near one of the roaring fires, drinking the whiskey and enjoying a feast of roast elk, the first one killed on the expedition and the first one Clara had ever seen. Though a member of the deer family, this animal was much larger than the buck she had shot downriver. Elk carried massive, branching antlers that John said were a measure of their age, the prime young bulls having as many as six to eight long tines that came up from a main trunk, which often arched for three or four feet over their back. They were magnificent creatures, with tawny coats that darkened to brown around their shoulders and neck. A large herd had been drinking along the river's edge, and John had killed two before calling on Clara to take one herself. This was the first of many herds they would see on their journey into the far mountains.

The feast continued, and they ate their fill of roast elk, while emptying two kegs of whiskey. Though she drank far less than the men, Clara still felt warm and relaxed. Not since her childhood had she felt such an urge to let go and enjoy herself. She laughed with the men as the hours passed and even joked in French with the *voyageurs*.

Clara could not remember laughing so much in all her life. The men had not realized how well she spoke French, and she delighted in telling them that she had understood every word they had said about her during the expedition.

Two of the *voyageurs* got up from the fire and came around behind Clara. Quickly each took her by an arm and lifted her to her feet. Clara, astonished, asked them in French where they were taking her, while the others laughed and followed, clapping their hands and singing a French river song.

Clara soon found herself being carried to the riverbank. There two *voyageurs* waded out into the water and, with a laugh, tossed her into the cold current.

"*Voyageur!*" they shouted. "You are a *voyageur*, a boatman!"

Clara gasped a few times and came ashore, squeezing the water from her long black hair. The chill had sobered her considerably, and she took deep breaths, fighting anger. John waded out to help her to the riverbank.

"They've finally taken to you," he told her. "They'll call you captain from now on."

"What an odd way to show respect," Clara said while she shivered in the cool night air.

"You've got to see it the way they do," John explained. "This here is the Platte River, the spot where all travelers stop to celebrate. Greenhorns get broken in here. It means they're on the way to the mountains, to be traders."

"You mean they were initiating me?"

John nodded. "Just fun. It means they think you can survive in the hills, be a sure-fire trader, like Manuel Lisa, or Astor, or the others. In all my days I've never heard of it being done to a woman before this. They'll stand by you now, through hell on the river or with the Indians. They'll give all they got for you. Stand proud, woman. They just called you a beaver hunter!"

4

AWAY FROM THE MAIN CAMP, Clara put flint to powder and brought a stack of kindling and branches to flames. She stripped off the wet doeskin dress and hung it on a limb to dry. Wrapping herself in a buffalo robe, she huddled on a log next to the fire.

Clara let the warmth from the flames spread through her and snuggled deeper into her robe. After a while, she pulled it above her knees to let the warmth flow over her legs.

"Such a lovely woman. So very beautiful."

Startled, Clara turned to see Jacques LaCroix make his way quickly toward her and sit next to her on the log. As his calloused hand touched her leg, she stiffened and pulled the buffalo robe down, pushing his arm away.

"LaCroix, what are you doing here?" she demanded. "Get away from me."

LaCroix's strange smile frightened Clara. "I have longed for you the entire journey, and I know you want me, also," he was saying. "Ever since the first day I saw you, I knew we would be together like this." He slid one arm around her waist, holding her to him.

"LaCroix, let me go," Clara commanded.

"For the first time we are alone," LaCroix whispered,

wrapping his other arm around her. His breathing was a heavy rasp in her ear, his lips were moist on her face and neck. She felt his hand fumbling beneath her robe. Then his fingers clamped savagely around her breast.

She tried to wrench herself away from him, but he held her robe, and she had to stop struggling or have it pulled from around her. LaCroix's hands again moved over her, and his breathing was a foul stench in her face. His weight was atop her now, crushing her beneath him.

In a surge of rage, Clara turned and swung her elbow with all her might, catching him squarely in the left eye. With a grunt he arched to one side and held a hand over his eye. Clara quickly clawed her way out from under him, clutching the robe tightly around her.

LaCroix was now on his knees, shaking his head and cocking it to one side as if to clear his vision. Clara quickly dropped the robe and pulled the partly dried doeskin dress over her head and shoulders, and down into place.

LaCroix was now on his feet, laughing wildly.

"The she-cat is good for Jacques," he said, starting toward her again. "She likes her love rough, I believe."

Clara dodged him as he made a lunge for her. She picked up a heavy piece of wood from near the fire and, as he turned to come at her again, swung it against his temple. It hit with a dull thud, and the wood cracked on impact.

LaCroix staggered backward and again shook his head. Clara quickly snatched up a thick branch and put all her strength behind another blow to his head. LaCroix growled like a bear and slumped to his knees while Clara, now breathing through clenched teeth, slammed another blow to the top of his head.

LaCroix began to whine, curling himself into a ball on the ground, his hands and arms covering his bloody face and scalp. Clara felt strong arms pulling her away, taking the heavy limb from her grasp. She kicked and struggled but the strong arms held her all the more tightly.

"Easy, Clara, easy." It was John's voice. "It's all over now. It's all over."

FIRECLOUD

Clara stopped trying to twist her way out of John's arms and let herself sit down on the log again. She ran her fingers through her long hair, trying to still the pounding inside her head. Some of the *voyageurs* had come and were helping LaCroix to his feet. Strangely, he did not seem angry with her at all. His face, through the blood, wore a chilling smile, as if her attack had pleased him greatly. A number of the men were standing around John, pleading with him to put his knife away and forget what he had seen.

Clara sat for a while by herself while the others, including John, went back to the campfires and talked among themselves. It would take some time to get over what had just happened. For now, she didn't feel like the same Clara Melton. A different person had just pushed through, a person she would have to get to know if she was to survive in this land.

THE WHIP MADE whistling slices through the air and curled across LaCroix's back and around his ribs like a thin brown snake. Red welts crisscrossed from his shoulders down to just above his hips, leaving trails of fresh blood that weaved their way along and over scar lines left by whips in years past.

John counted as each stroke sang its song. Seven lashes remained of the fifteen he had been sentenced to receive. Clara's fingers went to her face and neck, feeling again the sting of the rose and gooseberry branches during her deer hunt far downriver. The whip, she thought, must be a thousand times worse than what she had felt.

LaCroix gripped the trunk of the cottonwood, his fingernails biting deep into the soft bark, his teeth clenched tight to keep him from crying out. From the *voyageurs* standing nearby came no sign of anger or resentment; LaCroix's time had come, and it was surprising to them that it hadn't come sooner. He had been telling them ever since the beginning of the expedition that he would have the beautiful white woman before long. They had expected him to desert the night before after John Huston had found Clara beating him with a branch. No one doubted what his punishment would be. In their minds, LaCroix was lucky John Huston hadn't killed him on the spot.

When dawn arrived, to everyone's surprise, LaCroix had already stripped himself to the waist and was awaiting his punishment. With welts and cuts along his scalp and neck from Clara's blows, and with his left eye swollen completely shut, LaCroix had told Clara, "I am not angry with you, my she-cat. It will be good to have such a woman as you. A fighter is good. I, Jacques LaCroix, will gladly take the whip for you. The pain will be good; I will endure it for you." He had ignored John Huston's warnings to stay away from Clara.

"We can get another interpreter," John had told Clara. "No one is worth all this." But Clara had insisted that LaCroix not be released. "Don't dismiss him because of this," she had said. "I don't want it to look as if I can't handle severe problems."

As the expedition continued, the incident seemed to have been forgotten. Though LaCroix continued to stare at Clara, he never again approached her or spoke to her. The cold eyes of John Huston were more than enough warning, and he knew he would have been left behind if it had been up to Huston to decide his fate. Despite his obsession with Clara, he was sensible enough to realize that it was best to stay away from her for now, that time would be in his favor sooner or later.

The expedition moved ever onward, and John and Clara turned their thoughts to the task at hand. They had many miles to travel before they would reach the trapping grounds, and time was their opponent. Summer had passed, and the colors of autumn had invaded the leaves along the riverbank, bringing bright yellow patches to what had once been a solid deep green. They passed Fort Atkinson, near Council Bluffs, again without stopping. "Here's where a good many have deserted," John explained to Clara. "We need all the men we've got if we mean to see the Rockies before deep snow."

They passed Blackbird Hill, the resting place of an Omaha chief who had died of smallpox and was buried astride his horse overlooking the river. And they passed the grave of

Sergeant Charles Floyd, who had died in the late summer of 1804, on the Lewis and Clark Expedition. The men told many stories of earlier expeditions.

Clara shot her Hawken daily and learned to cook various plants and meat, and to recognize plants that were commonly used for food.

She knew she must master Indian sign language if she wished to receive respect from the tribes she wanted to trade with. It taxed her mind and brought from her hands and arms a coordination of movement that she did not know she possessed. John kept at her steadily to practice with him and to gain as great a facility as possible. Learning the various dialects and languages of the tribes would be impossible, John told her, but they all understood sign.

As the keelboats continued their journey upriver, the *voyageurs'* skin grew darker from the sun. Their hair was long, and they had taken to wearing only breechclouts, in the Indian style, for comfort and ease of motion. Except for the difference in facial features, they looked much like the people they were going to trade with.

As they journeyed, Clara saw a vast change in the landscape. The heavy woods that had reached from the river to the surrounding hills suddenly disappeared. The valley was grassland now, and the air had become dry. On the rocky cliffs along the river only scattered, low-growing shrubs and gnarled yellow pine and juniper could survive.

Game had become scarce since the cover along the river had grown less dense, and the few deer and elk found in the evenings coming down for water were never enough to feed the entire expedition. There could be no stopping for a major hunt, as time was passing quickly.

For the first time in her life Clara felt real hunger. The fall had been unusually warm on the plains, the hot temperatures persisting through September and well into October. Most of the game, John told her, had likely moved out of the lowlands along the river and farther west into the Black Hills, where it was higher and cooler. Plants no longer made good food, for their root systems had dried hard as wood, and one expended more energy in digging them than could be gained back from nourishment.

The men complained continuously as they pulled and sweated to move the boats upstream, their bodies aching and their stomachs empty. They might have complained more but for Clara and John, who ate almost nothing so that there would be more food for those who moved the boats. Clara had told one of the *voyageurs* to eat the food himself one night when he had offered her a last piece of venison. The result was a marked increase in spirit among the men, and they had traveled an additional three miles each day during that week.

Another week went by, and Clara's body began to adjust gradually to the poor diet, though she noticed her health in general to be suffering. She knew she was in no danger of starvation, but a full stomach was something she would not know until they either reached the Mandan villages or found game. She and John now walked to ease the load on the boats, and her feet soon became swollen and sore. To avoid the rocks and steep cliffs that formed the river channel, they were often forced to walk far from riverbank, through steep gullies and up along ridges above the river while the *voyageurs* struggled with the tow ropes against the current. After a while the days wore together, and Clara lost track of time and distance.

Just before daybreak one morning she was awakened suddenly by John's loud shouting: "I'll be damned! I'll be a damned prairie goat!"

John was still whooping when Clara felt an odd sensation creep over her. The ground beneath her was moving, and a steady rumble nearby grew louder and louder.

"Buffalo!" she told herself. "At last! Buffalo!"

John had told her she would know when they were near, whether she could see them or not. The ground under the great herds trembled for miles around, as if thunder beneath the earth were causing the ground to tremble. Now she could hear them grunting and could see the mass of them moving into the river some distance upstream. It was unbelievable. She had never heard or felt anything like it before. The herds were beginning their fall migrations into the southern grasslands.

By now the *voyageurs* had forgotten their weakness and were dancing and singing around fires that had sprung up everywhere. Clara, John, and a few *voyageurs* hurried to the top of a rise overlooking the river. The pink and scarlet of dawn streaked the eastern sky, and clear blue showed above it. Through the river channel surged a mass of brown, shaggy bodies, and as the sun crept up over the hills to reveal the vast open land, Clara could only stare. To the north and west, as far as the eye could see, was a river of buffalo.

"This isn't possible," she said to John.

John chuckled. "Oh, yes it is. Buffalo from sunup to sundown. Maybe longer. We might as well find us a stray cow or two and eat good," he suggested. "We'll get nowheres today, and to my way of thinkin' it's best we figure on stayin' here two or three days. This here's a sizable herd."

Clara shook her head in disbelief. "You mean there are more buffalo than we can see now?"

John nodded. "They'll keep comin' for a long time. Nothin' we can do but wait."

Though everyone was eager to eat, John ordered the crew to be patient and wait until the wind was right to make their kills. If the smell of blood reached the herd they would likely stampede and there would be no telling which way they would decide to run. With a herd that size, death would be a sure thing.

Finally in late morning the wind changed, and they took three dry cows and a young bull. John advised Clara to wait and shoot her first buffalo another time. The first shot had to be fatal; a wounded buffalo would incite a stampede in little time.

For three days they feasted on buffalo while they waited for the herd to cross. Clara never tired of watching the giant beasts make their way across the open prairie to the river, filling themselves with grass until the entire area was denuded. She watched with fascination as bulky calves butted at their mothers' udders for milk, and huge herd bulls with massive horns all made their way out into the water, frothing from their mouths and bellowing in low, contented sounds. It was an endlessly moving, flowing brown sea, and it made Clara dizzy if she watched any one spot in the herd for any length of time.

In late afternoon of the third day, the entire expedition gathered on a low rise overlooking the river, crowding each other for a better view. "Sacred medicine," John said to Clara, pointing down to the edge of the herd. "A white buffalo. Sacred to all Indians."

Clara could not keep her jaw from hanging. He was pointing at a large white bull with only a tuft of black hair atop its head. John gave strict orders to the grumbling *voyageurs* to keep all rifles down and not even consider going out on a chase that would surely stampede the herd. The skin of a white buffalo was valuable, and John knew the *voyageurs* would fight to the death over the animal if he gave them the chance. Clara watched until the unusual buffalo had crossed the river and became a white speck amid the dark sea far off to the south.

Again that night, Clara could not sleep. The incessant noise and tromping made rest impossible. It was late when she got up from her bedroll and made her way out of the sleeping camp and to the knoll above the river. The evening breeze was cool, and a near full moon shone down.

"As peaceful as you could ask for, ain't it?"

Clara looked up and saw John standing nearby. He strolled over and sat down in the grass beside her.

"Nothin' like a warm night just before the snows hit," he added. "A night like this has got a special feel to it."

Clara nodded in agreement. "I can hardly wait until we get moving again. There's so much to see out here. And I hope you're wrong about snow."

"Can't you feel it?" John asked. "Could come tonight."

Clara gave him a push sideways and laughed. "Don't tease me, John Huston." She pretended to club him with her fist. "We've got too far to travel yet before the snow comes."

Laughing, John pushed himself back upright. "It'll be a good spell yet before the snow sets in tight," he said. "But the early, wet storms could start any time. It depends on the wind."

"The wind," Clara said, with a teasing laugh of her own. "You ought to know a lot about wind, since you blow off a lot yourself."

John laughed, then looked into her eyes. "I never knew a woman could be so pretty," he told her, moving closer.

Clara let him kiss her, a gentle kiss at first that quickly became passionate. She was not surprised; she had known this would happen sooner or later. She had noticed a subtle change in him over the last few months. His eyes had grown softer each time he looked at her, and his actions had become more refined and gentlemanly, as if the manners of his early life in New England were resurfacing. As his kiss began to press her backward, she stiffened and he drew back.

"I'm sorry, John," Clara said. "It's just not right. It's not you, understand. It's me."

John took a deep breath. "I'm sorry. I guess I've been too long in the hills."

"John, understand, I like you very much. I owe you a great deal. I think you're very attractive. It's just, well, I don't know. I can't explain it."

"I'm too old," John said in disgust.

"Nonsense," Clara said quickly. "I see you as a valued friend."

"Has LaCroix been bothering you again?"

"No." Clara shook her head. "He hasn't spoken to me since the whipping."

"He stares at you, though," John said.

"Yes, but I've noticed he watches you closely, too. As if he thinks you're going to steal me from him."

"Then it is LaCroix, in a way, isn't it?" John asked. "You just don't want LaCroix and me slittin' each other's throats."

Clara thought for a moment. "Yes," she finally answered. "We don't need that kind of thing."

"Well," said John, "I'd get rid of him tonight but for the fact he knows Kainah Blackfoot tongue. Speaks it better than French, I sometimes think."

"How did he learn it so well?" Clara asked.

"He took a Kainah woman for his own for a spell, long enough to learn the tongue right well. I wish there was anybody else who could talk Kainah even half as good. I'd sure like to be rid of LaCroix."

"How long do we have to keep him?" Clara asked.

"Just long enough to get ourselves established," John answered. "Once we get to be friends with even a small band, we can send him a hikin' back to St. Louis. That's what he talks about, bein' in a card game in St. Louis."

Clara was silent a moment. She felt uneasy about trusting LaCroix with helping to establish the business. "If LaCroix thought he had finally lost me to you," she said, "would he turn the Blackfeet against us?"

John sat up a bit. "Now that you bring it to mind, I can see how we'd have more trouble than we could handle if LaCroix turned against us. Maybe we'd best take our chances with sign talk and send LaCroix off now. The Mandan villages are less than a month upriver. I'll see if he don't want to stay behind and take up with one of their women for the winter."

"Maybe it would be best if we wait until we reach the Mandans to tell him the news," Clara suggested. "We need no more trouble than we already have."

John took Clara to the camp and left her to think about the problem of ridding the expedition of LaCroix and about the arduous task of getting as near Kainah Blackfoot country as possible before winter made travel impossible. As the night wore on and she grew more restless, it occurred to her that getting this far would soon seem to have been the simplest part of the journey. All the planning she had done before leaving St. Louis was now going to have to be redone. Instead of taking the *Rosebud* and the *River Otter* on past the Mandan villages and then up the Yellowstone, it would be faster to trade with the Mandans for horses and ride cross-country through the northern edge of the Black Hills. A drought had made river travel a nightmare, with the *voyageurs* constantly pulling the boats off sandbars and snags. The closer they got to the mountains, the less water would be in the rivers and the time would surely come when they could no longer navigate.

A few days farther upriver, Clara was again sitting on a hill overlooking the countryside, remembering what John had said about securing horses from the Mandan. They would need very good horses that could take hard travel and little rest. Such animals were valuable to Indians whose success at hunting and warfare depended on them. Clara was worried about trading many of their most expensive items to the Mandan for horses before even reaching Kainah Blackfoot country, where their main trading efforts were to take place. Clara knew that all the tribes in the Plains and Rocky mountain regions had been trading and bartering for centuries, and they all recognized a good or a bad deal when they saw one. All the deals Clara offered would have to be good ones. The Indians knew what their furs were worth to these white-skinned people who came into their lands from so far away.

Early that morning, John joined her with a twinkle in his eye and her Hawken in one hand.

"Get your rifle ready to shoot," he said, handing her the gun. "We're goin' on a little huntin' trip."

Puzzled, Clara stood up. "We've got enough meat on the boats now to last us three more days."

"I didn't say we were after meat," John said, the twinkle even more evident in his eye.

They left the men hauling the boats upriver and made their way into the line of rugged hills that rose up from the river bottom. As they walked away, Clara noticed LaCroix glaring after John. His eyes then went to Clara, making her shudder, for his look was wild.

"That man is growing more insane with each passing day," Clara remarked to John as they walked. "I just hope things don't blow sky high before we reach the Mandan."

They walked through the hills for nearly an hour before

they topped a rise below which grazed a small herd of buffalo. John pointed to an isolated grove of yellow pine that stood on a bluff nearly a mile distant.

"Meet me there at those trees about midday," he told her. "I'll circle off left so that the two of us can cover more country."

Clara looked at him, frowning. "John, you still haven't told me what we're doing out here. Who or what are we looking for?"

The twinkle returned to John's eyes. "Just walk toward the hills and keep your eyes on the countryside as you walk. If you still don't know by the time you reach the pines, I'll tell you when I see you there." With that he turned and started off at a brisk walk.

Clara didn't know how to respond. It wasn't like John to embark on a foolish excursion, especially when time was so precious. With a shrug, she began to walk toward the distant trees, resigned to the fact that John considered this important.

The morning was pleasant, with a light breeze that cooled the skin and made the walk invigorating. The hills were covered with low, creeping juniper intermixed with lush grass that had cured a golden brown in the frost of the early mornings. Overhead a flock of geese formed a V in the sky, honking loudly as they made their yearly southern flight. Though they were quite high, Clara could see their outline against the pale blue of the sky, their floating motion carrying them through the sun's haze and into the vast distance. The meadowlark, so common on these plains, with its bright yellow breast and black throat markings, had already migrated, as had the tender-throated mourning dove and the dainty lark bunting that sang its shrill song and performed its aerial suspension tricks above the tall grass.

But still evident in great numbers along the ridges were the large prairie hens that fed on the coarse, pungent sage. They stayed in these hills all winter and were a blessing to travelers, for their meat was delicate and moist, as Clara had learned during an evening meal downriver. A flock of them flew up in front of her, and she watched their noisy flight over the crest of a hill and down into a meadow beyond, where a herd of buffalo grazed. Clara's eyes traveled to the edge of the herd, and her mouth dropped open in surprise at the sight of what John had taken her out to find, a prize that would surely bring them many fine horses.

A white buffalo.

Clara felt that this must be the same white buffalo they had seen crossing the river downstream. The markings were the same—a solid milky white with a black tuft of hair between the horns. He looked even larger now than he had when he walked among the immense herd.

She remembered the stories the men had told as they sat around the fires after seeing the white bull. Clara had learned that the white buffalo was a rare and priceless symbol to these Indians, and warriors had traveled thousands of miles in search of one after hearing that a herd had passed by with a speck of white in it. Battles had raged over robes made from the skin of a white bison, and Clara knew that bringing down this white bull could well mean success in acquiring quality horses from the Mandan.

Gathering her thoughts, Clara dropped to a prone position in the grass, looking down from the ridge to where the buffalo grazed below. She could feel the breeze as it touched her back and her hair, hoping it would not change directions and send her scent down into the peaceful herd. The white bull had moved into the herd, and Clara would need to wait for the right moment to shoot.

Clara lay for a time, impatient and eager for the bull to emerge from the herd. She knew her aim would have to be precise, for the lead ball would have to enter low and behind the shoulder and penetrate the heart. Any other shot would send the buffalo scrambling off to run for miles before going down, or not going down at all.

Suddenly the small herd began to move away from her, their heads raised in her direction and their tails curled up over their backs. Many were grunting loudly and began to swing their heads back and forth in irritation. Clara, in complete bewilderment, rose to her knees. Surely they could not have seen her, for she hadn't moved or made any sound. Nor could they have smelled her, for the wind had not changed directions. Feeling an odd sensation, she turned to look back over her shoulder. There, little more than an arm's length away, his cold eyes staring at her in curiosity, stood a wolf.

5

CLARA SHRIEKED IN FRIGHT and jumped to her feet. She brought her Hawken up and leveled it at the pair of yellow eyes that had startled her. The wolf barked loudly and backed away from her, moving quickly toward his pack, which was strung out along the ridge stalking the buffalo, their ears flattened tight against their heads.

Still dazed from the startling encounter, Clara stared for a time at the wolves, unable to move, and then turned to see the herd in a dead run, pounding headlong out of the grassy bottom and around the hill. The white bull was lost among coats of brown and black with no chance for a shot. In sudden fury she turned the rifle on the wolves, which had regrouped a short distance away and continued to stalk her threateningly.

Clara took a deep breath and watched the herd crest a small hill near the trees where she was to meet John. They had slowed down to a trot. As she watched them move out of sight over a far rise, her excitement returned, for the last of the herd disappeared at a walk. If she approached slowly and cautiously, she might still stand a chance of acquiring the prized white pelt.

Clara turned to see the wolves a short distance away, staring at her. After the expedition had reached the plains, the *voyageurs* had told her about the packs of wolves that trailed men pulling the tow ropes. Prairie wolves, the *voyageurs* called them, intelligent and curious brothers to the large timber wolves farther west in the mountains. The slow and weak members of the buffalo herd were their main source of food. Clara knew they would surely follow her when she began to stalk the herd, and she would have little chance of success with the competition they would provide.

She knew she would have to kill one wolf with a single shot—a very careful shot—but the wolves were impossible to see when they ducked into the tall grass.

Recalling a lesson she had learned from John, she started down the hill, watching the wolves closely as they began to follow. A large black male moved out in front of the pack, and one by one the others took their places in line. As leader, the black was obeyed without question. If she could get him, Clara knew the rest would mill about in confusion and make no effort to follow her farther. Quickly she ran down over the brow of the hill, momentarily out of the wolves' sight, and hid in the tall grass. The wolves quickly appeared at the top of the hill, their large ears darting about, their noses testing the air.

The lead wolf moved from one position to another, whoofing at the others, who crept through the tall grass in an effort to find Clara without endangering themselves. Patience was essential now, and she carefully brought her Hawken to her shoulder, parting the grass stalks slowly with the barrel. Slowly she raised herself to her knees, taking aim at the pack leader.

Clara sighted down the rifle barrel at the ears and head that stuck up above the golden grass. The head would be too small a target; she would have to rise up a little more to see the body. She quickly rose to a crouch and put her finger against the trigger. For an instant, as he detected Clara, the wolf froze. Clara fired, and the wolf let out a high-pitched yelp and began a headlong run through the grass at breakneck speed, tumbling and twisting as the life left his body.

Clara ran forward as the rest of the pack dispersed and sank to her knees next to the wolf. Tears flooded her eyes. The shot had been well placed, but why did such a noble animal have to

FIRECLOUD

die? These creatures clung to life so tightly, struggling to survive until the very last heartbeat.

Looking up, she saw John some distance away approaching at a run. She composed herself and reloaded. Then she stood and waited for him, staring down at the dead wolf. Her heart was still pounding, and the sickness was still with her.

John stopped in front of her and paused for breath. "I'm a sight happier to see it was wolves you've been shootin' at and not Sioux," he said.

"Sioux? What do you mean?"

John was casting glances in all directions, his eyes holding an intensity that Clara had never seen before. He pointed behind him, from where he had just come. "There's been a battle back there like hell rose to the top," he said. "Sioux and Mandan mostly, it appears. But there's a mess of Blackfoot arrows scattered around. Can't figure that this far out of the mountains. There's a mess of Indian blood over there. We'd best get back to the boats. Now!"

"A battleground?" Clara said.

"It's nothin' you'd care to see," John answered quickly. "Both sides got their dead picked up mostly. But the blood still ain't all dried, and there's hands and arms and such scattered."

"My God!"

"Indian warfare ain't pretty by no sight. And when you mix Blackfeet and Sioux, there's enough hate to boil a pot without a fire. Now we'd best head back."

"What about the buffalo, John?" Clara asked. "I saw the white buffalo."

John's eyes became wide. "What?"

"Isn't that the secret you wanted to show me this mornin'?" Clara asked.

"No." He shook his head. "I spotted some bighorn sheep at first light down by the river. They ran up here, and I thought maybe you'd like to see them and maybe get one. Their meat is sweet eatin'." Then he shook his head. "You didn't see no sheep, but you saw the white bull?"

Clara nodded. "I'm pretty sure it was the same one we saw

downriver." She turned and pointed to the pine grove where they were to meet. "The herd ran up there. I might have had a good shot if it hadn't been for the wolves. Don't you think we should find him? We could sure trade for a lot of horses."

John took a deep breath. "We sure could, but is he worth your hair?"

"He's not more than fifteen minutes from here."

John looked all around them again, his eyes still filled with concern.

"We'll go to the trees," Clara suggested. "If the herd has left, we'll give up and go back to the boats."

"Follow me, then," John said. "Let's just hope them Sioux have left these parts and didn't hear you shootin' wolves."

They started off toward the pine, staying below the tops of the hills and ridges. The herd had left an easy trail to follow. The grass was trampled, and the cloven hooves had left clear imprints in the black soil. As they neared the trees, they slowed their pace to avoid alarming the herd, if it was indeed still anywhere nearby. They stopped often to listen for the sound of approaching horsemen. John explained to Clara that if the familiar sounds of the prairie birds ceased, or if a flock of sage hens or turkeys suddenly rose up out of the grass, it meant something had disturbed them and danger of some sort was most likely nearby.

They reached the grove of pine and searched the small draws and hillsides nearby. There was no sign of the herd. The trail had led to the area, but the tracks indicated to John that the herd had never settled down.

"No doubt they're still headed south," John commented. "Once they get riled, it's hard to settle them. And a pack of wolves and a rifle is enough to strain the nerves on any critter." He laughed.

As they started back, John pointed to a small trickle of water coming down a draw just below the trees. Clara nodded. "Is there a spring up there?"

John nodded and pointed. "I'd say there's a good flow right about where them thorn apple are growin', and if your thirst is anywhere near mine, you'll follow me up for a cool

FIRECLOUD

swallow before we head back to the boats."

Clara followed John up the draw toward the spring, looking out across the hills in the direction of the river, praying that no Sioux riders would appear. Suddenly, as they approached the thorn apple patch, a flash appeared in front of them.

"John!" Clara screamed.

"God A'mighty!" he yelled, aiming his rifle and firing in one motion.

Clara stood stunned and speechless, unable to move her Hawken to her shoulder, while John cursed and desperately tried to reload his Hawken. His shot had gone wild, and there, scrambling to his feet after ducking John's rifle blast, was an Indian warrior.

Clara pulled the hammer back on her Hawken as the warrior rose to a crouch. He was dressed only in moccasins and a breechclout, and his body was a mass of red and black painted stripes. The lower half of his face bore large circles of red paint, with jagged lines of black through them, and his throat was painted solid black from his ears to a deep V on his chest. His muscles stood out like layers of steel over his trim frame, and the fingers of his right hand gripped a large knife.

For a long moment the warrior and Clara stood facing each other while John rammed the lead ball and patch down the barrel of his rifle. The warrior made no move toward them, and Clara noticed that his left leg was wrapped with a poultice just above his left knee. His sudden movements had broken a wound open under the poultice, and blood was running in thin streams down his inner thigh.

"Wait!" John shouted. "Don't shoot him unless he comes at us. He's Blackfoot! By all that's crazy in this world, he's Kainah Blackfoot!"

"How can you tell?"

"That's what you've got to learn yet," John said. "Any trader worth his beaver has got to tell one Indian from the rest. Those that don't can plan on losin' their hair before first snow hits."

"I just want to know how you can tell," Clara said.

"The cut of his moccasins," John answered. "The style of

his hair; the way he paints up for war; the way he wears his feathers in his hair. There's a lot of things to look for, and you've got to know 'em all." Then he pointed to the warrior's injured leg. "Appears to me he caught an arrow or a lance and has set to patch himself up."

Clara was intrigued by the warrior. For all his ferocious appearance, he retained a great measure of appeal. His muscles were sleek and trim, and he was the image of power and savagery. He reminded her of the bold black wolf she had killed, in that he was clearly unimpressed by the fact that he was facing a powerful weapon. He refused to be intimidated, and Clara was impressed by this.

"He knows I could kill him in an instant," she remarked to John. "Why doesn't he turn and run?"

"No true warrior will run from a fight, no matter the odds against him. This one knows better than to just light into us and get his head blowed off. But he's not about to back down, either."

"Why would he challenge us like this?" Clara asked.

"It's a matter of honor with them," John answered. "If we up and shoot him standin' still like he is, he dies a proud death. Then, in his eyes, we'd have lost our honor and would have to live our lives out as cowards. He goes to the world beyond to live happily as a brave warrior, and we've got no choice but to die in shame and pine away forever."

"You mean he wants me to shoot him?"

"No. He just wants us to know where he stands. But don't get no notions about lowering your rifle. He'll be on us like flies on a carcass."

"What'll we do?"

John took a deep breath. "If we can make him see we mean him no harm, we'll like as not all get something out of this. The way I see it, he's a long ways from his people without a horse or food. I'd just bet we can make a deal with him to take us to the mountains to trade some furs with the Blackfeet." He looked at Clara, and his grin broadened. "You tell him, Clara. Now's a good time to use your sign language. I'll keep my rifle on him. Tell him we're his friends, not his enemies."

FIRECLOUD

Clara stood for a time and stared at the warrior.

"Tell him." John nudged her. "Don't go gettin' scared now."

"I'm not afraid of him, John."

Clara continued to look at the warrior, who had not moved from his position with the knife raised as if ready to do battle, rigidly still, glaring at her, in the crouched position he had first assumed. His muscles remained taut, though his eyes showed that his leg wound tortured him, poised as he was. Never before had Clara seen such courage. Never had she seen the wild, untamed honor of a warrior ready to fight, to the death if need be.

"You'd best tell him we're friends," John advised, "or he's apt to leap at us. He's about out of patience."

Slowly, Clara shifted the Hawken to the crook of her left arm, where she held it a moment while the warrior watched her closely. Then she raised her right hand, palm out and fingers skyward, in the sign for peace. Carefully, she laid the rifle down and began to make sign to the warrior. Never faltering, she told him that they had come up the river in boats and that she and the man beside her had come into the hills to hunt the bighorn sheep. She told the warrior they had not come to fight and that they would take him back to the boats with them to treat his leg and give him meat. Her movements were convincing and her face sincere. She saw the warrior relax slightly, and his eyes lost their hard glare. Still, he did not lower the knife.

Clara turned to John. "Did he understand me?"

John nodded. "It's just gettin' him to believe it. He's been in one hell-hard battle, it appears to me, and it's most likely hard for him to believe someone still ain't out to take his hair."

Clara made more sign to the warrior: "If you understand me, you know we do not wish to fight you. When you point your knife at me, it makes me believe that you wish to fight us. Is this true?"

The warrior looked at Clara for a moment, then shook his head and lowered the knife.

69

"Tell him we will take him back to his people," John told Clara.

Clara made more sign to the warrior: "We wish to travel to your lands, to make friends with your people. We want to take you with us. Do you wish to go?"

The warrior nodded and put his knife into a buckskin sheath in his breechclout. Then he looked at John, his face puzzled, and asked in sign, "Why is it you have a woman to speak for you?"

John shifted from one foot to another and answered the warrior in sign: "No woman has ever owned me. This woman is from where the sun rises each day. You are the first of your people she has ever made sign to. I believe she does very well."

The warrior looked at Clara in amazement. He made more sign to John: "This woman is not of the Indian peoples; this I know. But she does not seem to be of the Long Knife blood. She is not afraid of these lands, as the Long Knife women are. Why does she wear skins from the deer, and not the colored cloth that the Long Knife women wear?"

"She takes this land as her own," John explained to him. "That is why she is not afraid of you."

The warrior's eyes began to study her, to try to understand. Just as Clara had, for the first time, seen the true, untamed warrior of the plains, he was seeing, for the first time, a woman such as he had never seen before. The women of his people were strong and often as brave as the men, but never were they so bold as to speak up to a man.

"I am Nighthawk of the Black Horse band of Kainah Blackfeet," he told them in sign. His movements were rapid, and Clara had trouble following him. Though she had practiced long and hard perfecting the motions of sign language, she knew that following someone who had talked in sign for many years would be extremely difficult. It would take her years to perfect the language.

"I couldn't follow all of it," she told John. "He's so fast."

"He just told you his name," John said, mild surprise evident in his voice. "That's a rare thing."

"What is his name?" Clara asked eagerly.

FIRECLOUD

"Nighthawk. And he says he is of the Black Horse band of Kainah Blackfeet."

Unashamedly, Clara made sign to Nighthawk: "When you make your sign, could you move your hands more slowly? It is hard for me to follow as I have not spoken with my hands before."

Nighthawk nodded. He began again to speak to Clara in sign: "Why does a woman of the Long Knife blood travel to these lands?"

"I have come to trade with your people," she answered. "I have brought many things from my homeland to give to the Kainah Blackfeet in exchange for the fur of the beaver."

Nighthawk nodded slowly. "Many come into our lands to take the beaver furs. Many of these Long Knives have died. The Kainah Blackfoot people do not want these Long Knives in their lands."

"I have heard about the trouble between your people and those who have come into these lands," Clara said. "And I am sorry for that. We do not wish trouble. We only wish to trade with you and be friends with you."

Nighthawk nodded. "I believe you have truth in your heart. You could have shot me with your thunder stick, but did not. You could have taken my scalp to show to your countrymen, but you did not. I believe you have come in peace. But it will not be so easy to make others believe this."

"We have presents for all whom we meet," Clara said. "We desire peace with all Indian peoples."

"That will be a hard thing to do," Nighthawk told Clara. "The different Indian tribes have been at war with one another since the beginning of time. If you are friends with one tribe, another tribe may not accept you."

John then made sign to Nighthawk. "You are in Sioux lands with a wound from battle with the Sioux. How is it you come so far to make war when it is so near to the cold moons?"

"We did not come to make war," Nighthawk answered. "We came to trade. I and others of the Black Horse band brought white skins from the mountain goat and feathers from the white-headed eagle to trade with the Dirt Lodge people, whom the Long Knives call the Mandan and the Hidatsa. We bring skins and feathers and other things they do not have here, and trade for corn and melons, which we do not have. We would not have fought with the Sioux but for a white buffalo."

Clara and John looked at each other. John asked Nighthawk, "Did you see a white buffalo out here?"

"We came to look for one," Nighthawk answered. "Five suns past a young Mandan woman told of seeing a white buffalo at the river while she was bathing. Many of the Dirt Lodge people joined us to find and chase down the Spirit Buffalo." Then Nighthawk pointed to the west, where John had seen the battleground. "That same day we were attacked by many Sioux. I do not know who won the fight, for an arrow went through my leg and into my horse, pinning me to him. My horse carried me for a long ways until he fell and died not far from this place. I have remained here until this day, when I began to find my way back to the Kainah."

"Let us take you back with us on our boats, which await nearby on the river," Clara suggested. "We have plenty of food. You must be hungry after five days without a good meal. You cannot hunt on that leg."

"I can hunt," Nighthawk said quickly. "There is nothing the matter with my leg. Do not think I cannot care for myself." He moved a short distance away and lifted a bow and a quiver of arrows out of the grass. "Yes, I can hunt and find a horse and get back to my people." He paused for a moment. "But I will go with you to the lands of the Kainah Blackfoot."

Clara was glad for his decision. She wanted to be his friend. As she watched him prepare to leave, she noticed that his eyes fell on her frequently. She knew they would have much to say to each other in the future.

6

NIGHTHAWK ACCEPTED NO ASSISTANCE during the walk to the camp on the riverbank. Clara wondered whether he had an extremely high tolerance to pain or whether he was just extremely proud and did not care to have anyone concerned about him. He made the long, grueling walk back without speaking again of the fight with the Sioux, walking with only a slight limp.

To Clara he appeared somewhat unsure of his decision, as if he had too hastily made the choice to accompany them into his land and to the Black Horse band of his people. She knew that he did not trust John, and being Blackfoot made him more uneasy. Clara tried to make him feel comfortable with them. But he spoke very little and that was only to point out Sioux war sign or comment on where he was going, and if he would be welcomed.

John told the *voyageurs* that Nighthawk would lead them to Kainah Blackfoot country, but they expressed concern about the remainder of the journey through the Sioux territory in which they were now camped. They, too, had seen Sioux war sign along the river, and Nighthawk's leg wound told them there had been conflict. That meant the fever for blood was running high among the Sioux. The presence of a Kainah

Blackfoot warrior among them would surely cause a fight if they encountered any war or hunting parties. Though the men's concern was justified, John convinced them that they were not much more than a week away from the Mandan villages and that they were likely to meet Mandans rather than Sioux. He also told them that they would pass by the Arikara villages at night, so as not to encounter that unusual and unpredictable tribe. This tribe, usually called Rees, lived downstream from the Mandan and Hidatsa and were a major source of trouble for fur trading parties. If the expedition could reach the Mandan without encountering either Sioux or Arikara parties, there was little chance of trouble along the river.

Nighthawk seemed comfortable only when he was around Clara. The curious eyes of the *voyageurs* followed him everywhere, and even John Huston seemed uneasy in his presence. John had noticed that Clara could hardly keep away from the Kainah warrior; she had even talked him into letting her shoot his bow. John shrugged all this off with the comment that it would help her to get to know Indians and their nature better, thus making her a better fur trader. It was easy to see, also, that Nighthawk enjoyed her company. He seemed pleased to speak with her in sign language and to tell her about Indian life and customs. Nighthawk and Clara began at once to spend most of their time together.

By the third day, Clara could not take her eyes off the strong warrior, who seemed to enjoy her company a great deal. Though the nights were cool and the frost stayed in the ground until the sun was quite high, she was always warm with the thought of Nighthawk. He was like no other man she had ever met, with his strong spirit and keen awareness of nature. He was kind and considerate, with none of the arrogance of the men she had known before. Instead, he showed respect for men and women alike, and seemed not to resent Clara's position as a leader of the expedition. He found it fascinating that she should be strong enough to influence men as she had. When she told him that she had been without a mother for

FIRECLOUD

many years and had assisted her father with the family business, he became even more intrigued. One evening they wandered away from camp, and he gave Clara a surprise.

"You and the Long Knife called John are the chiefs of these men," he said. "And you are the first chief."

Clara looked at him with astonishment. He had spoken in English.

"And your name, in the Long Knife tongue, is Clara," he added, a broad grin reaching from ear to ear.

"How could you have picked up our language in so short a time?" Clara asked, still unable to believe what she had heard.

The smile still broad, Nighthawk answered, "It is not so short a time. My mother taught me the Long Knife tongue when I was a small child. You see, she was a Shoshone, the wife of a Long Knife trader, before my father killed him and took her as captive into his lodge. I can remember some of the Long Knife tongue." He supplemented his speech with sign talk.

"That is amazing," she said. "Then you are not full-blood Kainah Blackfoot?"

"It is true," he answered, "I am not totally of Kainah blood. But my father was Kainah, and in the ways of the Indian peoples, a child is claimed by the people he lives with, whether or not his mother is of other Indian blood. Since my father is of Kainah blood, I am considered Kainah also."

Clara learned more from Nighthawk about his past. His mother, Shoshone, had married an English fur trader who had ventured down from Hudson's Bay into the northern Rocky Mountains. A few years later, a war party of Kainah Blackfeet, led by Nighthawk's father, surprised a group of English trappers. They spared the young Shoshone, and Nighthawk's father took her as a slave to his lodge. She later taught Nighthawk to speak Shoshone and English. Nighthawk's father was a fearless leader of the Kainah until he was killed during a raid on a Salish village. Before his death he had fathered another son by a Kainah wife, a son who had grown up to be Nighthawk's bitter rival.

"Soon after my birth, a half brother was born to my father and his main wife, his sits-beside-him wife," Nighthawk explained to Clara. "He is named Black Owl, and there is no fondness between us."

Conflict, Clara learned, had developed between the two at a very early age and had developed into bitter hatred by the time they had reached early manhood. Nighthawk, although born of a slave woman, had grown up to be even braver than the son born of the higher union. Though Black Owl would someday follow in his father's footsteps and become a great leader among the Kainah, it was Nighthawk who always won the foot races, shot his bow with the greatest accuracy, and excelled at all the games that helped a boy become a warrior of honor and courage. Nighthawk's triumphs rankled, and Black Owl did his best to discredit his half brother's achievements and relegate him to the role of slave woman's son, entitled to nothing.

"As a young warrior, I was first to count coup against an enemy," Nighthawk told Clara. "This angered Black Owl deeply. He told the council of elders that I lied and that it was he who struck first. Others saw it, but when the council asked them who struck first, they would only shake their heads and say that it was not clear to them. They did not want to anger Black Owl, for he will one day be the Kainah chief. Because of this, Black Owl has gained much influence with the council. He has made himself very powerful."

"But doesn't the council know otherwise?" Clara asked. "If you are stronger and can run faster, and fight just as bravely in battle, can't they see that you would make a better leader than he?"

"Black Owl has given them reason to doubt my competence," Nighthawk answered. "He has made the village believe that even if I am strong at times, I will not stay strong. He tells them that my children will be weak and not of good Kainah stock because my blood is mixed with Shoshone and white as well as Kainah. This is not true, for I have no white blood, but he has made the people of the village believe him."

"How can they believe him?" Clara asked. "They all know

you have no white blood in you."

"He has told them that the Long Knife husband my mother once had made her blood impure with his man-part when they lay together. Black Owl is slowly turning the village against me. Because of this, no young women in the village will look at me."

Clara shook her head in disbelief. It was sad enough that Nighthawk had incurred his half brother's jealousy but for him to have endured personal humiliation because of Black Owl's lies seemed entirely unreasonable. Looking at Nighthawk, Clara wondered how the young women of his village could shun him. He presented as fine a figure as any man she had ever seen.

"Why do you stay with the Kainah Blackfeet?" she asked him. "Why don't you go and live with your mother's people?"

"I will not dishonor myself by running from Black Owl and those who believe his false tales. I will stay and show all those of the Black Horse band that I am far more powerful than my half brother, and that his evil deeds cannot destroy me. Before my mother died two winters past, I told her I would gain honor in the village, for myself and for my sister."

"You have a sister?"

Nighthawk nodded. "She is called Spring Bird. She was born two winters after me. She and I are very close; few women in the village will speak to her. When my father was killed, his other wives and his younger brother shunned us. After that, my mother, Spring Bird, and I lived in a lodge of our own. Now our mother is dead, too."

"You should have left long ago," Clara said. "Anything would have been better than living as outcasts."

Nighthawk shook his head. "I cannot say what life is like in the country from which you come, but it is not easy for a Kainah to leave his home. It would be dangerous for us to leave. If we were to meet an enemy war party, I would not be able to defend my sister, and we would be killed. You see, the Kainah Blackfeet have many enemies. The tribes of the

Blackfoot nation have fought bitterly with many different Indian peoples, and all these peoples come into the Blackfoot lands to do battle and steal horses. For now it is best if we stay with the band."

"I am glad that we found you and that you are going back to the Kainah Blackfeet with us," Clara said. "John will be pleased to hear that you speak English."

"I cannot speak English to you when we return to the camp," Nighthawk said quickly. "No one must know I have told you my past. We must speak in sign, as before."

"Why?" Clara asked. "It would be so much easier."

"The other chief, John Huston, does not like us to spend so much time together. I believe he would like to have you for his own."

Clara was not surprised at Nighthawk's perception. He watched things in camp a great deal and said little to anyone but Clara. "Don't worry about John," she said.

"It would be no good to make trouble," Nighthawk said. "John Huston does not like me. I am not sure that he would cause trouble, but he does not like me to be with you. And there is one other Long Knife, the one they call LaCroix, whose eyes say he owns you. He is a dangerous man."

"Pay no attention to LaCroix," Clara said. "He does what he is told. He and John hate each other, so they will not side with each other on anything. Besides, we plan to leave LaCroix at the Mandan villages and go on without him."

"We have not yet reached the Mandan," Nighthawk remarked. "If there is trouble, I will stand alone, because I am an outsider. Even if they do not agree among themselves on most matters, they will not side with me against one another. No, I will speak no more English for now."

As they walked back to camp together, Clara wondered what difficulties they would face. Unlike the proper men of New England, who remained civil even in competition for a woman or in arguments about business, these men were straightforward and unrelenting. No one counted to ten before firing out here. Out here there were no rules of order, no

FIRECLOUD

laws of conduct that everyone followed. Women took their chances in the wilderness, and she had earned her place as leader of the expedition. But she was still a woman.

After the evening meal, Clara was cleaning the metal pots and plates when LaCroix approached her. He had picked an opportune time. John was off hunting, and Clara knew he was avoiding her as much as possible. Nighthawk had gone by himself to a hill to say his nightly prayers. Now, as LaCroix advanced on her, Clara saw the strange glint in his eyes.

"The lady, she is without company," LaCroix began. "Surely I can make the night complete for you. Yes?"

"I would rather be by myself, Jacques," Clara told him. "I have many things to do before we leave tomorrow."

"Oh, but I can help you," LaCroix insisted. His eyes opened huge and round, and he held his hands up in front of him with the fingers spread, as if he had just conceived a brilliant idea. "Yes, I could be of great service to you."

"I don't need your help."

LaCroix rubbed a hand through his unkempt beard, a crooked smile appearing on his face. "No, I insist." He stepped forward. "A man must do all he can for his woman."

Clara looked directly at him and said, "Jacques, I can accomplish more work by myself. I'm sure you have things to take care of also."

The smile faded from LaCroix's lips, and his eyes narrowed a bit. "You don't want my help?"

"No, Jacques."

"Ah, but my she-cat, I wish to help you. It is my job. No? Is it not what I was hired to do?"

"Your job is to help John organize the men, Jacques. You command the *River Otter* and make sure it is always in good sailing condition. You are to be our interpreter with the Blackfeet. You have a lot to do, I'd say, and I don't think you have time to stay by my side each minute."

LaCroix's eyes turned to hard slits. "Yes, but the Blackfoot, he is by your side each minute. He was not hired to help you. I was. No?"

Clara took a deep breath. "Jacques, listen to me. You were hired to do what John and I tell you to do. Now, I am telling you that I do not need your assistance at this moment. Do you understand?"

LaCroix stood staring at her through his hard eyes. After a time his eyes traveled from her face to her breasts, standing firm under her doeskin dress. The smile returned to his face. "You are very beautiful, my she-cat," he said, almost under his breath. "I am sure you must be tired of waiting for me to take you as mine. You must—"

"LaCroix!" came a booming voice from behind him. John Huston walked quickly over to where the two of them stood. "Are the men finished patching that hole in the starboard side of the *River Otter*?"

LaCroix shrugged. "I do not know."

"Then find out!" John barked. "If it isn't patched tonight, you'll do the work yourself by torchlight."

LaCroix gritted his teeth. "I will see if the work is finished. And maybe you can sneak the she-cat away before the Blackfoot returns. No?"

John's face flushed, and the muscles in his neck stood out like steel cords. Advancing on LaCroix, John growled, "You stinking river rat!"

In that instant, John grabbed LaCroix by his greasy flannel shirt and tried to get his fist through LaCroix's blocking forearms. Then LaCroix tried to hit John and the two men locked together, hatred blazing in their eyes.

The two men rolled on the ground, punching, kicking, gouging each other in uncontrollable anger. As the *voyageurs* gathered around in a circle and began to bet on the outcome, she asked them to stop the fight. They only shook their heads, telling her it had to be settled between LaCroix and Huston.

The two combatants were nearly equal in strength, and neither could gain an advantage over the other. John was the smarter of the two fighters, however, and managed to push himself loose from LaCroix and stand up. As LaCroix got to his feet, off balance for an instant, John landed a crushing blow to his face, opening a deep gash that immediately spurted

FIRECLOUD

blood down over LaCroix's nose and beard. Like a bull gone mad, LaCroix charged John and threw him down again before he could react, slamming him repeatedly with one fist while he held his head down with the other. John finally got a hand up into LaCroix's face and pulled hard on the beard, ripping some of it out.

LaCroix bellowed and released John's head. John pushed himself out from under LaCroix and, as LaCroix rose to his feet, slugged him savagely in the stomach. LaCroix groaned as the air rushed from his lungs, and doubled over in pain. John then grabbed LaCroix by the hair and forced his head down, at the same time bringing his knee up into LaCroix's face. Blood sprayed from LaCroix's nose and mouth, and he slumped forward into the dirt.

Clara quickly stepped in front of John, hoping to calm him. "Quit now, John," she ordered. "He's had enough."

Some of the *voyageurs* went to LaCroix's aid, propping him up against a tree and washing the blood from his face and beard. LaCroix looked at John and Clara through dazed, hate-filled eyes.

John stepped around Clara and faced LaCroix. "You scum! If you ever say anything like that to me again, I'll kill you!" Without as much as a glance toward Clara, he picked up his rifle and left the camp.

LaCroix had caught his wind and was now on his feet, grumbling under his breath as he went off with the *voyageurs*. Some of the men were laughing, others cursing as they exchanged coins or goods to settle their bets. Clara blew her breath out in disgust and went to her fire to continue washing the dishes. When she next looked up, Nighthawk was standing nearby, his arms folded across his chest. His eyes took in the sight of the men caring for LaCroix at a distant fire, then came to rest on Clara.

"Did you see the fight?" she asked him.

He nodded and walked over to the fire. "I told you LaCroix was trouble."

"It's over," Clara said, putting some pans into the water. "There is some meat left. Eat your supper."

Nighthawk accepted her invitation and sat cross-legged near the fire. He threaded some buffalo meat on a long stick and held it over the fire.

"It is very hard for you to lead these men," he said. "They are not used to it."

Clara continued to scrub a pot she had taken from the hot water. "As soon as we get rid of LaCroix, things will settle down."

"Can you be sure?"

Clara looked over the fire at Nighthawk. "Why shouldn't they be? LaCroix is the troublemaker."

Nighthawk nodded. "That is true. But all the others are now unhappy because of the hatred between the two men. Most of them care for both John and LaCroix."

"Mostly LaCroix."

"But they listen to John, also."

"They listen to him before they listen to LaCroix." She rinsed the pot and set it aside to dry.

Nighthawk was studying her now. "Why did you journey out to these lands?" he asked her. "Why would a Long Knife woman care to lead so many men into a land such as this?"

"To keep food on my table," she answered. "And a roof over my head."

"You do not need these men to do that."

"You do not understand," Clara said. "Life is very different where I come from. Once my home was open and full of game, as this land is, and people could live off the land. But now people cross over from other countries and have children, who in turn get married and have children of their own. There are many of my people back there now and many more are born or come into the country each new year. The land is no longer open, with game everywhere, and the people must work at a job or a business to earn them money to buy the meat that once could be taken during a hunt or the wood that once could be cut with an ax. I came out here to take beaver furs back to St. Louis to sell and get money, so I can buy food and clothing back in the land I come from. Now do you understand?"

Nighthawk took the meat away from the fire and cut off a

piece with his knife. "I hear your words, but I do not understand. I have seen this thing you call money. All Long Knives carry it—round pieces of metal. But what good is it? You cannot eat it, nor can you build a lodge from it. It is good only as an ornament to be worn in the hair, on the clothing, or around the neck."

"It is traded in our land as goods," Clara explained. "Just as you trade mountain goat hides and eagle feathers to the Mandan for corn and melons."

"We trade goods for goods. The round pieces of metal are meaningless."

"You can't carry goods with you in our land," Clara said. "There are too many people. We trade with one another continually, not just during certain times of the year, as you do. We must have something easier to exchange. Money."

Nighthawk continued to study her. "And if you have much of this money, you gain honor among your people?"

Clara nodded. "Just as many horses among your people bring honor, much money brings honor to us."

"Do the women seek the honor in your land? Do the men work?"

"Mostly the men seek honor in our lands," Clara said. "Women stay home and have children."

"But you are different. You seek honor."

"My mother died when I was young. As there were no sons, I helped my father to gain honor. Now my father is dead, and I must not lose the honor he gained."

"That is good," Nighthawk nodded. "But do you believe your father would be happy if he were here today, to see what has happened?"

"He did not want me to come out here," Clara answered. "He was very unhappy when I suggested it. But he was a good and understanding father and did not want to tell me no because of his own beliefs. He warned me that it would be hard. But I am not afraid of hard things."

Nighthawk watched her finish washing the last of the plates and pots, eating the last bits of meat from the stick as his eyes traveled over her. She was strong, and far better to look at than almost any other woman, Long Knife or Indian. And her words were spoken straight and true. She cared little about impressing anyone with silly talk that had no meaning, and it had not pleased her this night to see men fighting, as it would have pleased some Indian women, and probably Long Knife women, also. This Clara was different from any other woman he had known. She could get along well in any land, and she could conquer those things that were hard.

7

THREE DAYS OF TRAVEL passed and then two in which the sky filled with clouds and sent down such a torrent of rain that they had to take refuge in some abandoned lodges along the river. Clara hardly noticed the change of weather, for she was experiencing new feelings, warm and wonderful, that were taking her to a level she had never before reached. Each day Nighthawk spent more and more time with her, laughing often, his eyes following her everywhere. He told her about the mountains and how she would enjoy life there, describing for her the land and its compelling charm. She found herself being drawn to him more and more, enjoying the closeness they shared and the energy he released within her.

At the same time she felt a certain apprehension. This warrior was beginning to control her emotions in a manner she had never before experienced. He guided her daily thoughts, her nightly longings; she seemed to be losing control over herself. It was something she did not know how to confront. As a young woman in New England, two young men had caught her fancy for a time. One had even lured her into his bed, but neither man had inspired any lasting emotion within her. But now something deep within her had risen to life. This strong warrior was taking her far beyond that which she had known before.

E. P. Murray

During the third day of driving rain, Clara sat with Nighthawk in one of the lodges, built of logs and bark, which the crew had patched against the rain. They were far more comfortable than a lean-to made of buffalo hides would have been. Looking out into the rain, Nighthawk again spoke of his past, as if searching for a connection between it and his future.

"I have listened to the words of a very old warrior in our village," he said. "He is called Aged One and has counted more winters than any other warrior in the land. My half-brother, Black Owl, considers him a silly old man and pays little attention to what he says. I think Black Owl is foolish, for Aged One has foretold many things. There is one story that even he cannot understand. The story was told to him in a vision that he does not yet know the meaning of. It is about a horse, a wild stallion called Firecloud."

"Firecloud!" Clara said, her eyes lighting up. "What about him?"

"You know of the Thunder Horse?" Nighthawk asked.

"John told me of the legend. He must be a magnificent horse."

"He is the most powerful horse that has ever lived. There could never be another stallion like that one."

"You speak as if he were some sort of god."

Nighthawk looked at her quickly. "If you had ever seen this horse, you would know my words are true. He is without equal in any land. He could have only come from the Thunder Lodge above." Nighthawk held his hand up, the index finger pointing skyward. "I have seen him beat stallions to take their mares. He makes them look like children. I have seen him run from the horse medicine men of our village, warriors who hold special powers in the catching of wild horses. Firecloud runs from them and makes fools of them by then turning back and running their horses down so that the men must jump from them or be killed. Black Owl says the horse is evil. Aged One says this is not so. He says Firecloud is a powerful horse who takes joy in making fools of hunters. It would be a great honor to own such a horse."

FIRECLOUD

Clara looked out of the lodge into the rain and said, "I will find that horse one day. And I will tame him and ride him."

Nighthawk did not seem startled by the remark. Many others had imagined themselves riding the Thunder Horse. He did not shake his head and call her foolish. Instead he smiled.

"I expected you to tell me I was crazy," Clara said.

Nighthawk continued to smile. "Whether or not you are crazy is not for me to judge. Everyone who wishes to own the Thunder Horse is considered crazy. I do know that you are very pretty."

Clara blushed, embarrassed by his sudden directness. Still aware of his smile, she asked, "Have you seen Firecloud often?"

"At the beginning of the warm moons he comes into the villages," Nighthawk answered. "He is always adding new blood to his herd, leaving behind mares, which he replaces with younger, stronger ones, taking only those that will produce the strongest foals. He goes to many Indian villages. When he comes to our village, he must always fight a big black stallion that belongs to Black Owl. Firecloud always beats the black stallion badly. That, I believe, is the main reason my half brother believes the Thunder Horse is evil."

"Has Black Owl ever tried to catch Firecloud?" Clara asked.

"Many times," Nighthawk laughed. "Each time he is made to look like a child trying to catch a camp dog. He has stopped trying to catch the Thunder Horse now. He would like to kill the stallion, but fears the spirits would look on him with disfavor."

"Kill him!" Clara said, her eyes narrowing. "Your brother sounds like a wicked man, a man who would rather destroy something he cannot have than see it go free."

"He is such a man," Nighthawk said. "Aged One says that one day Black Owl will destroy himself. That day will have to come soon, before he becomes too powerful within the council and among the war chiefs. When that happens, he will destroy our band."

Clara looked into his dark eyes. "I believe you will someday be the most powerful chief in your village."

Nighthawk smiled and moved closer to her.

The rain had let up, and they could hear the *voyageurs* coming out of the other lodges. Nearby, they heard LaCroix and John Huston arguing. Then footsteps approached, and Nighthawk moved away from Clara as John Huston stuck his head through the doorway and said, "We'd best get on the river or we'll be pushin' ice before we reach the Mandan." He gave Nighthawk a suspicious look and disappeared.

"That man wishes you had not found me," Nighthawk said.

"He's worried," Clara said. "He's afraid we won't get to the Mandan villages before cold weather sets in."

Nighthawk smiled again. "Why do you speak in circles?" he asked. "Why do you not say what you feel? What you say is that John Huston is trying hard to bring honor to you by traveling to where you want to go as fast as he can, and that it is making him tired. Why do you not say that John Huston does not like to see us together, and the bad one, LaCroix, does not like us to be together. But you do not care what they want. You will stay with me because you want to. Why do you not say that?"

"I will say that to you," Clara said boldly.

"That is enough," Nighthawk nodded.

Clara wanted to stay with him longer, to have him move close to her again, but there was no chance of that. Not now. She got up and Nighthawk followed her out of the lodge. The men were waiting for them, staring. Clara looked straight ahead and climbed aboard the *Rosebud* with Nighthawk behind her. John ordered them to shove off, and the boat drifted away from the riverbank under the force of the poling and the two ropes. John had said nothing. He looked ahead, casting his eyes to the sky, where the clouds were parting and the sun was breaking through. After a time, Clara began to resent the silence. What business did these men have deciding what company she should keep? She was in command of this expedition, and it was time to remind them of that. The *voyageurs* had been hired to man the boats, and LaCroix and John were supposed to help her lead the men. Nothing else was required of them.

That night when they made camp Nighthawk went off by himself to eat his meal. Clara quickly went to him and stood above him with her plate.

"May I join you?" she asked. "Or would you rather eat alone?"

"Sit," he said. "You are a woman who does what she pleases, no matter what others think."

"Do you care what others think?" she asked.

"No. But I may have to kill the one called LaCroix."

"What? Why?"

"His eyes become more crazy each day. He did not learn from the beating he got from John Huston. Someday someone will kill him. He looks at me with anger. He believes you are his."

Clara looked around the camp. LaCroix was nowhere in sight. Some of the other men were glancing over at them, talking among themselves, but they were not staring as they had earlier and seemed to show little concern. John was in another group. He was laughing now and again. He seemed to have accepted Clara's friendship with Nighthawk. For the time being it seemed there was nothing to be concerned about.

"You will have to learn to be calm," Nighthawk told her. "In the Kainah lands there is always the fear of attack. But everyone must live each day without worry or grow old quickly."

"How can you be calm when you think someone wants to kill you?" Clara asked him.

"My spirit helpers are with me," Nighthawk said. "I will not die."

Clara frowned in thought. "Do they speak to you?"

He nodded.

"Do you hear them?" she asked.

Nighthawk smiled. He pointed to his head and said, "Inside. You must learn to listen for them." He pointed to his stomach. "Sometimes here. Usually if something bad is about to happen."

Clara pointed to her own stomach. "You don't feel anything here tonight?"

Nighthawk smiled again and shook his head. "Eat your food. If you want to walk ahead of the boats with me when the sun rises, as you said you did, then you will have to be strong. And you must sleep."

Clara shook her head. "I cannot understand how you could close your eyes after what you just said about killing LaCroix."

"Tonight is not LaCroix's night," Nighthawk said. "He has eaten too much and is already asleep."

Clara looked around camp again. "Where?"

Nighthawk pointed to beyond the farthest fire. "He has been asleep since before you came over here to be with me. Will you now eat and rest well?"

Clara nodded. It would take her time to become aware of her surroundings, as Nighthawk was. She guessed that his alertness had come with his training as a boy and his life in the wilderness. Nothing escaped his eyes, not even the direction toward which the ants were carrying food crumbs from the fires, or the direction the birds flew from the trees when they were scared. Noticing the minutest detail could save one's life in this land.

Clara ate breakfast with John and LaCroix the next morning, briefing them on the plans for the day. If they pushed hard, they could reach the Mandan villages soon. The men were eager to trade and enjoy themselves among these friendly Indians before pushing on overland to the upper Yellowstone. Throughout the meal, John emphasized to LaCroix that there were to be only brief stops to rest and eat. LaCroix said little, but eyed Clara, as if he wanted to know whether she really intended to walk ahead of the boats with Nighthawk. As the sun rose, the boats pushed off into the current, and Clara set out on foot with the Kainah warrior at her side.

FIRECLOUD

For Clara the day passed as quickly as the flight of a bird through a grove of trees. She followed Nighthawk along the trails and across the hills, learning to read the sign left by animals and Indians. She listened as he told her secrets of living off the land, even in winter when the roots of plants were buried in frozen ground and only the inner bark of trees and the dried fruit of shrubs and flowering plants remained. It was a time of learning to see detail clearly and training the ear to the language the land was speaking. Nighthawk showed her how to hide in the woods, how to become a part of the trees and the shrubs or the grasses and scraggly brush of the slopes and tableland. She had to force herself to be attentive, for many times she wanted to tell him to stop talking and to take her in his arms and hold her.

As the sun began to sink in the west, Clara and Nighthawk found a suitable place to camp for the night and sat down to wait for the keelboats and the crew to catch up to them.

She saw Nighthawk looking at her intently. "I have thought about this moment for as many days as we have traveled together," he said. "I can hold it within me no longer. I must tell you now."

Clara looked into his eyes with a warm anticipation. Nighthawk was holding a small leather pouch that hung around his neck on a rawhide cord. He had told her this was his medicine bundle, his most prized and powerful possession. In it were sacred objects so secret that he could not reveal them to anyone. They connected him to his spirit helpers; they were his link with the other world. To expose the objects would mean breaking that link and opening the door to serious harm. As he took two objects from the bundle, she knew that she was linked to him in a special way.

"Aged One made these for me at Spring Bird's request," he said to Clara, holding up two small figures carved from wood. One was a warrior and the other an Indian maiden; both were garbed in bright-colored clothes and both had real hair. Their hands were clenched into fists, their wrists crossed over their hearts—Indian sign language for love.

Clara stared at the two tiny figures, fascinated. She understood the meaning of the figures and knew Nighthawk must have carried them in anticipation of this moment, when he felt sure of what he was doing.

"Spring Bird felt that I would find love someday," Nighthawk went on. "It is now nearly three winters since these figures were made. Aged One told her that love would not come easily for me, nor would it come in the usual way. He was right."

Clara felt a strange sensation of warmth overwhelm her as Nighthawk leaned over and kissed her lips, putting the two small wooden figures between them as their bodies came together. Clara did not want the moment to end, so strong was the power of his kiss.

"Aged One told me that the two wooden figures would grow warm within my medicine bundle when I found love," he said. "The moment I first saw you I could feel the warmth begin. It was surprising to me, for at first I thought we would surely fight to the death. But then I saw that you did not want to shoot me with your thunder stick, and I suddenly felt no hatred for you and did not want to fight."

Clara sat listening to him, letting their closeness fulfill the longing that had been growing inside her for so long. "Somehow I have always known all this," Clara said. "Ever since that first day, something inside me said that you had been placed there for me to meet. And to love."

Nighthawk handed Clara the small warrior figure and told her never to part with it, for as long as he had the tiny maiden and she had the warrior, they would be able to find each other. Holding the figure in her hand, Clara had the feeling the tiny wooden warrior was almost human. It seemed to radiate warmth and was not hard to the touch, but soft and fleshlike. She had heard that love charms existed, but she had considered them little more than superstition. Now she was holding one and looking into the eyes of the man she had fallen deeply in love with. She knew there was much more than the two wooden figures between them. The charms served only to

FIRECLOUD

symbolize the fact that they had found each other. Love had come so quickly to her, and so decisively. She was now a totally different person than she had been three months ago in St. Louis, she realized, and she felt so wonderful being with Nighthawk that the past seemed only a memory.

Clara and Nighthawk stood up as a keelboat came into view on the river. LaCroix squinted at them from the deck of the *River Otter*. Clara wondered if John had stayed behind to hunt or to walk along by himself, giving command for the time being to LaCroix. The river had swollen from the rains, and the men had made good time by rowing. Now LaCroix ordered them ashore for the night, and a hearty cheer rose from the men.

Fires sprung up along the shoreline, and Clara took some skin water bags to a small inlet where the water passed through slowly, cool and clear. When she returned, she saw that the *voyageurs* had formed a ring around two men who were fighting on the ground: LaCroix and Nighthawk.

"Stop!" Clara shouted, pushing her way through the circle. "Both of you, stop it!" But she could not make herself heard over the yelling of the *voyageurs*.

Clara felt helpless, watching the two men roll on the ground, each holding a knife. They hurled insults at each other in the Blackfoot tongue and gripped each other's wrists, slamming knees and elbows whenever the opportunity occurred. Nighthawk's leg wound showed a small trickle of blood, and the sight of it seemed to encourage LaCroix. He bellowed and threw himself on top of Nighthawk, but the warrior was too agile and quick to be trapped for very long. He released LaCroix's wrist, letting the knife come down along his shoulder, scraping the skin. Then with a twist and an arch of his back, he slipped out from under LaCroix and jerked his knife hand free from LaCroix's grip. In one motion, the warrior thrust his knife toward LaCroix, who raised his arm just in time to keep the blade from entering his chest. Instead, the knife slashed through his buckskins and buried itself in his hip. LaCroix staggered back, screaming, seeing only the hilt showing from his blood-spattered leggings.

Clara quickly stepped in front of Nighthawk, who had come to his feet, and insisted he stay away from LaCroix. Nighthawk's eyes were filled with rage, and he was making sign to Clara that he must kill LaCroix, who churned on the ground while two *voyageurs* held him and another pulled the knife from his hip.

"No," Clara said. "I do not want you to kill these men."

Nighthawk turned his anger on Clara. "What right have you to interfere? That dog did not care to fight as a man, but instead drew his knife and tried to kill me without warning. He has no honor!" He spat.

Clara started to speak, but Nighthawk pushed her to the ground just as LaCroix fired a pistol. The ball whizzed over them and into a tree. Nighthawk quickly jumped to his feet, rushing LaCroix. A number of *voyageurs* stepped in his way, attempting to grab him. He swung and kicked in fury, knocking two of them over and breaking the fingers of a third. Then, suddenly, a rifle shot split the air.

"What is this?"

John Huston's voice was loud and filled with anger. The *voyageurs* moved away from Nighthawk and helped LaCroix to his feet, where he stood on one good leg and glared at Nighthawk, holding his bleeding hip.

"LaCroix!" John bellowed. "You again?"

LaCroix was cursing Nighthawk in the Blackfoot tongue, spitting at him and yelling. Clara held Nighthawk tightly by one arm, begging him not to go after LaCroix again. John had reloaded his Hawken and pointed it back and forth between LaCroix and Nighthawk.

"Any more of this and there'll be powder and ball mixed in."

Nighthawk looked at Clara and jerked his arm from her hold, making his way over to one of the fires. John walked over to stand beside Clara.

"You can't make a riverman like LaCroix respect an Indian," he told Clara. "Especially a Blackfoot. This was bound to happen."

FIRECLOUD

"LaCroix started it," Clara said quickly. "That man is nothing but trouble!"

"He's one of them!" John said quickly and emphatically, pointing to the *voyageurs* gathered around LaCroix. "He's a riverman, just like them and they stand behind him. And he ain't blind. He can see how you've taken to that Blackfoot!"

"So *that's* it!" Clara said hotly. "You and the others think I need your permission to live as I wish. Well, let me set you straight, Mr. Huston, once and for all."

"You ain't got a lick of sense!" John interrupted her. "You should have known takin' up with that Injun would be trouble. What do you expect?"

"God *damn* it!" Clara yelled. LaCroix and the *voyageurs* stared. John Huston took a step back, his eyes wide. "Understand something, Mr. Huston!" She was shouting, pointing his finger at him, backing him up farther. "I don't need approval from *anybody* for what I do! I don't give a *damn* about your petty convictions! I'm going to dock you and the rest of these louts two days' pay for your behavior; and if you want to leave now, you don't even have to wave good-bye!" She was breathing heavily, as if she had been running, and her body shook with rage.

John stared for a moment and then said, "Settle yourself down. Things will work themselves out." He looked out to the edge of camp where Nighthawk was walking westward along the river.

"Where is he going?" Clara asked. "He isn't leaving, is he?"

"Most likely," John answered. "You humiliated him by breakin' up the fight. By Indian ways he had every right to kill LaCroix without anybody steppin' in. He couldn't stay here after being humbled like that."

"No," Clara said. "He can't leave."

"Why can't you just let him go?" John asked. "I can't figure you. There's a pile of money tied up on those two boats—foofaraw for tradin' and traps for settin'—and all you got on your mind is one lousy Blackfoot. If that don't beat all."

"John, don't talk about him that way. I thought you liked him."

"Maybe at one time," he said, turning his head. "But it was plain things wouldn't run smooth with him here. Maybe it's best; things might settle down some among the men, and you just might be able to keep yourself in the fur business." He turned and walked away from her, seating himself near a fire to cook his evening meal.

Clara took a deep breath and looked into the cover of trees and brush along the trail where Nighthawk had disappeared. Suddenly she did not care if she lost the loyalty of the *voyageurs* by going after Nighthawk. They were only a day's journey from the Mandan villages. All that mattered was finding the warrior whom she had grown to love. The tiny wooden figure around her neck, the love charm she had so happily received earlier that day, seemed to be throbbing. She held the tiny figure in her hand, seeming to feel the pulsation. From within her mind came a voice. Was it the voice of the little wooden warrior? The words came to her over and over: *Listen to your heart. Listen to your heart* . . .

8

CLARA SET A POT over a fire and cooked strips of meat and a few vegetables. Each moment that passed seemed like an eternity in which Nighthawk was quickly making his way out of her life. Her mind and heart were troubled. To run after him, to ask him to come back, would surely make her appear foolish to the men of the expedition. And perhaps he did not care to come back. If what John had said was true, the chances were good that he would want nothing more to do with her. Still she could not keep her eyes from the spot where she had last seen him walking away.

Seating herself next to the fire, Clara took a wooden bowl and began to fill it with the meat and vegetables from the boiling pot. Her hands shook, and her heart felt heavy. In the west, clouds had begun to push their way out across the sky from the horizon, and she knew nightfall would come soon. Every moment counted now. She would have to hurry or risk having the darkness close in around her and take the warrior from her forever. Nothing else mattered now, not even the staring eyes of the men, watching her as she left the fire and put on a deerskin shawl to ward off the chill in the air. Nothing was important except finding Nighthawk. Even if she failed to persuade him to rejoin the expedition, she had to see him.

She wrapped some food in one oiled canvas and set off at a brisk pace along the trail. Soon she heard footsteps behind her and John's voice.

"Wait," he yelled. "What are you up to?"

"I am going to try to talk Nighthawk into rejoining us."

"He's long gone," John said. "You'll never catch up to him. Indians don't walk when they travel afoot. Injured or not, they run."

"We need him," Clara said. "He can take us into the Kainah Blackfoot lands."

"LaCroix speaks Blackfoot."

"We're getting rid of him," Clara retorted. "Or have you forgotten?"

"You'll never catch that Blackfoot."

"I've got to try!"

John moved closer to her, his face clouded with anger. "You've fallen in love with him. Ain't that so?"

Clara took a deep breath, looking up the trail, knowing each second that passed could be a second lost forever. She started out again.

John quickly grabbed her by an arm and spun her around. "Ain't that so?" he repeated.

Clara pulled away from him. "What is the matter with you? Didn't you understand me that night when we were together on that hill?"

"Maybe so," he answered. "But I can't see you goin' to no Indian."

"Well, then," Clara said angrily, "you had better stay away from Indian women. Can you do that?"

John gave her no answer.

"I am going after him," she said impatiently. "I will be back, with or without him, by morning. Keep things organized."

John looked at the sky. "A storm is movin' in."

"Can you take care of things here?" she repeated.

"Whatever you say, Miss Melton," he said sarcastically,

bringing his fur cap in front of him in a sweeping bow. "You run the outfit."

Clara turned and started along the trail once again. She realized that a display of anger would only work against her, and she broke into a run, thinking only of what she would say when she caught up with Nighthawk.

The clouds now masked the sun and shadowed the trees and river. In little more than an hour darkness would fall. The air was cooling rapidly around her and the cloud cover grew ever denser, but she continued to run. Her only concern was to find Nighthawk as quickly as she could.

Breathing heavily, Clara stopped at the edge of a small clearing. She leaned against one of the cottonwoods at the edge of the clearing, trying to get enough air into her lungs. She felt dizzy and nauseated. She did not know how far she had run, but she would have to slow her pace if she meant to continue.

Somewhat rested, Clara started walking. A short distance away, in another clearing, she found Nighthawk. He was seated at the edge of the river, looking out across the water. She wanted to cry out for joy. If he had no feelings for her, she realized, he would have been gone by now, and she would never have seen him again. He had traveled several miles from camp, perhaps to test Clara's love for him. As she approached, he made no sign to indicate that he knew she was there, but kept his eyes on the river, even as she set the parcel of food next to him and seated herself nearby.

"I did not mean to dishonor you, Nighthawk," she began. "I do not know your customs."

Nighthawk continued to sit and stare out across the river, as if he had not seen her. Then, without looking at her, he picked up the parcel of food.

"The meat is the best part of the buffalo, the hump," she said.

Nighthawk opened the parcel and began to eat. After a while, he said, "Why did you follow me? To give back the love charm?"

"You know why I have come," Clara said. "And I know

why you waited here instead of traveling on while it is still light enough to see."

"Do you want the wooden woman that I have? Is that it? Did you want to give it to another who waits for you in the camp?"

"Nighthawk, I came out here to find *you*. I brought food for *you*. There is no other waiting for me in camp."

Nighthawk was silent for a time. There was no doubt this woman cared a great deal for him. She had come a long ways along the trails by the river, and she had journeyed quickly. She had not wanted him to be lost from her. Again he was impressed by the physical strength and endurance she possessed. And her will would not bend; she would say what was in her heart, no matter what others might think of her. It was good to know that such a woman cared for him.

"I see that you choose not to talk to me," Clara said. "I will return to the camp."

As she got to her feet, Nighthawk quickly rose and gently took her arm. "Do not leave me," he said. "I do not wish to make you angry. But my words to you about the white dog, LaCroix, were true. The day will come when I shall have to kill him. It should have happened this day, but Huston stopped it."

"Nighthawk, don't you understand? If you had killed LaCroix, the others would have killed you."

"The others would have been afraid," Nighthawk said. "They have always been afraid of me. I am a Blackfoot; they are Long Knives. There has been much blood between us. They do not forget this."

"If you had killed LaCroix, the men would have tried to kill you sooner or later," Clara said.

"It does not matter now," Nighthawk said. "LaCroix is still alive, and it will be much harder for me to kill him now. The spirits gave me my chance, and Huston stopped me. Now, maybe LaCroix will kill me."

"He will be gone after we leave the Mandan villages," Clara said.

FIRECLOUD

Nighthawk looked into the darkening western sky. The sun had set, and the last rays of twilight were dwindling. Clara could see into his mind. She could feel what he was about to tell her.

"Why must you leave?" Clara asked him. "I thought you were going to lead us to your people."

"That would not be wise," Nighthawk answered. "I have too many enemies in your camp. Besides, you must still travel through the lands of both the Assiniboin and the Crow peoples, both bitter enemies of the Blackfeet. You would have to fight your way past the Assiniboin and the Crow, for they would surely try to kill me if they saw me."

Clara looked up into his eyes. "But it is so far for you to travel alone."

"To travel alone is to travel in silence. It is true, I have many lands to cross before I reach my people. But I will travel at night and I will light no fires. I will follow the river the Long Knives call the Missouri, until I reach the Great Falls where the Black Horse band of Kainah Blackfeet camp during the cold moons. The Dirt Lodge people will give me a horse, I am sure. Before the moon is full again, I will have reached my people."

Clara took a deep breath. "Will I ever see you again?"

Nighthawk looked at her as if she had asked a very silly question. "Did you forget my words about the love charms? As long as you wear it, we will be sure to come together again. Maybe the next time we can stay together, if there are not too many Long Knives with you."

Nighthawk took her hand and led her into the trees, where darkness had now fallen completely. She resisted lightly at first, wondering if she dared to follow him, but his strong hand sent a warmth racing through her and she could not stop the desire building within her. His strong arms were around her, pulling her to him with a gentle force that made her heart pound. She felt her own arms coming up around his broad shoulders, feeling the rock-hard muscles swell to her touch. His lips met hers, and the warmth swelled the passion within her. She felt her body tremble as his lips found her cheek and neck, his tongue probing and flicking around her ear.

Effortlessly, the warrior picked her up and carried her to a patch of soft grass beneath a large cottonwood. He took off her deerskin shawl and spread it on the ground.

Again she thought of camp, and a pang of worry came over her. Uncertainty again began to work on her. "Nighthawk," she said. "Maybe we should wait until another time."

Nighthawk said nothing. His strong arms again went around her, and his lips began to work their magic once more, removing from her mind everything but the pleasure he was giving her. His strong hands found their way beneath her dress, and his fingertips traced patterns along her back and then around to her breasts. He rubbed them gently and traced their contours, bringing the nipples to fullness, all the while talking to her in low tones of her beauty and grace. His words were like the sound of sweet water falling all around her as he continued to stroke her with his hands and his lips. She arched her back as he slid her dress up and off, and she felt his breechclout brush her leg as he removed it. The touch of him, warm and naked, against her sent her desire spiraling high. She let her hands find their way along his sleek, strong body, feeling a love so strong that it took her breath away. She forgot everything but the passion she felt for the strong Kainah warrior.

He moved himself over onto her, and she felt him thrust into her, slowly at first, and then deep into her farthest reaches. His motions were smooth and effortless, his manly power filling her to capacity. She locked her legs around him, matching her own motions to his. Within her, she felt the intensity of her passion building quickly toward the threshold. Losing control, she felt her body reach the peak of ecstasy, and heard his cries mingling with her own. Clara felt his massive power surging within her, throbbing in uncontrolled release. Then together they breathed deeply of the cool night air, lying in each other's arms.

Nighthawk rolled to his side, leaning over her. His fingers

FIRECLOUD

stroked her cheeks, and his voice was soft. "Never before has there been a night like this one for me. I did not know a woman could give so fully of herself. I cannot go from this land without you."

"Will you come with us?"

He shook his head. "No. You must come with me. There is nothing back there for you."

"I must preserve my father's honor. For that I must go back."

Nighthawk continued to stroke her cheek.

"You belong here in these lands," Nighthawk told her. "Your heart is like the eagle, soaring high and free among the clouds. Your heart is like the wild stallion I have told you about, the Thunder Horse, Firecloud."

"Someday you and I will own that horse," Clara said. "He will be ours, and the entire land will call you a great warrior."

"Yes, and I will have the most powerful wife any warrior could dream of."

Clara held him tighter. "Yes, I want that to happen, but you must help me. You know it will be hard for me to go into a land I do not know and be successful at trading furs."

"You have shown me this night that you have a deep love for me," Nighthawk said. "I will do what I can to make it possible for us to live together as husband and wife. I have never wanted anything so badly before. Not even to own the Thunder Horse, Firecloud."

"The day will come when you have both of us." Clara smiled.

"It will be very hard to make things happen so that we can be together," Nighthawk said. "It will be even harder to catch Firecloud."

"Why? He is only a horse, not a ghost."

Nighthawk shook his head. "He is more ghost than horse. You do not understand his power. You cannot understand what he is until you have seen him. When he appears, he is like a vision before you, his legs moving above the ground, his white mane flying in the wind. He lives at the top of the earth, deep within the burning Mountains, where the fires of the underground spirits cause the waters to boil and the skies to fill with hot breath. Firecloud's land is very beautiful, but strange things happen there. That is why people fear the wild stallion. They believe he may be one of the earth's evil spirits in a horse's body."

"Do you believe this?"

"I believe only that he is a very powerful horse. I have never felt the presence of evil when I have seen him. I feel only the certainty that this stallion has no equal."

Clara envisioned the strong, proud stallion standing alone atop a hill, his mane and tail moving in the wind. "And no one has ever ridden him?" she asked.

"There is a story of how he was caught once, when no more than a yearling. But he escaped and has never been caught since. He knows what the rawhide rope means now."

"Maybe there is another way to catch him," Clara suggested. "All he has ever known is riders trying to run him down and tie him up. A horse does not have to be a spirit to know that to preserve his freedom he must stay away from riders with ropes."

"Yes, but he does *not* stay away. He challenges all those who go after him. He then makes a sport of the chase, and many riders have fallen from their horses and been injured. Others have lost control of their horses. For this reason, people believe that Firecloud is able to speak to the other horses, to control them, and to fill them with terror. Even the older and wiser members of the council simply shake their heads and say they have never heard of a horse with such powers. Only Aged One believes the horse is good and not evil. Therefore some people say he is losing his senses. The stallion is feared in our village. Whenever he comes, he brings trouble to our people."

"I must see this horse," Clara said. "Will you take me to him?"

"There is not time to journey to the Burning Mountains before the snow lies deep on the lands where the Thunder Horse lives."

FIRECLOUD

"Is the snow so deep that no one can get in or out of there?" Clara asked.

"Those lands are very high," Nighthawk explained. "The snow would cover a man on a horse very easily. It is said that the Thunder Horse can live there because he is a spirit, but I believe the words of Aged One, who says that where the underground spirits live, their hot breath rising into the air melts the snow. There is always green grass for Firecloud and his herd to graze."

Clara nodded in understanding. The land where the horse lived during the winter had to be the place described by John Colter, who worked for Manuel Lisa shortly after the Lewis and Clark Expedition. No one had believed Colter, and the area had earned the name Colter's Hell. Colter had described vast basins of boiling mud and water, which poured into a river the Indians of the region called Firehole. To the Indians, the area appeared to be eternally on fire. They spoke of the Burning Mountains where the fiery underground spirits breathed into the sky. The wild stallion could live there, safe from the Indians who were afraid of the area. The constant underground heat melted the snow, and the vegetation stayed green and lush throughout the year. The wild stallion had merely taken advantage of a natural wonder.

"When the cold moons end," Nighthawk said, "the Thunder Horse will journey down from the Burning Mountains. Then I will take you in search of him."

Before Clara could say anything, he disappeared into the darkness. She sat up in bewilderment, hearing only the murmur of the river nearby and the hoot of an owl overhead. The love charm around her neck was warm, and she remembered what he had told her earlier, knowing she would again find him. She lay back down and wrapped the doeskin shawl around her against the night air that had grown steadily cooler. Deep within her she had a gnawing feeling of want. She misssed the warrior already. But she would see him again soon; she had no doubt of that. The warm memory of their lovemaking lingered, and everything else seemed unimportant. In so short a time her life had changed completely. She knew she must establish a fur trading company, but this would not stop her from sharing her love with Nighthawk. She closed her eyes and relaxed, a smile forming on her lips. Nighthawk would be forever in her life.

9

THE SENSATION OF MOISTURE against her face awoke Clara suddenly at dawn. Large feathery snowflakes were floating in slow, irregular patterns all around her. The air was heavy and so still that a whisper would echo like a falling rock.

Clara dressed quickly and wrapped herself in the deerskin shawl. She walked quickly, wishing she had journeyed back to camp the night before. As she made her way along the trail, now starting to collect snow as the cool air lowered the temperature of the ground, she thought of John, no doubt thinking she had abandoned the expedition to go with Nighthawk. He had finally given up on his dream of winning her love, and had not come looking for her this time. She remembered his sweeping bow and callous remarks about her running the expedition, all the while trying to conceal the hurt in his somber eyes. It was hard for her to see why a man nearly twice her age could be so determined to win her over despite the odds against him.

Clara continued to hurry, occasionally breaking into a run. In her anxiety, time became distorted in her mind until she thought the morning must have passed, although the light had barely changed since she awoke. Not knowing how far she had come in the semidarkness the night before to find Nighthawk, she could only continue onward.

The snow continued to fall, and Clara strained her eyes for any sign of the keelboats or the men. Onward she went, wanting to call out through the storm, but knowing that no one would hear her. Confusion took over. Still she went on, the stillness broken only by the soft pad of her moccasined feet on the damp snow. She was sure of nothing but the storm, that was now covering the entire land with a blanket of snow. Her confusion grew. Then a flock of turkeys scolded her for her intrusion and flapped noisily from their perches in the branches above her, knocking snow and twigs into her path. This first sign of life had broken the menacing stillness. She had seen no deer or elk, not even the occasional herd of buffalo that had stayed for the winter. Maybe all the animals had taken shelter from the storm. The woods seemed too still, and snow fell noiselessly.

Clara kept walking, no longer feeling the wet flakes that now bathed her face in tiny rivers of moisture. In a small clearing beside the trail, she stopped and turned a slow circle, looking all around her. Could she have traveled in the wrong direction? Her confusion increased. She walked to the riverbank and saw that she had been following the river downstream, toward the spot where the men had made camp the night before.

Relieved, Clara continued downstream. She found the camp a short distance farther on. The fires were out, and most of the men were aboard the keelboats, holding their rifles at ready. Clara stared at them all for a long moment, realizing they were prepared for an attack. They had probably been up most of the night.

"Are you fixin' to stand there now the rest of the day?" John hissed.

He was beside her in an instant, holding her and escorting her nervously to the *Rosebud*.

"What's going on?" Clara asked.

John's irritation increased. "You're so taken with that Indian that you can't use your senses. Can't you feel the air? Damn, it's tight! We've got Sioux all around us."

A cold fear rushed over Clara. John's urgency told her the

FIRECLOUD

reason why there had been no deer or elk or buffalo along the river. Her blood froze. Had there been Sioux watching her all the time? Maybe they had spared her for fear of giving themselves away to the rest of the expedition. What was aboard the boats was far more important than a white woman. Then she thought of Nighthawk, but realized he most likely had traveled far upriver before the Sioux arrived.

The snow began to fall more heavily than before. John yelled at the men to get the boats out into the current. LaCroix and his crew pushed against the bow of the *River Otter*, groaning and cursing. Finally it scraped free of the gravel bottom and began to float out into the river. Clara felt the deck of the *Rosebud* rock to and fro as the men strained to move the craft free of the bottom to join the *River Otter*.

"Move it! Move it!" John was shouting. "Let's get out of here!" The *Rosebud* lurched and rocked wildly. The hull was caught on a rock beneath the water. "Keep shoving!" John shouted, using a pole to push away from the bank. Clara tried to help, but he told her to stay back; the men were in each other's way as it was. Then a *voyageur* standing next to John let out a choked scream and clutched at the shaft of an arrow that protruded from his throat. His eyes rolled back in his head, and he fell forward from the deck into the shallow water. More arrows came, and Clara heard the slicing thud of their points pushing through flesh and bone.

Conquering the fear that threatened to numb her muscles, Clara raised her Hawken and aimed at one of the painted Sioux who emerged from the trees like ghosts, making their way through the storm with leaping strides toward the *Rosebud*. The rifle slammed back against her shoulder as the blast sent a warrior reeling into the snow, holding his blood-smeared chest. John shot a warrior who was trying to climb aboard, and clubbed yet another with the butt of his rifle. Now the Sioux were like ants crawling over a log, trying to pull themselves onto the deck of the keelboat. The air was filled with screams and shouts of agony and terror, mixed with the shrill war cries of the Sioux. Many of the *voyageurs* were jumping overboard, screaming for the *River Otter* to wait for them. LaCroix ordered the men to pole and row harder, and his boat picked up speed as it reached the main current of the river. Sioux warriors on horseback rode into the river to spear the swimming men with their lances or to shoot them with trade muskets or arrows. The snow continued to fall silently as blood soaked the deck of the *Rosebud* and stained the water of the river.

John fired at another Sioux warrior. The small swivel cannon on the bow of the boat was useless now, for all of the crewmen had either jumped into the river or were lying dead or dying on the deck. Soon the warriors would return their full attention to the boat, and there would be no hope of survival.

"We've lost her," John told Clara. "It's over if we don't swim for it."

"We'll try for the opposite shore," Clara said. "Away from the men. We could never reach the *River Otter* now."

"That bastard LaCroix," John said. "All he had to do was fire his swivel cannon at them once, and they would have run like chickens. Instead, he left us to get butchered. He's most likely laughin' at us right now."

"It's too late to think about him now," Clara said. "We've got to hurry. The cover of this storm will help."

"We can't sail this boat no longer," John said. "I'll set it afire, and we'll use it to help us get away."

Clara lowered herself over the side into the cold water while John dumped kegs of gunpowder over the deck, spreading it on everything. Powder fell on *voyageurs* who would never breath again, some of them already scalped by the Sioux warriors, and lay in piles all along the deck. Then he dipped a rag in lamp oil and set it on fire before lowering himself over the side next to Clara.

Clara waded away from the boat and John tossed the burning rag onto the deck. The explosion blew wood and pieces of bodies in all directions and the flames filled the dense, stormy air. Thick black smoke shrouded the boat. There were shrill cries of alarm from the Sioux, who were still trying to find all the *voyageurs* who had tried to swim toward the *River Otter*.

"Hang on to one of those logs and kick hard," John yelled.

FIRECLOUD

The current was cold and swift and Clara felt her body steadily growing numb. She held tight to the log and kicked with all her might, trying to keep her head down as far as possible. Once they reached the opposite shore, they could hide until the Sioux left the area. She looked behind her and saw John close by, kicking his way through the water as fast as he could. The smoke continued to rise from the *Rosebud* in heavy, billowing clouds, blanketing the entire area in thick black haze. The heat from the fire had turned the snowfall into a misty rain, and the river took on the colors of dawn. John's plan had worked.

Clara felt the gravelly river bottom beneath her feet and waded through chest-high water to the bank. Suddenly John began to yell. In the shallow water at the river's edge, she saw a warrior on horseback facing John, and she watched in terror as an arrow left his bow. John arched his back, his face distorted in pain and horror. Leaning from his horse, the warrior then grabbed John by the hair and pulled his knife.

Rushing toward them Clara pulled the surprised warrior into the ankle-deep water by his tunic. As the warrior slipped off the horse's back, Clara slammed her foot into his exposed crotch. She heard his muffled groan as he doubled over in the water. She pulled John up onto the riverbank, struggling to maneuver his heavy body over the rocky ground. The horse was now far out into the river, but the warrior was making his way through the water to the shore.

Frantic, Clara pulled John into the shelter of a fallen tree and laid him on his side. The arrow had entered his back at an angle, coming out high on his chest, its pointed head just under his chin. She turned to see the Sioux warrior, still in pain, struggling through the shallows on his hands and knees. He would recover soon, she knew, and though he had lost his bow and his knife, there were still arrows in the quiver slung over his back.

Clara picked up a large stone from the shoreline, heavier than she would ordinarily have been able to throw. Wanting to get as close as possible to the Sioux, she waded back out into the shallows and edged boldly up to the warrior's lowered head. With blinding quickness he seized her ankle and pulled. She shrieked and fell backwards, letting the rock splash into the water beside her. As the Sioux began to pull her to him, he twisted on her ankle, spinning her to her back. Pain shot through her leg as he continued to twist on the ankle.

Screaming with rage and pain, Clara brought her other foot up, kicking him repeatedly in the face. He took the blows, continuing to twist and pull on her leg. Clara stopped trying to pull away from him and sat up. In surprise, the warrior looked up to see what had made her quit fighting. Through the streaks of paint, Clara could see the dark hate in his eyes, made worse by a deep scar that ran along his cheekbone. Before he could react, she grabbed his hair with both hands and pulled herself toward him with all her might.

The warrior groaned in rage. He released her leg and tried to grab her hands. In that instant, Clara let go of his hair and quickly pulled an arrow from the quiver draped over his back. As he rose up to jump forward on her, Clara thrust the arrow into the soft hollow at the base of the warrior's throat. The momentum of her thrust carried the shaft far in, and she felt the hot blood bubble out of his throat against her clenched fist.

Forgetting the pain in her ankle, Clara scrambled away from the warrior, who knelt upright in the water, his eyes dazed with shock. His chin bobbed up and down and the muscles in his throat contracted spasmodically, as if he were trying to swallow something that would not go down. His hands were pressed tightly against the base of his neck around the shaft of the arrow, his blood surging through his fingers and down over his chest in pulsing streams. As Clara reached the shore, the warrior slumped sideways into the shallows and began to writhe and kick the water into a bloody foam. Then he was still, face down in the water.

Clara, weak from fright and horror, went to the fallen tree where John lay. He had managed to prop himself against the tree. He was conscious and in extreme pain. The ground was now covered in a thick blanket of fresh snow. The black smoke from the burning keelboat had spread out over the

FIRECLOUD

river. Shouts from the opposite shore told her the Sioux were still looking for stragglers. She shook her head, as if to revive her senses and convince herself that she was living this nightmare, not dreaming it. John was still alive and needed help. She had to get him into the cover of the trees and brush before the Sioux crossed the river.

Suddenly Clara heard shouting behind her and turned to see three Sioux warriors coming into the shallows on horseback. Wild with fear, she screamed at them, shaking her fist in the air. Startled, the warriors reined in their horses. Clara rushed over to the dead warrior lying near the shore, splashing through the water, continuing to scream. Straddling his back, she grabbed a handful of his wet, matted hair and pulled the slain warrior's head from the water, exposing the arrow through his throat. She pulled another arrow from the quiver on his back and raised it high above her head.

"Come ahead, you killers!" she screamed. "Come on! Come to me, so I can stick this in one of you!"

The warriors turned their horses and began to yell and wave at other warriors behind them. Confused by their retreat, having expected them to kill her, Clara dropped the warrior and struggled back to shore, sobbing and trembling. Her ankle was now completely numb from the cold water, and she had lost most of the feeling in her lower leg. As she tried to drag John into the trees away from shore, she stumbled and fell heavily.

"You . . . plan to kill . . . kill them all?" John asked her, trying to laugh through his horrible pain. "They sure left in a hurry. Crazy woman . . . Scared of . . . crazy woman."

A sudden queasiness nearly overcame her. "Don't talk, John," she said. "I'll get you away from shore."

John insisted on rising and trying to walk, with her support. He had regained some strength, it seemed to Clara, but she worried about him using it up and having nothing left.

"Got to . . . hear me, now . . . Clara," he managed, as she helped him sit down on the ground, resting against a tree. "My time is . . . short."

"John, don't talk that way."

"Truth . . . Clara. Got to face . . . up to it."

113

Clara's eyes filled with tears. "It's all my fault."

"No. I had . . . a feelin' about today. Nobody's fault." He winced in pain, the blood rattling in his lungs. "Get . . . it out," he said. "Please . . . It burns."

"John, I don't know how."

"Break it . . . in the back. Pull forward."

"Oh, John—"

"Please, Clara. Hurts . . . Oh, God . . . burns."

Clara took hold of the arrow where it came out of his back. With the other hand, she gripped the shaft where it protruded from his chest, the warm, fresh blood wet and sticky against her hand. She struggled to keep from gagging.

"Do it, Clara."

With a quick downward twist of her wrist, Clara snapped off the arrowhead and pulled the remaining shaft from his chest. He yelled and nearly fainted. She threw the shaft away as if it were a hot ember.

"Better," John managed to say, breathing hoarsely.

"Rest now, John," Clara said. "I'll melt some snow."

"No, don't leave me . . . alone. Don't go . . . Please."

Clara fought back the tears, but they fell despite her efforts.

"My time . . . to go. That's all. You've got . . . to get away. To the Mandan. Promise?"

Clara covered her face with her hands, the tears streaming through her fingers.

"Clara. Promise?"

"I promise, John."

He continued to struggle with his words. "Get . . . to the Mandan. Catch boat . . . back. Forget fur trade. You'll just get . . . killed out here." He tried to laugh. "My time," he said. "Don't hear no . . . bugles. Just gone. Like . . . like floatin' away." Then his eyes cleared for an instant, as if he had to retain his senses a while longer before dying. He tried to reach into a pocket. Clara reached into the pocket for him and brought out seven animal teeth strung together. "Elk . . . eye teeth," he said to her. "Good luck. Wear the . . . bracelet. For me."

FIRECLOUD

Clara, hardly able to see through her tears, slipped the bracelet on her wrist.

John's eyes began to fade again. Quickly this time, with tears forming in them that spilled onto his face. "Love . . . you, Clara. Don't . . . forget me." Then his head slumped sideways, and he let out a long breath of air.

"John, John," Clara sobbed uncontrollably. "John, don't die like this."

She couldn't shake him back to life. It was over, with only the black smoke mixed with the falling snow to show that anything had happened here. The Sioux warriors had retrieved their dead and ridden away, leaving the crazy Long Knife woman behind, the one who had killed a warrior with her bare hands.

Clara found a low spot in the ground where some animal had created a wallow. She dug deeper into the muddy soil and laid John to rest, covering him with soil, logs, sticks, and rocks. He was now a part of the hills, like the rocks and the trees and the buffalo that grazed there. He had become one with the earth.

Now Clara was alone. She would have to survive on her own, using all that she had learned from John and from Nighthawk about living in the wild. And with the snow coming down harder and the air turning icy, she was facing the season of the cold moons.

10

THE PAIN IN HER ANKLE became a pulsing throb as she made her way through the tangled growth along the river, trying to put as much distance as she could between herself and the nightmare she had just fought her way through. She would have to hide for the remainder of the day, for the Sioux would certainly across the river to look for any who might have escaped. By now their surprise at her behavior had likely turned to anger, and they would no doubt try to find her and take their revenge.

As she walked, she thought of LaCroix. Her anger brought her added strength as she thought of how he had left the crew of the *Rosebud* to die. She wondered where he was now. Was he grinning happily? Did he now consider himself the sole owner of the *River Otter* and all the trade goods on board? He would no doubt continue to the upper Yellowstone as planned. He undoubtedly planned to enjoy the profits of the trading and trapping. Though John had told her before he died that he wanted her to forget about trading furs and just return to New England, she knew that was the last thing she would do. One way or another, she intended to get back what was rightfully hers.

Farther along the riverbank, Clara came to the mouth of a

small stream. Here she found clumps of chokecherry and Juneberry. On the hill above her a flock of prairie chickens rose from the gray, thorny branches of the buffalo berry and lost themselves in the storm. Though most of the berries and rose hips along the bottom were now shriveled and dry, the moisture from the storm would soften them somewhat.

The storm began to let up, and the snow fell less heavily. The black smoke from the *Rosebud* had lifted, and Clara found herself in a world of bleak white. The air had cooled even more, and the wind sent a chill through her doeskin dress. She was wet and cold, and she knew that she must find cover. Her strength was leaving her, and she realized she must rest until the shock of what had happened wore off.

She followed the stream until she came upon a rock ledge, beneath which was a cave. Her teeth chattering, Clara made her way through the snow to the mouth of the cave and peered in. She jerked herself back as a large, round-eyed owl suddenly flapped past her face and settled into an effortless glide across the stream, coming to rest in a snow-covered tree on the other side, a spot of brown in a world of white. She peered into the cave again, searching for other surprises. Satisfied that it was empty, she dragged herself inside and curled into a ball. She had no food and no warmth, for a fire would reveal her hiding place to eyes that looked for curling smoke. None of these things seemed to matter. Exhaustion had left her without the energy to remain alert for danger, or to care about the pain in her ankle and lower leg. She reached inside her dress for the tiny wooden warrior that rested between her breasts. Her fingers encircled it, and the thought of Nighthawk eased her tension and brought a sense of warmth to her. A smile parted her lips and, as darkness approached, her eyes closed.

SHE AWOKE JUST AFTER DAWN. The storm had blown past during the night. Already the air was warmer, and a blue sky promised a sun that would burn through the snow and again bring the land back to the orange and gold of late autumn.

FIRECLOUD

Winter had not yet come to stay. There would be more time before the bitter cold set in, making travel nearly impossible. She would need every precious moment of decent weather to reach the upper Yellowstone before the end of the year. For now, she thought only of reaching the Mandan villages.

By noon she was slipping and sliding in mud. She had developed a cough that shot pain through her chest, making her steps slower and sending chills over her. To stop would be out of the question, she knew, for she needed food, shelter, and rest to regain her strength.

She pulled some berries from a bush, tasting their sweetness and gaining back a measure of her lost strength. Still she continued to tremble with chills, and her cough was becoming worse. As she continued to eat berries, she became aware of a noise among the bushes near her. An animal of some sort was moving about, snorting and grunting, smacking its lips as it fed. For a moment, Clara stood frozen with fear. Though she could not see the animal, she knew that it was one of the giant bears that roamed this land. The bear with the long silver-tipped coat was more powerful than any other creature that lived here. John and the *voyageurs* had told stories about this bear and the awesome strength it possessed. It could kill huge buffalo bulls with its powerful teeth and claws. And now she was only a few steps away from the most powerful creature in the wilderness.

Clara heard the bear make its way out of the berry patch, and suddenly it loomed over her. She had no time to turn and run; the bear was too close and moving too fast. In terror, she threw herself to the ground and rolled herself into a ball. She covered her eyes, but she could hear the beast grunting. Within seconds he was sniffing the ground around her and poking his nose at her. Paralyzed with fear, Clara lay rigid and held her breath, feeling the hot breath of her attacker close to her face. Then, without warning, the bear grew motionless, and the sound of its heavy breathing stopped. Cautiously Clara opened one eye just in time to see the bear rise up on its hind feet with its nose in the air, seemingly confused. Had he

E. P. Murray

picked up another scent? Was there another animal nearby whose presence was more familiar and whose smell was more tempting to him? Breathless and terrified, Clara watched as the beast sniffed the air. Then with a loud snort, the bear lowered itself to all four feet and ambled off down the trail.

Clara came to her feet slowly, thankful for whatever distracted the bear and sent it off into the trees. On another day, or perhaps even at another hour of this day, the bear might have killed her. There was no way to predict what these bears might do at any given time, and as she stared at the clump of bushes she had just been eating from, she resolved to be more careful of berry patches in the future.

Clara turned and walked on, making her way through the thick cover with an extra caution now, forcing herself to be attentive, and to travel as Nighthawk and John had shown her. Another chance encounter with a bear, or perhaps with a Sioux or Arikara warrior, could end her life, and she would no longer need to be concerned with finding LaCroix. As she walked on, she watched for anything that seemed out of place or unusual. Instead of losing herself in her thoughts, she listened and watched the trail ahead of her and the brush around her. Her frequent coughing fits forced her to walk slowly and stop occasionally to rest and to listen for movement and sound. It was a slow way to travel, but she felt safer.

Evening had set in when she came to the mouth of a river that flowed into the Missouri. On the riverbank stood a group of large earthen lodges that looked like brown domes. She knew she had at last found a Mandan village. Finally she had reached the home of the Indians she had heard of so many times since leaving St. Louis. Weak with fever and hunger, she stumbled into the village, hardly noticing the hordes of naked brown children who gathered around her and the packs of camp dogs that yapped and barked and nipped at her heels. Her only concern now was to find one of the chiefs, someone who would listen to her story and possibly give her a horse on which to travel to the Yellowstone.

As Clara made her way into the center of the village, she

saw several hanging strips of meat or bowls of wild berries and corn on poles to dry in the sun. The women clustered together as they watched her pass. Near the center of the village, a group of men stood talking among themselves and gesturing toward her. From their midst a single warrior broke and quickly made his way toward her.

It was Nighthawk.

Clara stopped, unable to believe her eyes. As Nighthawk ran toward her, Clara forgot about her weakness and hunger and rushed into his arms. He received her, his strong arms encircling her and bringing her close against him. The torment she had suffered the last two days seemed instantly gone.

"My heart is very glad this day," Nighthawk told her, holding her even tighter, not caring that nearly the entire village had gathered to look on curiously. "I had feared the worst."

"You know of the Sioux raid?" Clara asked.

"This village learned of it soon after it took place. Our scouts knew the Sioux had come back into these lands, and we were watching them, in case they should attack this village. When I came here to get a horse to travel back to my people, I was told a Long Knife boat was burning on the river. I wanted to go back, but it was too late. The fighting was already finished. I knew that you would come here if you lived. And now I have you in my arms again."

"I am so happy to see you," Clara said. "John and the others were killed; only LaCroix and the men on the *River Otter* got away."

"Yes," Nighthawk said. "LaCroix and his men went to the nearby Hidatsa village and traded for horses. The chiefs here would not let him enter this village. They know him from a few winters past, when he took one of their women, the sister of a medicine man, and later killed her. LaCroix will never again be welcome in this village."

Clara again felt her anger rise. Everywhere LaCroix went, he brought trouble with him. It was easy to believe that he had killed the Mandan woman for no reason. Knowing he was just a short distance ahead of her invigorated her, and she was eager to acquire a horse.

"We need not leave this village at once," Nighthawk told her. "Now you need rest and care."

"I am not that sick," Clara argued. "I can't wait. I have no time to lose."

"LaCroix has many men and many supplies. He cannot travel nearly as fast as two people," Nighthawk said. "We will leave soon. But first you must rest and get over your coughing sickness. If you do not, you could die in the cold weather that will surely come." He took her again in his arms. "I could not bear to lose you." Then he looked at her with eyes that sparkled. "Besides, you are to be honored."

"Why would I receive honor?" said Clara.

"One of the Mandan scouts told of a Sioux singer who prayed for the spirit of their war chief, who had been killed in the battle. The words of the singer told of their chief dying at the hands of a crazy Long Knife woman. I know of only one crazy Long Knife woman in all of these lands." He smiled proudly at Clara as he finished. "The Dirt Lodge people are grateful, for over many winters they have lost warriors in battle to this chief, who was known as Cut Face. I wish to hear the story of how you killed him. It is said he could not sing his death song, for an arrow had gone through his throat. What you have done is brave and you will receive many presents."

"I would rather forget it," Clara said. "I was never so afraid in all my life."

"Yes," said Nighthawk, "but you were victorious. And that is most important. Now, worry no more about LaCroix and let me take you to where it is warm and you can rest."

Clara was soon in one of the round earthen Mandan homes. A fire in the center of the lodge brightened the room and filled it with warmth. Clara immediately began to relax. Nighthawk helped her out of her damp clothes and into a bed of buffalo robes and soft antelope skins. He knelt beside her, his eyes smiling and his face alive with happiness. His lips found hers and she wished he would remove his own clothes and climb into the robes beside her.

FIRECLOUD

"A shaman, a medicine man, will come to you soon and make you well," Nighthawk said. "Sleep now. He will make you strong again. Then, when you have received honor from the village, we will go."

"Where will you be?" Clara asked.

"Close," he answered, squeezing her hand. "Always close."

Soon the shaman came into the lodge, painted with red lines across his face and forehead, and across his arms, chest, and thighs. He wore the headdress of a pronghorn antelope, with owl wings tied to holes drilled in five places through the bone. On a belt under his coat of pure white mountain goat skins, he carried rattles made from dried and hollowed-out melons. He dispersed leaves of dried sage liberally through the fire and began to chant. Instantly the lodge was filled with the strong, pungent odor of the burning sage. Clara then drank from a bowl of brewed herbs; the taste was strong, yet quite flavorful. Taking a yellow paint from another bowl, the shaman drew lines across her cheeks and nose. He pulled the robes back, smearing a sticky mixture of plants and bear grease over her throat and chest. Over the mixture he placed a large red trade cloth. Then he rearranged the robes over her.

The sage fragrance filled the lodge, settling the cough she had fought for nearly two days. The shaman's chanting continued, and Clara found herself relaxing into a deep sleep. Over the next three days, she was fed a soupy broth, and sage was continually thrown into the fire. The poultice that had been applied to her throat and neck felt like fire against her skin. She saw Nighthawk frequently but was too drowsy to converse for very long at any one time. He kidded her endlessly about the shaman "sending her into another land" to cure her cough and clean out her lungs. She would laugh at his remarks, but felt quite certain the effects of the sage smoke and all the herbs she was taking in the broth were altering her physical and mental state. More often than not she felt disassociated with her surroundings and in a surrealistic world of warmth and softness. Her fever had broken, and her cough was clearing up.

But no amount of comfort could keep her mind off LaCroix and the trade goods he was taking to the upper Yellowstone. If she could succeed in getting the items back and having a successful trading season, she could break even on the venture and possibly even make some money. At this point not only her money but also the investments of George Whittingham and Martin Folmon were very much in jeopardy. As part of her agreement with the two men, Clara had pledged some of her personal business assets against what they had invested, so great was her confidence that this business would work. If she now lost all that remained of the expedition, her entire investment would be gone and she would be forced to forfeit her pledges to the other two investors to satisfy their losses. She knew she must find LaCroix as soon as possible. How she would get her property back, knowing full well LaCroix would resist her, she did not know. But she had to find a way; there was too much at stake.

The next day Clara was on her feet and anxious to leave. She did not want to be discourteous to the Mandan Indians, who had shown her such hospitality, but the thought of LaCroix getting farther and farther away distressed her.

"We will leave the village soon," Nighthawk told her, "when the sun rises tomorrow. This day is for feasting and for smoking the pipe with the council of this village. This is the day you will be honored."

Clara listened as Nighthawk explained to her that the feasting and the smoking of the pipe showed peace and brotherhood. Clara would show that she had enjoyed the company of her hosts and was happy to accept their food and drink. Pipes were smoked on religious or seasonal occasions and also when unusual events had occurred. To the Mandan, seeing a Long Knife woman who had killed an enemy war chief constituted an unusual occasion. Usually, women were not a part of a pipe ceremony, or a gathering of a council, but they saw Clara as a special woman worthy of honor, a woman of great medicine. It had been surprising to them when they heard from Nighthawk that Clara was the leader of the large Long Knife party that was to have journeyed to their village to trade boats for

FIRECLOUD

horses. When the Mandan people learned that she had also fought her way past the terrible Sioux, they were amazed at her power. Though she did not understand what was to occur or why, Clara saw this day's events as a chance to gain a greater knowledge of this land and its people.

Inside the lodge where Clara had recovered from her sickness, Nighthawk helped her prepare for the ceremonies ahead. He spoke to her over the drums that had sounded continuously since the rising of the sun.

"You are to be honored as no other woman here has ever been honored," Nighthawk told her as he parted her hair in the middle and, with ochre, colored the part, from front to back, a bright red. "You are now one with Earth, the All Mother. What I have done to your hair tells all that this is true. You must now forget all the Long Knife ways you once knew, for you have never before lived through a ceremony by Indian people. You must not think what to do; I will help you. You will not understand, but you will learn."

"I don't know whether to be afraid or not," Clara told him as he helped her adjust her doeskin dress.

Nighthawk laughed. "It is they who will be afraid of you. That is why I tell you not to think, but only to let things happen."

Clara soon found herself being escorted through the village by the leaders of the Mandan tribe. "Remember what I have told you," Nighthawk reminded her as they walked. "Do not think; do not speak unless asked. Just watch and do what seems natural." She walked all through the village while the drums continued to sound and the people watched her pass. Many of them, wishing for some of her power, ran up and touched her, screeching and looking at their hands. Warriors brought their weapons and asked her to touch them and thus give them a power that they could carry into war against their enemies. Clara touched shields and lances and bows, trade guns and war clubs. She handled the scalps fixed on a large coup stick, its owner believing she had the power to cause more scalps to grow from it. She watched while warriors cut themselves and asked her to touch their wounds, thus inoculating them with her medicine and great power. It went on for a long time, and she listened to Nighthawk and said nothing. She gazed upon the people with as much awe as they showed her. Never before had she seen men and women so transfixed on the supernatural. It almost scared her.

Later she sat cross-legged in a circle with Nighthawk and the Mandan leaders. She had been placed to the right of the chief, with Nighthawk on her right. The chief lit a pipe and held it up to the sky in reverence. He then puffed and blew smoke to the earth and the sky, and to the four directions, signifying his respect to the powers that ruled the earth.

Clara took the pipe from him and imitated his actions. She drew on the pipe, slowly at first, and then more heavily. She found the contents to be a smooth-tasting blend of herbs and bark, quite unlike what she had expected. Without understanding why, Clara felt an overwhelming serenity as she passed the pipe on to Nighthawk, who took it with a nod and a smile.

When the pipe had passed completely around the circle, the chief placed the pipe in a special leather pouch and began a long oration in Mandan that Clara could not understand. As he spoke, all those in the circle, including Nighthawk, made sounds and gestures of awe and approval, showing the speaker that they were very impressed with what he was saying. When he had finished, he looked to Clara.

"He was telling about one of his brave deeds in battle," Nighthawk explained to Clara. "Now it is your turn. They are all waiting to hear about your fight with the Sioux war chief, Cut Face."

The eyes of all the council members were on her as she moved her legs to ease the cramps that were beginning to make her uncomfortable. This was an experience she had never had before, and she wondered what they expected of her. Should she be dramatic and play up the fight, as they surely wished her to do? Or should she be very modest and claim that she had gained strength only through instincts? It then occurred to her that the telling of this story could well raise her status among these people and thus help her acquire good horses for the trip to the Yellowstone. Nighthawk had warned her that she would have to tell them how a Long Knife woman had come to have so much power. She knew then what she would tell them about power, and how she had come to dream of it. Her story would be one they would always remember.

11

CLARA BEGAN IN SIGN to tell of the morning that the Sioux attacked the expedition. She told of the deaths of John and many of the *voyageurs*, and how she had to cross the river to escape with her life. She told of the Sioux warrior, the one they called Cut Face, who had shot John in the back with an arrow, and how she had pulled the warrior from his horse and fought with him to save her own life. She told how she had killed the warrior with the arrow she had taken from his quiver.

All those in the circle looked upon her with awe and great admiration, yelling war whoops when they heard of the Sioux war chief's death. Then she began the part of her story she knew they could understand, for all Indians who excelled in battle paid homage to a spirit helper who had looked down on them with favor, having given them the power to accomplish their feat.

"Ever since I have come into these lands," Clara told them in sign, "I have heard of a special horse who rules the lands where the mountains begin. He is the Thunder Horse, the one called Firecloud. My thoughts have been filled with a vision of him. My one desire is to ride this beautiful stallion and call him my own. The thought of him filled me with the power to conquer the Sioux war chief, Cut Face. The spirit of the Thunder Horse gave me this power."

Nighthawk looked at her and smiled. "You will never be settled until you have ridden that horse," he said. "Perhaps you are right about the horse filling you with power. If this is true, you are a special person, chosen by the spirits to come into this land and ride a horse no one else has ever been able to catch for very long."

The others in the council looked to each other and pointed, making signs that meant she was bestowed with great power, that she had strength and courage rarely seen in a woman. And to have the confidence needed to ride the Thunder Horse was a sign that she was special among all those who lived in these lands. Each of them looked upon her for a long time, as if to remember her and to know her every feature, for they would repeat the story they had heard from her to others, and one day they would be able to say they had sat together in ceremony with the Long Knife woman who had killed the Sioux war chief, Cut Face, and who was bestowed with power from the Thunder Horse, the one called Firecloud.

The chief talked to one of the other council members, who got up from his seat and hurried to another lodge.

"He is sending a messenger to the Hidatsa village," Nighthawk told Clara. "They want the Hidatsa to see you, also. You are someone special."

"In all the winters I have seen," the Mandan chief told Clara, "this is the first time my eyes have beheld a woman such as you. This is a day I shall not forget. But I wish to know why you did not take Cut Face's scalp."

"I am not used to fighting," Clara answered. "I meant only to save myself."

The Mandan chief nodded. "If ever you were to prepare for war, your power would be very great."

A delegation of Hidatsa arrived, dressed in ceremonial costume, singing songs of war deeds. They were honored to have been invited to meet this powerful Long Knife woman, and they too bestowed on her many presents, including skin dresses adorned with shells and beads, and an assortment of clay cooking and storage pots. They also wanted to hear her story, and when Clara had repeated it, they cheered her and nodded in admiration. They believed the Sioux had meant to attack their village, and by killing their war chief, Clara had single-handedly driven them away. On a buffalo hide, one of the men began to draw a series of stick figures, one with a dress, holding an arrow above her head over a fallen enemy. Nighthawk explained to Clara that the men considered this ceremony an important event in their year. It would be the subject of their winter count, a drawing of the most outstanding occurrence to happen to them from the passing of one winter through the passing of the next. She would be a part of their pictorial calendar, which was passed down from one generation to the next.

After a song was sung honoring her, a Hidatsa leader paid her a special tribute. He gave her two eagle tailfeathers, each one tipped with a tuft of hair from the tail of a horse, symbolic of a special victory in battle against an enemy.

"Few men among a tribe of Indian people are ever honored in this way," Nighthawk told Clara. "This is a day any warrior would be very proud to have lived."

"But I am no braver than you," Clara told him. "It is strange that I should be honored this way when you and many of these warriors have fought many battles and have faced far greater danger."

"Yes," Nighthawk said, "but you killed a Sioux warrior thought by many to be invincible, and your being a woman makes the feat even more astounding. Killing an enemy hand to hand, after first striking him while he is alive, merits great honor. You have done all these things to a great enemy war chief. This village will always remember you."

After Clara had been honored and presented with the gifts, the Hidatsa joined the Mandan council, and they repeated the pipe ceremony. Then, in honor of the Long Knife woman, Hidatsa as well as Mandan orators took turns in describing deeds of valor they had performed on the battlefield, mostly against the Sioux.

It was late when the assembly broke up and the Hidatsa

returned to their village. Nighthawk helped Clara load her presents on three horses the villagers had given her, and prepared the horse they had given him for the journey west. She and Nighthawk made their way to a special lodge that had been decorated for them. The fire inside had been built up, and pots of meats and vegetables awaited them.

"We could eat for the rest of our lives," Clara said jokingly, "and it may take that long for the muscles in my legs to relax. I have never sat so long in one position!"

Nighthawk laughed. "You will need to get used to sitting like that for long periods of time. If you are going to trade, there will be many sessions as we had today."

Clara stretched out on a pile of robes along one curved wall of the lodge, moving about in discomfort as the aching in her legs persisted.

"I will ease the agony in your legs," Nighthawk said, kneeling beside her. "I do not like to see you in pain."

Clara turned over on her stomach, and Nighthawk knelt over her, one knee on each side of her legs. His strong hands moved rhythmically, massaging her muscles in a slow, even motion that soothed the hurting within. She felt her dress sliding higher and higher as his hands moved up and down her legs, his fingers bringing warmth and comfort to her. Soon his hands were making long, even strokes over her skin, his fingertips trailing to her inner thighs and finding their way up under her dress. Desire began to mount within her.

Nighthawk continued to massage and stroke her legs, moving his fingers deftly and increasing the inner warmth that was pouring over Clara like a flood.

"You are under my care," Nighthawk said softly. "I know the best treatment for you."

Clara began to indulge herself in the pleasure Nighthawk was bringing to her. She lifted herself up as he slipped her dress higher and higher until he had eased it over her head and shoulders. She let him turn her over and pull her up to a sitting position, where he looked at her naked form as the flickering light of the fire danced against the walls of the lodge.

FIRECLOUD

"You are the most beautiful woman I have ever seen," he told her, gently moving his fingers along her face and neck and down across her breasts. Clara let her hands wander over him, feeling his sleek frame, his gracefully contoured muscles that bunched hard as iron when he moved. Her lips met his, and she let him take her once again into the world he always created when he touched her. Gently, he pushed her down on the warm robes, his kisses moving from her lips to her face and down her neck. His lips found her breasts and nipples, which he caressed with his lips and tongue until the fire within her had pushed past her conscious senses to something far deeper. His tongue flicked downward, into the curves of her lower stomach and abdomen, and she heard herself cry out.

Lifting herself up, she brought his lips again to hers, pulling his breechclout free. Her hands found him, and the wanting within her rose to an unbearable height as he arched himself over her.

She gasped as he pushed deep into her, filling her and moving in a controlled, powerful rhythm that took her breath away. She pressed herself up into him, falling into the rhythm and climbing higher with him until their uncontrolled passion exploded within their bodies and the surge of release overwhelmed them.

Clara lay in his arms while he spoke to her softly of the future and their happiness together. He told her of the Kainah Blackfoot lands again and the beauty of the mountains he wanted to share with her forever. Soon he was asleep, and she carefully slipped from his arms and put her dress on. Outside the night was cool, with a clear sky thickly dotted with glittering stars. The village was quiet, and only the occasional snort from a horse tied next to a lodge could be heard through the stillness. Clara paced back and forth in front of the lodge, trying to decide what to do. Nighthawk wanted her to go with him directly to his people; he was becoming possessive of her already, wanting to control her thoughts and desires. Maybe it would be best if she left him and let him return to his people while she attended to her business. Could a warrior with a wild and fierce pride exist in harmony with an independent woman from the white culture? She felt the tiny wooden warrior around her neck, knowing that harmony would be difficult to achieve. But she also knew they had built between them a love that would endure through any conflict, a love that would endure forever.

THE SWEEPING PLAIN WAS cut by rugged badlands of clay and rock that contained steep, rugged trails. Since Clara and Nighthawk had left the villages, a cold rain had turned the trails into greasy mud that stuck to the horses' hooves and made traveling slow and tedious. They lived only on dried meat and pemmican, traveling only at night and camping without a fire. They were now crossing lands that belonged to the tribes Nighthawk had told Clara about, the Assiniboin and Crow peoples, bitter enemies of all the Blackfoot nations. They ruled the high northern plains, marked by the meeting of the Missouri and the Yellowstone. These tribes were fierce fighters and would give no quarter to an enemy; they would torture with relish any Blackfoot captives.

Clara preferred to travel at night, for the day's warmth allowed comfortable sleep. The sun's arc had become increasingly lower, and the nights were heavy with frost. It was better to be riding on a horse after dark than lying on the cold ground. The trees were bare now, the cottonwoods with their towering, crooked branches standing gray-white and stark in the crisp air. Though late fall had given way to the season Nighthawk called the cold moons, there had been no heavy snowstorms since the one during the fight with the Sioux. But storm and cold could come at any time. Nighthawk told her the weather in these lands had been known to change from very warm to extreme cold in less than the passing of one sun. They had been lucky so far, and Clara hoped their luck would continue.

Throughout their journey, Nighthawk had spoken often about his people and the land they lived in. He had told her many stories about his sister and his deceased mother, and also of Aged One, the old warrior who was his best friend. He spoke angrily of his half brother. Black Owl, he believed, had talked the rest of the Kainah warriors into leaving the Sioux battlefield as quickly as possible in the days just before John and Clara had found him. The thought that Black Owl had left him to die made him bitter. Usually the members of a war party would risk their own lives to find and save one of their comrades. Nighthawk suspected that his half brother was rejoicing at the thought of having finally disposed of the only other young warrior in the village who could challenge him for the honor of becoming a war chief and member of the council.

Clara detected the fierce determination in his face. She knew he looked forward with confidence to meeting his half brother and the rest of the villagers. He seemed to be ready to make a strong bid to overturn Black Owl's influence in the village and gain greater respect for himself. With Clara as a symbol of strength, he hoped to show his half brother and the other villagers that he was worthy of higher esteem. Clara's concern was that she would not be readily accepted by the Black Horse band of Kainah Blackfeet, some of whom had undoubtedly never seen a white woman before. She knew that women were considered unimportant by the Plains Indians, and Nighthawk, although he loved her, still wished to gain control of her.

They made camp but a few days' journey from where the Yellowstone emptied into the Missiouri, the Big Muddy, as the Indians called it.

"The spirits have looked upon me with favor," Nighthawk told Clara as he studied the surrounding hills and ravines from where they had camped at a place along the river, hidden among the cottonwoods and willows. His eyes studied the surrounding land, looking for signs of anyone else in the vicinity. "Yes," he continued, "the spirits have been very good to me, for I have found a woman who is both beautiful and powerful. It is hard for me to understand such power in a woman. If we were to meet with the Assiniboin or the Crow, I believe that your power would be too great for them."

"Nighthawk," Clara said, "I am no different than I was when you first met me after you had been hurt in battle. I was just as frightened when I killed Cut Face as I was that first day. I cannot do all the things that others now believe I am able to do. I was just fighting for my life."

"I know of very few other women who would have the courage to fight as you did. And there are no other women with the power to conquer death, as you did."

Clara had noticed that Indian men considered themselves lord and master over their women, but they took for granted the daily work done for them by their wives. The women were expected to perform all the lowly tasks of daily life, even moving the lodge and all the family's possessions when the village changed camping sites. Preparing food for winter use, making different types of clothes for different occasions, and preparing buffalo hides for lodges and clothing were foremost among the duties of the women. Clara had been able to understand this when Nighthawk explained it to her during their stay with the Mandan. The men protected the village, provided the food, and gained honor by fighting against tribal enemies. Now Nighthawk was placing her above the other women and on an equal with the warriors among his people. The women would certainly resent her, which would damage Nighthawk's attempt to gain the respect of his people.

"I do not want to be anyone special," Clara told him. "I wish I had never seen the Sioux and Cut Face. Things would be much easier for me now."

Nighthawk looked quickly at her. "We would not have found each other as we did. Maybe not for the passing of many moons. Do you regret seeing me again?"

"No, of course not," Clara said. "Don't be silly. I only meant things would be easier for me. I would still have both keelboats and all my provisions and trade items. John would still be alive, and I would be rid of LaCroix by now."

"Maybe the time will come," Nighthawk said, "when trading for the fur of the beaver is no longer important to you. Maybe other things will become more important. Maybe I will then be more important."

"Nighthawk, I wish you would understand. I have never known anyone in my life, outside of my father, who was more important to me. You have done more for me, as a woman, than I could have ever dreamed. You know that. I would never have come after the fight with LaCroix if you hadn't become special to me. And you would not have waited for me on the bank of the river if you hadn't hoped I would try to find you. Isn't that true?"

"Yes, your words are true," Nighthawk nodded. He put his arm out and Clara snuggled close to him.

"If you ever do that again," Clara said with a grin, "please don't go so far before you decide to stop and wait. I thought I would never find you!"

Nighthawk laughed with her. "I would stop and then decide to go again, stop, and then go again. Finally I pulled the petals off a flower, saying to myself 'stay' and 'go on' with each petal. You are lucky; the last petal was 'stay.'"

"I know," Clara said with a smile. "I'll bet you planned it that way."

Nighthawk shrugged. "Well, maybe there was one time when I pulled off two petals at once."

Clara held him tight. "Don't get mad at me any more," she said. "The flowers are gone until spring, and you could get too far ahead of me by then."

The sun crossed the sky twice as they traveled west, warming their sleep and bringing the sounds of birds in the leafless trees that lined the sweeping flow of the Big Muddy. The moon grew round as it rose a deep yellow-orange. The moon of change, Nighthawk called it, the moon that meant all the berries should be in and dried and all the roots dug, for the cold was coming and there was no more time to gather.

To Clara, the full moon seemed sad, even though it was so spectacularly beautiful as it pushed through low clouds adrift above the eastern horizon. For all its brilliance, it meant that every tree and bush, every blade of grass, must be ready for the tormenting cold. It meant that every creature in this land must have grown long shaggy hair, or turned its coat to white, to settle in the snow when its life was threatened. It meant that all life had gone into a state of transformation, the leaves and the green of the land all lost until the time when the sun would again climb higher and once again bring a new season to the land. "It is the test that comes to all creatures and peoples who live in these lands," Nighthawk said. "Sun turns his back on us, and life is very hard."

As the orange moon rose high into the night sky, to shrink back to a smaller circle and again become white, Clara wondered how she would face her test as the cold came to the land. Confused and tormented, she wondered how she would manage to get her property back from LaCroix and again gain the loyalty of the men. She wished in every way that Nighthawk would help her, and not leave her to settle her problems herself. This warrior now meant a great deal to her, and the last thing she wanted was to enter into conflict with him.

One morning Nighthawk spoke to her as they prepared to sleep for the day. They had reached the place where the Yellowstone flowed into the Missouri.

"When the sun falls and the night again comes," he said, "we will cross the Yellowstone and follow the Big Muddy on to the Great Falls, where my people are camped for the cold moons." His spirits were high as he discussed his plans for the two of them. "Soon, when the Mountains of the Big Snow come into our sight, we can again begin to travel by day. We will then be close to the lands of my people. We can again have the warmth of a fire. Then the days will all be good."

Clara looked into Nighthawk's eyes and took a deep breath before she spoke. "All the time we have traveled you have talked only about going to your lands and people. Never once have you asked me how you could help me get my trade possessions back. I have yet to hear you say that you would like to help me with my problem before we decide about our future together with your people."

"You do not need the Long Knives' money to live in these lands," Nighthawk said. "I will provide for your needs. Why do you want to be a Long Knife trader? Why can you not be happy as my wife?"

FIRECLOUD

"You know it is not a simple thing," Clara reminded him. "If I do not trade for furs, I will lose all the money and honor my father worked for all his life. I cannot do that. I must save his money and his honor. After I do that, then I can think about my life with you. I hoped you would help me."

"I cannot go with you to find LaCroix," Nighthawk said. "I would kill the dog, or he would kill me before the sun set on the first day. And the others could never accept me in their camp. Never."

"LaCroix will be no problem after we arrive," Clara said. "I will send him away immediately. Then I will again be in charge. I will increase the men's wages and give them more whiskey. They will stay. And they will accept you."

Nighthawk shook his head, silent for a time while he studied Clara. Finally he said, "What has happened to the mind that was once so clear and sharp? Did your head strike a rock in the river during your fight with Cut Face?"

"What are you talking about?"

"You do not speak with good thought. LaCroix will not leave so easily. Why would he travel so far from the land of the Long Knives to be told to leave by a woman?"

"I will pay him well before he leaves," Clara said. "Much more than was decided upon for the entire length of the expedition."

"He will know he has far more to gain by staying," Nighthawk argued. "Why would he agree to accept your offer when he knows he could have much more by keeping that which belongs to you? And you know he wants you for his own. Why are you so foolish as to think that he will leave you alone? His eyes are those of a man who has evil spirits in him. I look at you now and see that your senses have failed you."

Clara realized that Nighthawk was right. LaCroix would resent her intrusion now that he considered himself leader of the expedition.

"Why do you not let me lead a war party against them?" Nighthawk suggested. "You would have your possessions back and be rid of LaCroix also."

"But your warriors would then divide my possessions among themselves as spoils of war," Clara said. "Isn't that right?"

Nighthawk nodded. "That is our custom."

"That would do me no good," Clara said. "I must have the possessions to trade for furs. In St. Louis, the trade items are worth very little. The furs are extremely valuable."

"Then we will wait until the snows have gone and LaCroix has traded for the furs. We will then attack him and take the furs."

Clara nodded, becoming somewhat excited. "That might be the best way," she agreed. After thinking awhile, she added, "But I still think it would be good to be sure that he has gone to the upper Yellowstone and hasn't built the fort in some other location."

"We will do that," Nighthawk said. "We will journey to find him. But first we will travel to my people."

"It would be better to find him now," Clara said, "while he is still traveling and hasn't yet settled for the winter. If he does decide to build the fort in another valley, it might be harder for us to locate him later in the winter. Maybe the weather will be so bad that we won't be able to travel at all."

"You must do as I say," Nighthawk insisted. "I am your man and you must grant my wishes."

"I have wishes, too," Clara declared. "And I see no reason why we can't work together to make each other happy. I am very worried about LaCroix and my possessions. As soon as I am relieved of that worry, I can settle down to learning life as it is lived out here. But first, my concerns must be taken care of."

Nighthawk set his jaw in anger. "You will do this without me! I cannot be husband to a woman who must gain her own honor. That is not the way I have lived. I will not live in that manner now!"

"I do not mean to gain honor," Clara said disgustedly. "I thought I made you understand that. And I am not trying to take honor from you. I am doing only what I feel I must do at this time. Your plan to take the furs from LaCroix in the spring is a good one. I only want to be sure he is where we can keep an eye on him. I don't understand why you can't help me find him before we go to your people."

"I wish for us to go to my people first," Nighthawk said. "If you will not come with me now, then this is where we must part." He looked at Clara hard for her answer.

"I cannot."

Nighthawk picked up his things and strode angrily to his horse. "I will leave the food with you, all but a small amount I will need to reach my people. And all of your presents from the Dirt Lodge people can remain on the horses. I will need but one horse now." He mounted and called to her before he left. "And you can also have this." He pulled the small wooden figure of the woman from around his neck and threw it to the ground, urging his horse into a gallop out of camp.

Clara watched him disappear from view, and the sound of his horse's hooves died away. There would be no going after him this time. And he would not stop this time, for he knew she would not change her mind. She was now alone, with only the icy wind that rattled the bare branches of the trees and the occasional chatter of squirrels and birds. She made herself walk over and pick up Nighthawk's wooden love charm from the ground. She reached for the tiny warrior that hung around her neck, but she could not snap the rawhide thong, and her neck burned from the effort. She slumped to the ground, looking at the figure Nighthawk had once cherished as a symbol of his love for her, tears dropping from her cheeks. Clutching it tightly, she wrapped her arms around her knees and buried her head, feeling the hurt that tore at her heart. Beside her the Yellowstone murmured. Its trails led to high in the mountains, but no matter how far they took her, she knew her every thought and dream would be filled with visions of the Kainah warrior and the love she would always have for him.

12

THE DAYS CREPT BY, and Clara traveled closer to the Rocky Mountains, passing through the Badlands and into the broad valley of the Yellowstone. The stark beauty of deep gorges and knobs of hard clay had given way to rolling hills and majestic cliffs of white sandstone topped with stands of yellow pine. This land, so strikingly different from any she had ever seen before, held her in its grasp, its timeless face molded by the wind that snapped and howled through the arches of rock that stood like the castles of a thousand kings. This was the home of eagles and hawks that circled the twisting river, and the small falcons that sailed through the air on narrow, sharp-tipped wings, taking their prey with blinding swiftness.

Travel had been easy for her, and she had made good time along the trails through the valley. The robes the Mandan had given her were more than adequate against the frost of the night ground, and the pemmican, with it's mixture of fats and meat and berries, kept her strong. She knew she was near the upper Yellowstone. She had passed the mouths of two large rivers that emptied into the Yellowstone, and she was certain that the Powder and Tongue rivers were behind her now. Another week's travel would take her to LaCroix.

Now, as the sun moved up into the hazy morning sky, Clara

got the horses ready to travel again another day, noticing a drop in the temperature and the sudden shifting of the wind to the north. A thick bank of whitish-grey clouds was moving across the sky, and the reluctance of the horses to move told her a storm was approaching. Blocking it from her mind, she struggled against the will of the horses and began to travel, pulling hard on the pack line rope repeatedly to keep up the pace. She could not afford to be slowed in her efforts now, not after having come this far. In only a week she would know for sure if LaCroix had stuck with the original plan. If he had decided to build that fort elsewhere, she did not know how she would find him.

Mixed with her concern for the business was an Indian warrior whose face would not leave her mind. Where was Nighthawk now? Had he safely reached his people? Each night his face had blocked her view of the sky, the desire for his warm caress taking her mind from sleep. She longed to feel his strong arms around her and to see the soft, loving eyes as they had been before hurt and anger had turned them cold.

The tears had come often, and her hands had clasped the two wooden figures that now hung around her neck. The love charms were warm to her touch and eased her loneliness to a degree. But nothing would take the place of Nighthawk's strong, muscular body against hers, his arms holding her close. She must see him again and be with him. The more she thought about him the more she realized that, despite their differences, she had become a slave to his powerful love.

At first, the snow came in flurries, rushing at her from the darkening sky on a wind that numbed her face and hands. She drew herself deeper into the robe, urging the horses along at a faster pace. They tossed their heads and snorted repeatedly. The storm grew worse, and heavy snow soon formed banks as the wind sculpted it around the trees and over fallen logs. The horses held back ever more strongly against her, and she realized there was little sense in fighting them.

She found an old stream bed, lined with a thick growth of cottonwoods and willows, abandoned by the current in years past when the river had changed its course. It formed a shelter from the whipping wind and snow. The horses edged themselves into the protection of the willows, their backs to the storm as she watered and fed them. Clara brushed snow from the brush and branches and set flint to a small pile of powder she had wrapped in a piece of torn blanket. As she had seen Nighthawk do, she placed tiny slivers of wood over the burning cloth and larger branches, ends outward over the igniting kindling. As the fire grew, she added wood until the fire blazed warm. Then she set about collecting more wood; there was no telling how long the storm would last.

An unending rush of wind and snow howled and cried out as it slashed through the trees and sent wailing echos through the rock cliffs and spires at the edge of the valley. Clara stayed awake throughout the night, feeding wood to the fire and rubbing the numbness from her hands and feet. Her ankle, though now completely healed, began to ache with the intense cold. Even as the light of a new day arrived, the blinding white of the storm persisted. Finally, as midday approached, the wind let up, and the snow eased. By early afternoon the snow had stopped, and a deep cold had settled in its place. The sun finally broke through into the valley, finding the land still and silent under a frozen white blanket.

Clara again built the fire up with large logs and ate a meal of pemmican and melted snow. The added warmth and the appearance of the sun comforted her. Two large black and white magpies alighted on her stack of firewood, cocking their heads and yapping, as if asking for food. She threw them some pemmican scraps and watched them fight over the food before bouncing into the air, their long tails spreading to give them balance. The horses moved around in the willows, snapping off branch tips and chewing them into a pulpy mush. Exhausted, Clara slumped down in her blankets and let her eyes close.

CLARA AWOKE WITH A START to the crunch of snow beside her.

Staring at her and talking among themselves was a group of Indian warriors. They were not prepared for war, for they were not painted nor did they carry buffalo hide shields and lances. Instead they were dressed heavily against the cold, and their faces and hands were smeared with grease as protection from the wind. The top of their hair was cut in a high roach, combed back, and packed with grease, but the back hair fell down over their shoulders and back, unusually long and heavily adorned with small animal skins and trade items. Clara knew with certainty that she was meeting the Absaroka, the Crows. This group was no doubt from a band of River Crows, for the Mountain Crow people would be found higher up in the valley.

Clara stood up and made sign to them. "I have come in peace. I wish to travel through your lands."

"Have you lost your man?" One of them asked in sign. "Was he killed and you became lost?"

"No," Clara answered. "I am not lost. I must travel through your lands to find a party of Long Knives who might have traveled through here when the moon was full."

The Crow spokesman nodded. "Indeed, a party of Long Knives traveled through here when the moon was full. They gave us cloth for our women and steel knives for our warriors in trade for the fur of the beaver."

Clara became excited. "Was their leader a large Long Knife with hair on his face?"

The Crow spokesman nodded and asked, "Is he your man?"

"He is not my man," Clara answered. "My man is not with me." She was careful not to mention anything about Nighthawk. The Kainah Blackfeet were the Crows' bitter enemies, and these men might think she was spying on them.

"You are strange to us," the Crow spokesman said, advancing and eyeing her closely. "Only a few of our people have seen a Long Knife woman, and never have we seen one, such as you, who is dressed as an Indian woman."

"I have come to find the Long Knife party," Clara said. "I am their true leader. We were separated when the Sioux attacked our boats near the villages of the Dirt Lodge people." She pointed to the east. Then she took from her skin pouch the coup feathers she had received from the Hidatsa council. "This I received from the Dirt Lodge people for killing a Sioux warrior named Cut Face." Clara knew the Crow and the Sioux were enemies and hoped to gain the favor of these men by displaying her honors.

The Crow warriors began to talk among themselves excitedly. Finally the spokesman said, "You must be a powerful woman to have done such a deed. We are grateful that you have killed one of our enemies. You must come to our village and feast with us."

The Crows had made their winter camp along the broad valley plain adjacent to the river. It was a huge camp, with clan lodges clustered in small groupings for over a mile in length. As in the Mandan village, many dogs and children rushed out to greet them, and Clara was immediately made the object of intense curiosity. She was immediately made comfortable at a large fire near the center of the village, and dishes of steaming food were presented to her. A circle of men quickly assembled, and a pipe ceremony ensued.

Again Clara recited in sign the story of her struggle to the death with the Sioux warrior Cut Face. Never having heard a story like it ever before, the Crows were impressed, and she was again bestowed with presents. She was given two more horses to carry her added possessions and a coup stick adorned with a single feather and painted with a yellow stripe in honor of her courageous deed.

Politely declining an invitation to spend the winter in their village, Clara left the next morning, anxious to reach the upper Yellowstone. She was told the Mountain Crows would also welcome her if she went to their village, for they also respected a courageous war deed against an enemy. But Clara's sole purpose was to find LaCroix, mark in her mind the place where he was building the fort, and then strike north to find the winter camp of the Kainah Blackfeet, and Nighthawk.

Encouraged by her knowledge that LaCroix had followed

the original plan and would establish trade outward from the upper Yellowstone, Clara traveled steadily through the cold. Soon she would be united with the man who had given her so much love. She knew Nighthawk must feel as she did, for the tiny wooden love charms were always warm, as if the fires of love were ever present and would never go out.

Though the land lay frozen and white, its spectacular beauty touched her. She had now reached the mountains, their jagged peaks towering high above the surrounding plain. The Crows had told her she would first see the mountains of the Bear's Tooth, named for a pinnacle that curved up near a high pass used during the warm moons of summer. The peaks soared high and blue below the thick crown of white that adorned the towering peaks. They were in the homeland of the Mountain Crows, the vast mountains of the Absaroka, home of the Sparrow Hawk people.

Along the river there was plenty of food for the horses. They found thick groves of willow to supplement the dried grass and thin slivers of cottonwood bark Clara had cut for them from the trees along the shoreline and in the bogs along the valley floor. She could eat fresh meat whenever she chose, for the valley teemed with deer, elk, and buffalo. At her nightly campfires she was never alone. A flock of magpies collected on the limbs of the cottonwoods, making a racket, and the squirrels darted about, their fluffy tails bouncing and curling behind them. An occasional ermine, or white weasel, padded softly through the snow with little hunter's feet, chasing mice out from under fallen logs, or just sitting upright, staring with tiny black eyes and a nose that wiggled constantly. And there were the chickadees, with which she had become the best of friends, fluffy little birds with a bouncy, cheerful nature and miniature black feathers that looked like tiny caps on heads that were never still but always pecking and looking about while their feet made delicate hopping tracks in the snow. These little birds would flit about her, from branch to ground and back, chitting among themselves and singing their song, as they passed the evenings and early mornings with her.

FIRECLOUD

As she continued her journey, she learned more each day about the land and the creatures who lived in it. She would watch with fascination the movements of the ever present packs of wolves and coyotes, their noses in the air. She knew that she provided many of their meals, leaving for them the scraps of the game she had killed for food. She now understood the constant communication that went on between animals, telling of contentment or the approach of danger. She knew the whoof of a startled elk and the low, guttural bawl of an angry buffalo. She now knew when the birds were singing happy songs, or scolding, or giving cries of warning. She stored all these sounds deep in her memory so that she could pull them out when she needed them to warn her of danger. It was important to know when the land spoke, and what it was saying.

Finally, as one morning broke into afternoon, she saw smoke rising above the cottonwoods from a point upriver. With renewed vigor and enthusiasm, she urged her horses along at a brisk pace. The smoke was farther away than it had first appeared, and she traveled until late evening before she could make out a fort being built on a small flat above the river. Leaving the pack horses behind, Clara rode closer, staying in the cover of the trees along the river. From the thick cover of a chokecherry bush, Clara was able to see LaCroix giving orders to a number of the *voyageurs*, who were lifting logs into place to form the walls of the fort.

Clara started back toward her pack horses, satisfied that she had found LaCroix at last. She would bring Nighthawk here with a war party when spring arrived. No doubt LaCroix would secure as many furs as he could to take back to St. Louis. She reached her packhorses with uplifted spirits, knowing she could now make way north to the Great Falls and the man she could not forget.

Clara dismounted and secured her horse to a cottonwood tree. Suddenly she heard a voice from behind her.

"Ah, it is the lady, Clara," the voice said. She turned to see a young *voyageur*. He went on before she could speak. "We thought you were dead, Miss Clara. But no, you have come to this place. LaCroix he will be very happy to see you."

Two other *voyageurs* appeared beside him as if from nowhere. They all held rifles cradled in their arms.

"Where did you come from?" Clara asked them.

"It is only by chance," said the one who had spoken to her, "that we find your horses. We have been hunting. We have a good catch. No?" He laughed, and the others laughed with him.

"I am once again in command," Clara told them. "We will all go to the fort and meet with LaCroix. I plan to give you all a bonus in wages if we have a good year."

The three were still laughing among themselves. The one said, "Yes, we will meet with LaCroix. But, no, I do not believe you are in command. You see, it is good to work for LaCroix. He gives us whiskey." They all laughed louder. "Now, it is for you to ride with us to the fort, for LaCroix he is waiting. And when he sees what we have brought, he will give us much whiskey."

Clara mounted her horse and rode between two of the *voyageurs* while the third led her pack animals, telling the other two in French what a good store of articles and supplies she had brought them. Clara took a deep breath, trying to control her anger, knowing she had to keep her thoughts clear if she hoped to save herself from LaCroix.

As they drew near the site where the fort was under construction, she began to fully realize the extreme peril she was in. Two of these three *voyageurs*, before escaping the Sioux, had been loyal to her. Now they acted as if she had never commanded them, as if they had never shown her respect, as if they had never even *known* her before. They seemed so different from the happy young men who had thrown her into the water to initiate her, to tell her they recognized her as one of them, to call her a true fur trader. They did not seem like the same men she had sat around the campfire with, trading stories and jokes, laughing and sharing the evenings until the next day came and they moved the boats again into the river.

FIRECLOUD

These could not be the same men, yet they were, and now they relished the thought of seeing LaCroix's face when they reached the fort. Clara knew that these three were typical of the men who had stayed with LaCroix; none of the others would be loyal to her either. She would be their captive, and she would probably be treated far worse than most prisoners.

The men told Clara to rein in her horse while one of them took her pouch from her horse. He looked into it and laughed.

"It would be good if you had something to make you look your best. No? It would be good, yes, very good, if you had the sweet smelling mint to rub on your neck. Or the meadow rue. Yes, something sweet. LaCroix would like that. Yes, we would get more whiskey." The three of them laughed heartily.

The *voyageur* continued to snoop in her bag, pulling out a bar of trade soap and the fingernail file she had brought with her from the East. He threw them and other items to the ground, intent on finding some vermilion or a pouch of crushed plants to be used as perfume. He grumbled as he looked, then laughed with glee when he found the Hidatsa coup feathers.

"Put these in your hair," he ordered. "LaCroix, he likes his women to be fancy." The other two cheered and laughed.

Clara placed the feathers in her hair while they nodded their approval. Then she pointed to a large skin pouch tied on one of the pack-horses.

"You will find some paints and perfume plants in that bag," she said.

"Ah, yes," one *voyageur* said. "You know what LaCroix wants." He ordered his two companions to get the bag from the horse. They cheered as they dismounted.

"I have to look my best," Clara said. "Did you have some whiskey already today?"

The *voyageur* broke into a silly grin. "We were to have gone hunting. But we steal a jug. Just one. You will not tell LaCroix, will you?"

"Is your whiskey gone?"

He nodded.

Clara pointed again. "On that horse you will find a skin of whiskey."

The *voyageur* went to find the whiskey.

Clara waited until he had reached the other two men, who were now tearing into her possessions and claiming ownership of her things. As soon as the three of them began to quarrel, Clara kicked her horse into a gallop and headed for the cover along the river. She leaned low over the stallion's neck, urging it faster through the snow, hearing shouts of anger from the *voyageurs* behind her. They had mounted and followed her. Her only chance of escape was to find cover in the thick undergrowth.

Clara dismounted and sent her horse off at a gallop. Then she pushed her way through the branches, and heavy growth. Like the whitetail deer, she would have to follow a zigzag path along the trails until she found a hiding place. She could hear two of the *voyageurs* shouting to each other as they started into the cover after her, the third running his horse on toward the fort to alert LaCroix and the others. Clara did not become alarmed, for the sun was now her ally. It had dropped low in the west and would soon disappear. She continued to run through the trees and brush, hoping to reach a point upriver where the timber came down a slope to meet the cottonwoods. There she could lose herself in the rocks and pines above the bottom. She knew if she could evade them until dark, they would give up the hunt, but until then they would search in earnest.

Through the tangled growth, Clara could see riders galloping their horses up the river to the line of adjoining pines and cottonwoods she had hoped to reach. Others were taking positions all along the valley at various places, dismounting and standing at the edge of the trees. It was obvious they meant to search for her both upstream and down, coming together in the middle. If the searchers on the bottom land flushed her out, those on the flat near the trees would see her. They had surrounded her on three sides, using the river to hem her in. There was no escape.

FIRECLOUD

Clara stopped and sat back on her heels to think, hearing the shouts and curses of men fighting brush all around her. They had forced her into a game of cat and mouse, life and death. She pulled her knife from its sheath and tested its edge. Her mind went back to the Sioux warrior, Cut Face. She could see him again plainly, and now each one of these men was another Cut Face. They were all Sioux to her now, her enemy.

The sun began to drop behind the mountains to the west, and the men hunting Clara cursed it. The shadows, already long, began to turn black. Picking her spot carefullly, Clara edged her way into a heavy tangle of wild roses that formed a screen along a sharp embankment. The plants were nearly head high, and their stalks were twisted together like loose knitting. It would take an extremely keen pair of eyes to spot her in such heavy cover, and soon the dim light would make it virtually impossible for the men to see her.

Clara nestled herself down into the roses, pushing the thorny branches aside and rearranging them over her. She thought back on the first time she had gone hunting and had come upon the burial ground. The sight of it had sent her into a panic-stricken run through the prickly undergrowth that had left her face, neck, and arms a crisscross of cuts and slashes. Since that time she had learned to make her way through the undergrowth with much more skill. She could now travel at a trot, ducking and moving her arms skillfully, and avoid being scraped or cut to any great degree. She had learned to use trees and cover to her advantage, and she was now testing this skill to the limit.

The sun continued to sink, and Clara sat silent, scarcely breathing, her knife in her hands. She could hear the men coming ever closer, cursing louder and more frequently now as they pushed their way through the undergrowth. They were walking too fast, trying to locate her before darkness put an end to their hunt. They were near her position and, moments later, past her, one of them brushing the edge of the rose tangle that hid her. They talked among themselves about the cold and the approaching night, and the warm fire at the fort.

They shook their heads and spoke of the uselessness of continuing the search, wishing one of the others up ahead would find her and yell out. They rubbed their hands and faces in the cold and asked each other repeatedly if anyone had found her.

Soon their voices grew faint, and she could hear them talking with the others about not having found her. She could envision them pointing to the timber and rocks and assuming she had escaped into the lower reaches of the mountains. Then they were out in the open, joining the other men at the edge of the trees, speaking of Crow women and the trading season ahead, and the whiskey and warmth that awaited them at the fort. They mounted their horses and, like a group of schoolboys released from class, raced one another to the fort.

Clara breathed a sigh of relief and worked her way out of the rosebushes. The sun had set, and it was twilight. Through the cold air she could see the line of smoke from the fires where the men were already laughing, yelling, and fighting over the gifts she had received at the Mandan and Hidatsa villages. The silence of evening hung over the river now. Her horses had undoubtedly joined the herd near the fort, and she would have to travel afoot. As if by impulse, she reached for the two wooden figures around her neck. Their warmth radiated through her hand and sent waves of longing through her. How she wished Nighthawk could be with her this night, holding her beneath a warm buffalo robe next to a cheery fire. But she was happy that she had escaped and that she could now travel north and find her Kainah warrior. The loss of her gifts and horses was not important. She was alive, and the tiny love charms gave her a measure of inner peace in knowing someone cared for her.

Clara left the cover of the trees and walked out onto the flat to begin her journey north. She knew she must cross over the divide to the west and enter the valley of the Gallatin River. It would take her to the Valley of the Three Forks, where the Jefferson and the Madison flowed into the Gallatin to form the headwaters of the Missouri. She was glad she had studied her maps with the attention she had; it made her journey through this vast mountain paradise a joy rather than a nightmare of guessing and concern about being lost. The reports of the Lewis and Clark Expedition had described this land and had mapped it in detail. Though their narratives had discussed the terrain, no words could convey the staggering beauty that lay before her. Glad to have escaped the searching *voyageurs*, Clara took a deep breath and headed for the mountains.

She had traveled only a short distance when she heard the snort of a horse behind her. On its back was a rider with a rifle pointed at her.

13

"LaCroix!"

The name stuck in Clara's throat. She had no chance to run; he was already upon her, and his eyes said he would not hesitate to fire the gun.

He jumped from his horse and pointed the barrel of the rifle at her head. "Ha, ha! My she-cat!" he yelled gleefully. "I knew you were in there, and I waited with patience, no? Now you are mine!"

"You will have to kill me, LaCroix!"

"That would be a shame." He grabbed her arm and held it tightly. "But if that's what my she-cat wishes, well, then, we shall see. But I think you will please me first."

He removed his buffalo skin capote and dropped the rifle in the snow. He lunged at her, his arms encircling her as she fell backward. His weight knocked the air from her, and he laughed, forcing his mouth and greasy beard down into her face. She turned her head, but his lips searched for hers, his breath rank and hot. With his left arm, he reached under her back and took her wrist, pulling it under her. She groaned in pain, and he laughed, pushing himself against her with even more force. Pinning her under him, he brought his free hand up under her dress. She screamed in rage, and he laughed again. She struggled to free her arms but he held her fast. He pulled her dress higher, and she screamed louder for him to stop. His laugh was breathy, lusty, and guttural. His hand came out from under her dress, and he grunted as he loosened his pants.

An intense wave of hatred and anger flooded Clara with sudden strength. Arching her back, she twisted sideways under him, forcing him to release her arm or lose his balance and topple over on his side. She quickly brought her free hand up, clawing downward over his right eye with all her might. Her nails bit deep, and as she raked his flesh, she felt his eyelid rip and the squish of the eyeball under her fingers.

LaCroix rose up with a howl, holding one hand over his bloody eye. Clara lunged for her rifle. She heard yelling from the direction of the fort and, glancing over her shoulder, saw several men on horseback racing through the snow. She turned and quickly aimed the rifle at the screaming LaCroix, who was now rolling in the snow with his hands over his eye. She pulled the trigger and the hammer fell, but the pan was full of snow, and the powder did not ignite. In rage and frustration, she took the rifle by the barrel and slammed it across LaCroix's shoulders and back, breaking the stock loose from the barrel. He let out a heavy grunt and rose to her knees, his injured eye a mass of blood. With a quick lunge, he caught her doeskin dress and ripped it as he fought to pull her to him. With her knife, Clara slashed the outside of his wrist, feeling the blade grate as it plunged through flesh and tendons and reached the bone.

Knowing she now had little time before the rest of the men would be upon her, Clara snatched up LaCroix's capote, mounted his horse, and headed west toward the pass. Behind her she heard the shouts of the men as they stopped to look after LaCroix. It was almost totally dark, and she would soon be but a shadow among the trees. They would not come after her now. LaCroix would not die, but he would think about her every day while he saw the world from one eye and used a weak and deformed hand.

Clara rode into the silent, forested hills. The moon rose,

FIRECLOUD

nearly full once again, providing light from a clear sky that shone down on the glistening white below. She now had the buffalo capote to keep her warm. The young mare she had taken from LaCroix seemed strong and capable of making the long, hard journey ahead. Once again she relaxed and set her thoughts on reaching the Kainah village and rejoining the warrior whom she loved so dearly. As the tension in her body seeped out and her blood calmed, she realized her journey to Nighthawk and his people at the Great Falls of the Missouri would be far harder than she had first envisioned. While fighting LaCroix, she had not noticed the considerable drop in temperature. The snow beneath the mare's hooves crunched and cracked, and the sky around the moon was a deep blue. There was no food in LaCroix's saddlebags, but she did find a pistol in a small leather pouch, complete with powder and ball. She would need to use the ammunition carefully and make every shot count, for she no longer had an unlimited supply of pemmican and jerky, or a collection of blankets and robes for warmth. The journey would be difficult, and there would likely be no hospitality such as she had received from the Crows. Ahead was only snow and deep cold.

NIGHTHAWK finished his evening prayers and sat atop a giant rock formation high above the frozen Big Muddy River. He looked out across the rugged hills and steep ravines, watching the sun move slowly down over this lonely land filled with cold and snow. He could shout as loud as he wished, and no one would hear him, not even the beautiful Long Knife woman whom he had left far away, nearly a full moon past. He could see her in his mind, but he could not touch her, nor could he forget her tender love.

The memory of her had been with him ever since that first night, and he had told himself over and over that he never should have left her; he should have traveled with her, to defend her against the crazy LaCroix. Once again this night, as in all nights since he had left her, he would get little sleep. It was not because of the cold, or because he dared not light a fire in enemy lands. It was not because of the constant need to be alert to the presence of Crow or Assiniboin warriors, enemies who would like to capture him alive and cut his heart out.

As a warrior, he was used to danger and discomfort. He was used to traveling far without leaving the back of his horse, or knowing the fires of a warm lodge with robes. A warrior could do without physical comforts. Something within him gave him a misery he had never before known. He had known physical pleasure with young Indian maidens, but the Long Knife woman who now rode with his heart had shown him a passion beyond any experience he had ever dreamed of. She had found him wounded and had helped him heal. She had laughed with him and talked with him about things he had told no one else. Each night he remembered her. And he remembered the love charm he had thrown to the ground beneath his horse. He longed for it now, and he hoped he had not shattered the love this Long Knife woman had had for him. If he could only have that moment back.

The next morning, with the cold settled deep into the land, Nighthawk passed the white cliffs and saw to the south the Mountains of the Big Snows and the buffalo grounds near the Mountains of High Woods. Finally he came to the Great Falls, where the water descended over rocks and turned the river below the falls into a spectacle of mist and foam. The water never froze here or at the Giant Springs nearby. It was a good place for a winter camp.

Nighthawk rode into his village, causing a great stir and bringing people out of their lodges. The first one to greet him was Spring Bird, his younger sister. Tears streamed down her face as she clutched him tightly.

"I thought you were dead," she told him. She held up her left hand, where a tiny portion of the little finger was missing. "I mourned for you."

"Couldn't you feel that I still lived?" Nighthawk asked her. "Did your spirit guardian not tell you I had not died?"

FIRECLOUD

"I did feel that you were alive," she acknowledged. "But Black Owl told the entire village that you had been killed, that he saw you with a Sioux arrow in you and your horse dragging you."

"I never fell from my horse," Nighthawk said in disgust. He showed her the scar on his leg. "Only a wound! Why did he lie?"

"I see you have returned."

Nighthawk turned to see his half brother standing with his arms folded across his chest. Many Kainah warriors stood around him. Black Owl spoke to Nighthawk through a sardonic grin. "What did you do, run and hide while we fought the Sioux?"

"You know very well what happened," Nighthawk said evenly. "Yet you lied to the people of the village. You told them I had died."

"We could not find you. What else were we to think?"

"How long did you look for me?"

Black Owl grunted and walked away.

"Nighthawk," Spring Bird said, turning him around to face her again. "I do not care what Black Owl and the others think. I know the truth. Do not worry about them. I am glad that you have returned and I am sure Aged One will be overjoyed as well. I will tell him, and we will feast this day."

Shortly Nighthawk sat next to a fire in his lodge, feeling warmth against his skin for the first time since leaving the Mandan village with Clara nearly a full month before. He ate meat and wild turnips until his stomach bulged, thinking he would never get enough. Spring Bird laughed all the while, telling him of the events in camp and of the successful buffalo hunt that had been conducted while Nighthawk and the other warriors had been away trading with the Dirt Lodge people.

Aged One sat with them, eating and nodding and studying Nighthawk closely. He was the last of his generation, having counted more winters than there were stars in the sky, people said. He told many stories of his childhood, when the Kainah Blackfeet and all the Indian peoples lived far different lives. It was before the coming of the horse, which he had called an Elk Dog, and it was before the people with white skin had come into the mountains.

Because of his age and because he valued the old ways, some of the villagers thought he was losing his senses. They said his stories came out of an old head that was drained of its wisdom. But Nighthawk respected Aged One and thought he exhibited more sense than the council members now in power. Nighthawk often went with the old man to speak with the spirits and build a fire of sacred sage to pray over. They had become very close, and Aged One was fond of his young friend. Because his hearing was failing, his discussions with Nighthawk were mainly in sign talk. Nighthawk had asked him repeatedly to come and live with Spring Bird and himself in their lodge, but the old man was too proud.

"Why do you look at me so curiously?" Nighthawk asked Aged One, as the old man continued to stare.

Aged One reached over and touched Nighthawk on the arm, as if to convince himself he was indeed real. His eyes became damp, and he spoke hoarsely.

"My heart is filled with joy this day, my young friend," he said. "I did not want to hear the words that circulated throughout the village. I did not want to believe you had passed to the Other World. My heart grew sad to hear your sister in the hills above the village crying to your spirit. I am glad this day has come. I wish to hear the story of how you were saved from death."

Nighthawk watched Aged One take a red stone pipe and fill it with tobacco, then make the offerings before puffing on it and passing it. Nighthawk puffed on the pipe and handed it back to Aged One, beginning his story of the white buffalo, the subsequent hunt, and the battle with the Sioux. He showed Aged One his wound, and the old man nodded proudly and told him he now had a battle scar around which he could paint circles of honor for all to see. Nighthawk went on to tell how he had been rescued by Long Knives, but he did not mention Clara. He told how the Long Knives had taken him back to

FIRECLOUD

their boats and nursed his leg wound until it had healed.

Aged One shook his head. "The Long Knives come into our lands more and more, like fish who have found a new stream. They will soon tell other fish, and one day our stream will be filled."

Nighthawk again took the pipe from Aged One. "I was on their boats during the passing of many suns. They wanted to come into these lands, but after I left them, the Sioux attacked and killed many of them. It is said that some of the Long Knives escaped on one of the boats and have traveled into the lands of the Crows, to the south."

Aged One took back the pipe and puffed strongly. "It is strange that the Long Knives would treat you as a brother. Our people have killed them, and they have killed us. There is no bond between us. They fear us and send the Crows and the Assiniboin against us. I do not understand why they treated you so well."

"They wish to trade with us. They want to come into our lands as brothers and trade for the fur of the beaver."

The old man quickly shook his head. "They do not speak truth. They do not care to be our brothers; they wish only to take the beaver from our lands. Do not believe them."

Nighthawk began to eat again, his mind going back to Clara. He swallowed the food, staring at the bowl in front of him.

"Did you see the Thunder Horse?" Spring bird asked, "the one called Firecloud?"

Nighthawk shook his head. "We did not see him. Maybe he has already gone to his lands high in the Burning Mountains."

"It is not yet time for him to go up there," Aged One said. "He will take mares from a village soon and go up to his lands before the deep snows fall."

"I passed through a village of our brothers, the Piegans," Nighthawk said, "at the foot of the big round butte near the Mountains of High Woods. They told me they had seen the Thunder Horse while hunting near the Three Forks. They said they did not chase him, for he was running too fast."

"How long will it be before you catch him?" Aged One asked.

"I do not know," Nighthawk answered.

"Maybe you do not want to catch him. Maybe you do not have enough faith."

"I *do* want to catch him," Nighthawk insisted. "But he is very powerful, and my task will not be easy."

Aged One nodded. "That is true. He is a very powerful horse."

"Where are your love charms?" Spring Bird asked. "Did you find love in the Mandan village?"

"What nonsense!" Nighthawk snapped. "Why do you bring that up?"

Spring Bird, startled by his sudden irritation, looked at him in bewilderment.

"You ask many questions," Nighthawk continued. "It is not good to ask so many questions of a man. Maybe the charms will not work now."

"I am sorry," Spring Bird said. "I only wish for your happiness."

"That is good," Nighthawk told her. "But do not speak of it again."

Aged One grinned. "Maybe you could tell her about the charms. Have they become warm yet?"

"Why is it funny?" Nighthawk asked him.

"I am smiling because I am glad to be with you," Aged One said, his grin widening.

"It is not a good day for me to speak of charms," Nighthawk said.

Aged One nodded and went back to eating. "We will speak of them no more."

Nighthawk finished his meal in silence while Aged One and Spring Bird talked quietly. Again Nighthawk saw the face of the Long Knife woman and remembered the love she had held for him. He longed to feel her arms around him and her lips against his. He was happy to have the company of his sister and Aged One once again, but without this white woman whom he had come to love so deeply, there was a deep emptiness within him, an aching that kept him from being contented. Finally his restless urge made him rise to his feet and leave the lodge.

"I have never seen him like this," Spring Bird said. "Do you suppose he is sick?"

Aged One grinned again. "The sickness is not from his wound," he said. "I think the love charms have become warm."

THE DARKNESS BROKE, and the new light found the valley floor as still as the end of a deep breath. The cold had settled into the very core of the land, and the smoke from Clara's campfire spiraled through pine needles flocked with slivers of frost. She pulled the last bits of meat from the breast of a roasted grouse and shared company with a pair of tiny chickadees who had been with her since the sunrise, poking for seeds in the melted snow around the fire.

She had climbed the summit of the pass during the night, seeing the sweeping valley of the Gallatin in the glow of dawn. Now, along the twisting flow of the river, she had stopped to rest through the day, regaining strength for the push onward to the Three Forks and farther to the Great Falls of the Missouri. There she would find Nighthawk, the warrior she could not keep her thoughts from.

The sun climbed higher, now encircled by a ring of white. A sun dog, the circle of cold, announcing that the land was destined to lie under very low temperatures for a long time. It was not a good sign, for it meant that she would need more wood to keep warm and more food to stay alive. Clara decided she would spend the morning resting before she pushed on toward the Three Forks. She released the young mare she had taken from LaCroix so that it could wander among the cottonwoods and willows for food.

Later in the morning Clara awoke when the young mare began nickering. She stood up to see the horse gallop out from the willows and onto the flat above the river, where a large group of wild horses stood facing her campsite in a long line. When the young mare joined them, they turned and faded like spirits into the timber above the valley floor.

Her heart jumping, Clara walked away from her campfire and toward the hillside. A herd of such strong, healthy mares, and of such size could only belong to one stallion. So excited was she that her mind did not register the fact that she no longer had a horse. All that mattered was to catch a glimpse of the fabled Thunder Horse, the one the Indians called Firecloud.

As she watched the timbered slope where the mares had disappeared, a flash to her left caught her eye. On the crest of another hill not far away was the most magnificent stallion she had ever seen. He held his head high and his tail straight out. His beautiful coat of deep red and white seemed to sparkle in the cold. Turning, Clara began to walk toward the hill, staring, her eyes transfixed on the big stallion. She continued to walk, looking at the horse she had dreamed of so many times. When she reached the base of the hill, the stallion snorted and, with a toss of his head, was gone.

Clara looked up at the top of the hill and the blue sky beyond, wondering if she had seen an apparition. But the spectacle held in her mind. She labored up the slope and found, in the layers of powdered snow, the tracks of a horse. He had been real! The tracks disappeared into the timber where the mares had hidden. Then, from the pines tinged white with frost, the stallion again appeared. He looked at her and shook his proud head, the steam rising as he blew his breath out in loud snorts. He began to prance along the ridge, his hooves raising puffs of snow with each step. The herd joined him, the young mare lost among them. The stallion's prance became a gallop, and the mares followed him off the ridge and down into the vast valley below. They continued, weaving out from the timber in a long, trailing column that seemed to stretch out into the valley forever.

Clara stood on the ridge, watching the stallion until he had become a moving red spot in a vast expanse of white. She remained there even after the stallion had gone and left behind only the silence and the frigid air, which she seemed not to feel. She trembled with a vibrant excitement. The horse was magic! Never before had she seen such a creature, nor did John and Nighthawk's descriptions do credit to his magnificence. Little wonder Nighthawk was so determined to catch him.

Clara made her way back to her campfire, wondering how she and Nighthawk could someday catch this magnificent horse. It would take all her skill to tame this red and white stallion. She would need patience to ease the horse into trusting her. It would be the greatest challenge of her life, the most difficult task she had set herself to do. This stallion was beyond imagination, and someday she would tame him, and he would be hers!

14

THE SUN DOGS came every day, and Clara continued her journey toward the Kainah village. Afoot now, she traveled slowly, and she grew far more tired than she would have if she had still been on horseback. She walked sideways or backwards sometimes to shelter her face from the freezing north wind. She kept the buffalo skin capote closed tightly at her throat and the hood up over her head. She was almost thankful that LaCroix had been waiting for her that night. Without the warm buffalo capote she had taken from him, she would certainly have already frozen to death.

With LaCroix's pistol, she killed grouse and rabbits that fed on the dried grasses and berries that hung from the bushes along the bottom and at the base of the slopes. When she reached the Three Forks, her spirits were lifted, for she knew she was coming ever closer to the Kainah winter camp at the Great Falls. She could see why the Indian band had chosen this land. It was filled with game and wild berries and could easily sustain a large villlage. Food was everywhere for the taking, but the bitter cold hung on.

As the days went by, Clara's senses grew hazy. She could not afford to stop and eat as often as was necessary to gain the extra strength she needed to fight the cold and walk great distances each day. Even the slightest warmth would have been a great relief. The icy wind was hard on the wildlife as well, keeping the deer and elk clustered together in large herds and the grouse and smaller birds huddled in the boughs of trees, their feathers ruffled up against the penetrating frost. As the cold endured and the land remained locked in a struggle to sustain itself, Clara found herself facing an additional problem: A pack of wolves had found her.

Day in and day out they followed her at a short distance, staying back from her nightly fires. Clara did not immediately become alarmed, for she knew they were curious by nature. She knew they considered her far more dangerous than any other animal in these lands, for they were well aware of the superior intelligence of the two-legged creature. Clara continued to make her way along the frozen Missouri, day by day, ignoring the wolves' watchful stares, trying to show that she was unafraid.

Still, though, she was unable to keep an occasional chill from running through her. There was no way to tell how long the deep cold would last or how much longer she could keep her pace up and sustain enough energy to stay strong. Each day was the same: She would kill a grouse or a rabbit while the wolves watched, their tongues hanging out. When she was finished with her meal and moved on, the wolves would eat the bones and scraps. As the days passed and Clara continued to make her way through the snow and cold, she began to awaken more often during the night, knowing the wolves were coming ever closer. She could imagine them running at her, their vicious teeth plunging into her throat. She wondered if there would ever be an end to the cold and if she would ever reach the Great Falls of the Missouri.

Two days later she came upon three buffalo, their legs trapped in the ice. The wolves rushed ahead of her to begin the killing. Though the buffalo were still strong and did not die easily, they apparently had been trapped in the ice for days; the skin on their legs was raw from thrashing in earnest to free themselves. As the wolves tore at the throats of their victims without mercy, death seemed almost welcome to the trapped buffalo.

FIRECLOUD

Clara walked out onto the ice toward the three fallen buffalo, now being torn to pieces by the hungry wolves. She was met by the leader, who arched his back and bared his fangs in a loud growl. Clara brought her pistol out and pulled back the hammer. Her life depended on getting a good supply of fresh buffalo meat to take with her as she progressed toward the Kainah village. It would give her renewed strength and save her the time she would otherwise have to spend hunting small game. At this moment, the wolf pack was claiming the three kills and if she challenged them without being sure her weapon would fire, she would pay with her life.

As the lead wolf continued to snarl, Clara took a few more steps forward, to be extra sure of her shot. Holding the pistol steady, she fired at his head. He fell immediately and lay still. Clara quickly reloaded, but the remainder of the pack retreated off the ice into the cover of the brush and trees along the shore, reminded of the power this two-legged creature possessed. Clara hoped the reminder would keep the wolves away throughout the rest of her journey.

As Clara moved on along the river, the wolves began to slink out of the trees to finish the three buffalo. She knew they would eat every scrap of their prey before moving on to find another source of food. It was likely she would never see this particular pack again, but there were many others to be watchful of.

The land along the river had now changed from open valley to walls of rock. She traveled on the ice much of the time, for the terrain along the shore was often very steep. Game grew scarce. Even the grouse that had been plentiful farther back were to be found only in very small numbers here. If she had not come upon the three buffalo, she would have been forced to turn back to the valley, or risk starvation while crossing through this land of rock through which the river had gouged a path.

The days went by slowly and drearily. Her supply of buffalo meat was now gone, and food became even harder to find. The river continued to be hemmed in by rock walls, now covered with ice and snow. She had passed through a channel of towering rock spires that had held her with fascination for a time before she realized she must move on. This land, so strikingly beautiful and yet so quick to take life from those who sought to live here. She knew she had passed the area of the Missouri called the Gates of the Mountains; she was now more than halfway to where she would again meet the warrior she longed for. The thought of Nighthawk pushed her on day after day, fighting frostbite and hunger, moving one foot ahead of the other, though walking had become ever more difficult. At times, her spirits soared at the thought of seeing Nighthawk again, but at other times, discouragement almost made her give up. What if he had not made it safely back to his people? What if he had now forgotten her and had taken another for his wife? Did he even want to see her again? These questions plagued her constantly. But her heart drove her forward, past the last high cliff of rocks and out again into wide, sweeping country.

Clara, realizing she was close to the Great Falls, tried to raise her spirits. Another pack of wolves began to follow her as she came out into the open from the dense timber along the river. She had cut strips of buffalo hide from the capote and wrapped them around her moccasins to keep out the cold, but they were wearing through. Each day it became increasingly difficult to leave her warm fire and again face the bitter-cold air. She found a few grouse and some small game, but not enough to bring back her strength; and her supply of powder and ball was now but enough to fill one hand. Her fingers and toes tingled constantly now, and she rubbed them in an effort to keep them from freezing. Each day it took more effort to travel a fraction of the distance she had once been able to cover. She had no way of knowing how much farther she had to travel to reach the Kainah village and the man who had changed her life completely. It was Nighthawk whom she struggled toward each day. It was Nighthawk who was keeping her alive.

Finally she came upon several hunting lodges similar to the ones in which the expedition had taken shelter during the heavy rains. She tore one lodge apart for firewood and built a

FIRECLOUD

warm fire inside another. She shot two grouse and ate them, wishing Nighthawk could share the meal and the love that had driven her toward him. She would rest in the lodge for a time, regain her strength on the plentiful berries and small animals nearby, and then resume her journey to the Great Falls. She knew she must be patient, though, for her strength was very low, and it would take time to build it up again. She put more wood on the fire and wrapped herself inside the buffalo robe capote to sleep. Her head swam with thoughts of the warm summer days she would spend with Nighthawk. She awoke to find that the fire was nearly out, but she was too weak to add more wood to it. The cold seemed not to matter, somehow, for she felt at peace, and a warmth had come over her. Had the weather broken? Had the warm chinook winds finally come to break the terrible cold? She struggled to focus her eyes on the dying embers. How odd that she should still feel so warm and comfortable! Again her thoughts drifted to Nighthawk and the time they had spent together. Sleep came easily.

IT WAS STILL DARK as Nighthawk wrapped his bearskin leggings and tied them tight. He chose his three best horses from the herd. They were strong and could travel many miles in extreme cold. He packed them with food, robes, and blankets. Then he slung his bow over his back, along with a quiver filled with arrows. Aged One and Spring Bird watched him with concern.

"Must you leave?" Spring Bird pleaded, tears streaming from her eyes. "At least wait for the snow-shrinking winds."

"I cannot. She is somewhere out in the snow and cold. She cannot wait for the snow-shrinking winds. I must go."

"Maybe she is inside the fort of the Long Knives, where you said she wished to go," Spring Bird suggested. "Maybe there is no need to worry."

"That may be so," Nighthawk said. "But I do not think she would go to the fort now. I must find her. I wish I had gone with her."

Aged One had said little about Nighthawk's love for a Long Knife woman. Nighthawk had finally told them about Clara, and it had made Spring Bird happy to know her brother had found love. Aged One had been quiet, however. Nighthawk knew what the old man thought and tried to convince him that this Long Knife woman was far different from the others. Aged One could see what feeling this woman had put into the young warrior he loved as a son.

"If you must go," he said to Nighthawk, "then listen to the signs of the land. If the trees begin to pop and crack, do not travel. You will freeze your lungs. And do not go out of the river bottom. Do not go where there are no willows and cottonwood bark. The horses cannot paw beneath the snow for grass. Are you listening?"

"I will listen to the trees," Nighthawk said. "I will be safe."

"Have you enough food and furs?" Spring Bird asked.

"The pinto is nearly overloaded," Nighthawk answered. "Don't worry. I will be safe."

Spring Bird dried her eyes and gave her brother a final hug. "Then go. Your spirit helper will be between you and the wind."

The sky was deep scarlet in the east as the sun rose over the mountains. The land was silent, as if all creatures had left and only the ice and snow remained, with the trees and the brush hidden beneath, stiff and brittle to the touch. The air was haze-blue with bitter frost, and the horses' breath froze into ice-needles around their muzzles. They struggled through the ice-crusted snow. Ahead, the Big Muddy, now a frozen curve of ice and snow, coursed through the barren land.

Nighthawk's eyes searched the white land, looking for movement, sign that he was not alone, hoping the woman his heart cried out for would appear as a speck against the winter background.

As the days passsed, his mind grew feverish with worry and anxiety. He began to cry out, calling her name. But in answer he heard only the sullen hush of a land buried beneath winter.

The sun rose and crossed the sky for the fourth time when

FIRECLOUD

he awoke. Thin wisps of clouds streaked across the sky above the far mountains, painted red and orange by the rising sun. The blue haze of cold was gone. Nighthawk left his fire to burn itself out. Today would bring change, he knew. Today something good would happen. The sky had changed; the warm winds were coming.

Late in the afternoon, as he was nearing the part of the river that pushed through high rocks, he saw a thin column of smoke ahead. Someone had built a fire in one of the hunting lodges! He shouted triumphantly, and the sound echoed through the land, which was growing steadily warmer as a wind began to push its way into the valley. The column of smoke grew thinner, as if the fire was going out. He urged the horses through the snow.

"YES, YOU HAVE EATEN many times since I found you. And you have slept much. You don't remember. You were close to death. Rest more, for you are still very weak."

Clara relaxed in the warm robes in which Nighthawk had wrapped her. She could not believe he was here. She remembered wishing for his strong arms and the pleasure he gave her. And she remembered wondering if he still cared for her.

"Do you want this back?" she asked, taking from around her neck the wooden love charm he had thrown on the ground. "Or did you mean what you said back there?"

Nighthawk took the charm from her, ashamed. "I do not deserve a woman such as you, who forgives me when I am a fool."

"Maybe I am the fool," Clara said. "Maybe I should have listened to you. LaCroix has taken everything, even the gifts I received at the Mandan villages. And he tried to kill me."

Nighthawk reached into her hair and removed the feathers she had been given in honor of her battle with Cut Face.

"You still have one very important gift. We will get all the other gifts back, as well as the furs the men trade for this winter. I will help you keep your father's honor."

Nighthawk built the fire up, his face alive with happiness.

E. P. Murray

He had chased wolves from the door to the lodge and had found Clara nearly unconscious from hunger and cold. Spring Bird had spoken truth when she had said his spirit helper would be with him during his search. If he had come just a short time later, the wolves would have reached her first. The thought made him feel empty and hollow.

Clara, her energy returning, rose, and Nighthawk kissed her slowly. She wished their lips would never part and his arms would embrace her forever. She turned and snuggled close, her back against his chest, as they sat near the fire talking. He was eager to take her home with him, to meet his sister and the old warrior.

After a time they went out of the lodge so that she could feel the winds that had chased the bitter cold from the land. Already the trees and shrubs along the river's edge were bare once again, and the snow underfoot was soft and slushy. It was hard to believe so great a change had happened so quickly.

Back inside the lodge, Nighthawk and Clara sat cross-legged next to the fire, facing each other.

"This is a special day," Nighthawk told her, "a day that neither of us will ever forget. On this day we shall become one, joined together as one spirit. I wish to take you as my wife. Forever."

With his knife, Nighthawk made a small cut in the palm of Clara's right hand. He did the same to his own right hand and then joined their palms where the incisions were made.

"Our blood has mixed together," he told Clara, a deep love in his eyes. "We have joined ourselves and will always be as one."

As they continued to hold their hands together, Nighthawk leaned over, and Clara met his lips with her own. His kiss erased all the fear and worry from her mind. Her days of cold and loneliness, of hunger and sorrow, were gone. Her longing for his gentle touch and his loving smile was fulfilled.

They enjoyed each other while Clara regained her strength. The hollows that had developed in her cheeks and along her back and ribs disappeared, and she regained some of the

FIRECLOUD

weight she had lost. Nighthawk killed an elk and collected berries and rose hips from the bushes along the river. The dramatic change in the weather contributed greatly to Clara's quick recovery. In a week she was ready to go with Nighthawk back to his people.

The villagers watched them ride in, standing in groups around their lodges, pointing and talking. Nearly everyone in the village had seen the British traders who had been settled for some time in outposts far to the north, and many had seen the new white traders from the east, whom they called Long Knives, but none in the village had seen a Long Knife woman. Though she was dressed as one of them, she appeared very different.

Clara had little trouble picking Black Owl from among a group of important-looking warriors in the center of the village. He stood out from them all, his arms folded in front of him. He wore only thin leggings and an elkskin shirt trimmed heavily with ermine tails. Most of the others had wrapped themselves in skins and robes against the biting wind. Black Owl seemed to defy even the weather.

In front of Nighthawk's lodge, Spring Bird hugged Nighthawk and made sign to Clara, saying "My brother brings home a sister for me. My heart is glad, and I am proud that he has found such a wife as you. I have heard much about you and wish you happiness among our people."

Clara smiled and made sign back. "I am happy Nighthawk has a sister such as you. I will be happy helping you in this lodge."

Beside them stood the old warrior Nighthawk had spoken of often. He was studying Clara closely.

"Aged One thinks you are very brave," Nighthawk told Clara. "He says you must love me very much to come into this village with me."

"I am honored to meet the warrior you have told me so much about," Clara said. "I hope to become his friend."

From the center of the village came Black Owl and the other young warriors. Spring Bird translated their words into sign for Clara.

"Why do you bring a stranger to our village?" Black Owl asked Nighthawk.

"Our people have always opened their lodges and offered food to strangers," Nighthawk said. "That custom has been handed down from our ancestors."

"Long Knives do not belong here," Black Owl answered emphatically. "Man or woman, a Long Knife is not welcome in our village."

The other warriors nodded. These people harbored a bitter hatred of the whites who were coming into their lands to establish fur trading outposts. Clara had noticed many items in the village that had obviously been taken from white trading and trapping parties. The Kainah people hung the objects from lodge poles and wore them for adornment. Traps, horse tack, knives, beads, awls, hammers, and other goods were visible in great abundance throughout the village. Clara knew these were not trade items and had been taken during raids.

"Not all the Long Knives are enemies," Nighthawk said to Black Owl. "This woman is now my wife."

Black Owl's mouth twisted into an evil grin. "You have proven my words to be true. You have the weak Long Knife blood in you, and now you take a weak Long Knife woman as your wife."

Spring Bird reluctantly translated this when Clara insisted she do so. "Black Owl insults you and my brother," she explained afterward. "I did not want to tell you, for I feared it would make you angry."

Clara gritted her teeth in anger, but she knew Nighthawk would not let his malicious half brother get the best of him.

Nighthawk took the two Hidatsa coup feathers from her hair. He held them up proudly for all to see. The villagers began to talk among themselves, for all Indian peoples recognized feathers of honor.

After showing the feathers, Nighthawk faced Black Owl. "Have any of your wives or any of the other women in this village killed an enemy warrior in battle, hand to hand?

Black Owl was silent, staring at the coup feathers and then at Clara.

FIRECLOUD

Nighthawk went on. "You have never done a brave deed such as this yourself. She has killed a mighty warrior of the Sioux nation, our bitter enemies, near the villages of the Dirt Lodge people. The warrior's name was Cut Face, and the Dirt Lodge people were very happy that their enemy had been killed. In honor, my wife was given these coup feathers, as a symbol of her courage, and the pipe was smoked."

The villagers again began to talk among themselves.

Black Owl grunted, "How many white mountain goat skins did you have to trade for the woman and the feathers?"

Nighthawk clenched his jaw in anger. "You speak of trading skins for war honors," he told Black Owl, "because that is the only way you could ever obtain a coup."

Black Owl stared at Nighthawk, his eyes alive with anger, but Nighthawk knew there would be no challenge. He had always been able to beat Black Owl in matches involving speed, strength, or marksmanship, and he knew Black Owl would not risk another defeat.

Black Owl could only stand and be silent in his anger. He would have been wiser to have allowed Nighthawk to bring Clara into the village without comment.

After Black Owl had turned and stomped away, Clara asked Nighthawk why his half brother had tried to make trouble.

"It is a good sign," Nighthawk answered, hugging her. "It means that Black Owl is afraid that you will bring me favor in the eyes of my people. He wishes to dishonor us so that the people will mistrust you."

"You have also caused him concern," Spring Bird told her brother. "The people say that you were very brave to leave the village during the intense cold."

Nighthawk smiled. "Soon the people will see what sort of a man Black Owl really is." He started toward the herd with his three horses.

While Spring Bird busied herself preparing food inside the lodge, Aged One spoke with Clara in sign. He told her about the enmity between Nighthawk and Black Owl. Much of it she had heard before from Nighthawk, but the old warrior's comments gave her an even greater awareness of the vengeful power possessed by Black Owl and the great lengths to which he would go to destroy the people's admiration for Nighthawk and, if possible, to drive him from the band.

"Black Owl's hatred for Nighthawk seems to overpower his common sense," Clara said.

Aged One shook his head as if he did not understand Black Owl's hostility. "Never have I seen a hatred endure for so long. Black Owl wishes for power. He is not content to share the burden of leadership with other warriors. He wants us all to follow him and listen to him only. Someday his hunger for power will destroy him."

"Many villagers think as Black Owl does," said Clara. "Too many. Life will be hard for Nighthawk."

"Nighthawk is brave and strong," Aged One pointed out. He looked hard at Clara as he continued. "I do not like the people of your color. They are greedy and selfish. But I cannot blame you for this trouble between Nighthawk and Black Owl. With or without you, Nighthawk would have faced his half brother in anger. The time of enmity has come. Maybe you are a gift from the spirits. Your love for him has given him new life. In the end, he will become the most fearless and respected warrior our people have ever known. And much of his success will be because of you."

"The two of us cannot overpower all those who listen to Black Owl," Clara said.

"Not all those in the village think highly of Black Owl," Aged One told her. "Black Owl is most respected among a powerful band called the Brave Wolves. On hunts and when we move camp, they have the power to punish those who do not obey their orders. They are even permitted to kill during those times. For that reason, many do not speak up against Black Owl for fear of the Brave Wolves' retribution. If they can see that Nighthawk is a better leader, they will denounce Black Owl. Nighthawk must make this happen, and you must help him."

Clara looked into the old man's eyes. "Nighthawk wishes to catch the Thunder Horse," she said. "He believes that owning Firecloud will bring him honor and recognition."

FIRECLOUD

Aged One smiled. "To dream of the stallion and to catch him are two entirely different matters."

Quietly Clara said, "I will tame Firecloud, and I will ride him. The horse will belong to us, and the village will see the power of Nighthawk and the Long Knife woman he took for his wife."

Aged One was silent for a short time. Finally he said, "Why do you believe you can do what no man or woman has ever been able to do before you? Do you speak with the spirits? Are *you* a spirit?" He reached out and touched her, to assure himself that she was real.

"I am not a spirit," Clara laughed. "I am different only in that I can tame and ride the stallion."

Again Aged One studied her in silence for a time. "Why do you laugh at the spirits? Do you wish to be looked upon with disfavor? Maybe, as a Long Knife woman, you do not understand the spirits and the power they possess."

"I only laughed to think that you would see me here, in flesh and blood, and call me a spirit. Like you, I believe that a Great Power controls us all. I pray to that Great Power for guidance. The Great Power is responsible for all life. I would never be so vain as to think I could possess any of his powers."

Aged One nodded. "You are indeed strong, and worthy of the honor you have received from the Dirt Lodge people for killing the Sioux warrior. But now you must help Nighthawk overcome his enemy. It will be a hard task."

"All I want is happiness with my husband and those he loves," she said. "We face a great struggle. But we will win."

15

AS THE WINTER PASSED, a bond of love formed between Clara and Aged One. The old warrior soon looked upon her as a daughter who had made his son very happy. Clara would listen with wonder and fascination to his stories of the days before the horse. His gestures and speech were more eloquent than any she had ever experienced.

Spring Bird opened up to Clara a door that had been closed all her life because she had never had a sister. The young woman, eager to share her knowledge of Blackfoot life, spent many long hours teaching Clara the Blackfoot tongue and the different methods of sewing and adorning clothes and lodges. Clara learned to mix paints and became proficient at bead and quillwork, as well as cookery. To Clara, it was like coming home to the family she had been looking for so long.

Soon the storms passed and the night breezes grew warmer. The geese flew overhead once more, and the dogs and horses began to shed their shaggy winter coats. Along the river, the pussy willows had popped into fluffy balls of silver. The ice in the river broke, and the water beneath it pushed it into huge jams that crashed and tumbled and piled up on the shores. A crier went through the village, announcing that the keeper of the sacred beaver bundle had declared it time to move camp.

The warm moons were approaching.

Clara helped Spring Bird take down the lodge and pack their belongings on a travois. The villagers would travel south along the river to the Valley of the Three Forks, where the river was born. This sent a shiver down Clara's back. She would once again see the country that had almost taken her life, but this time the land would be green and beautiful and filled with new life. The bushes would be heavy with clusters of flowers, and the chickadees would no longer have to probe in the melted snow around the fires in search of food. Fear and cold were of the past.

The villagers moved out in a long, wide column, led by the Medicine Pipe warriors, distinguished by their long hair pulled forward into a coil over their foreheads. The women, children, and old people walked or rode in the middle of the column, with the young warriors and the horse tenders on either side or behind with the herd. At the extreme edges of the column were the Brave Wolves, chosen by the council to keep order and protect the column against attack. Painted brightly and dressed in colorful costumes, they held supreme authority now. Black Owl, a leader of the Black Wolves, took full advantage of his chance to wield power.

"Nighthawk," he ordered, "you are to travel with the horse tenders, to assist them with the herd."

"I am a warrior with coup honors!" Nighthawk protested. "I am not a horse tender!"

"You will do as you are ordered!" Black Owl said sternly. "Or face death!"

Clara and Spring Bird were sent to walk at the end of the column among the poorest families of the band. Defiantly, the two women walked proudly along in their beautiful new antelope dresses, their hair adorned with beads and shells.

Clara was well aware that the conflict between Nighthawk and Black Owl would soon become more deadly. She had learned some revealing facts about Black Owl's personal life. Though she had never been inside his lodge, she knew that he had three wives, all sisters, the oldest of whom was his sits-

FIRECLOUD

beside-him wife. She was aptly named Eyes-Like-Black-Stones. Her dark eyes seemed to glare constantly, and Clara had often felt their hatred. This wife seemed to control Black Owl's life, and he tried to keep her content, a task that seemed to be insurmountable. Spring Bird, like the other women of the village, had little to do with Eyes-Like-Black-Stones. She and Black Owl were two of a kind.

This knowledge made Clara far less intimidated by Black Owl. She tried to understand Eyes-Like-Black-Stones so as to gain an advantage over her and thus be better able to assist Nighthawk in the feud with his half brother.

The band traveled onward toward the Three Forks, watching the snow recede up the slopes, seeing the hordes of spring flowers display their brilliant yellows and reds and blues. The land soon became a sea of color, and the villagers sang joyful chants as they moved.

Upon reaching the wooden lodges where Nighthawk had found Clara, the two of them crept away from the camp during the night and made love in the lodge where they had joined their blood together as man and wife. They built a fire where the embers had once died and left Clara alone in the numbing cold that had tricked her senses. They spoke to each other softly, knowing that nothing could ever part them again.

Before them now were the mountains and the rock cliffs that Clara remembered so well from the past winter. They followed a trail out of the valley and through the mountains away from the river. Clara had wished to see the Gates of the Mountains, the rock spires she had passed through in her search for the Great Falls, but she was not allowed to leave the column. Black Owl told her the safety of the village was all that mattered.

They reached the Three Forks Valley, and set up their village. Activity was intense as they erected lodges and pulled the buffalo-hide covers into place. Families placed their lodges together, and the wealthy and honored took special places. But Clara, Nighthawk, and Spring Bird were ordered to erect their home at the edge of the camp, in a solitary location near that of Aged One, as a mark of isolation, lack of family, and absence of esteem.

"I cannot live this way any longer," Nighthawk told Clara as they sat alone in the lodge the next day. "The laughter and the talk when our backs are turned fills me with anger. To kill Black Owl would only bring death to me and sorrow to you and Spring Bird. I don't know what we are to do."

"We will tame the stallion, Firecloud," Clara said.

Nighthawk shook his head. "The time is not yet right."

"You told me when the warm moons came, you would take me to the Burning Mountains to find Firecloud. The warm moons are here."

"I must first talk with the spirits, and I must make a special rope of rawhide."

"Nighthawk," Clara said in disgust, "no special rope will catch that horse. Don't you think that has been tried before? Many, many times?"

"That is how I must do it. To go after him without special preparation would only make the spirits angry. Failure would be certain."

"Maybe there is another way," Clara suggested. "Maybe it would be best to use an ordinary rope and not let the stallion see it until you have gained his trust so that you can touch him."

"You cannot walk up to that stallion and touch him! First you must catch him and secure him."

"I don't want to *catch* him," Clara emphasized. "I want to *tame* him. If we journey to the Burning Mountains, I can tame him. We can bring him back to the village, together with his herd of mares, and you would own more horses than any warrior who has ever lived. Black Owl will stare in disbelief. You will have all the honor you want. You—"

"Wait." Nighthawk held up his hand, interrupting her. "You are telling me that *you* will tame the stallion. I do not want that. No."

"Why not?"

"*You* would gain the honor, not me."

FIRECLOUD

Clara blew her breath out in frustration. "Nighthawk, I am your wife. We would do this thing together. When he is tame and trusts us, we will both be able to ride him."

"It is not the same as if *I* tamed the stallion," Nighthawk protested.

"Must you stand so defiant in your belligerent pride?" Clara asked, her fists clenched. "What good has your pride done you so far?"

"I do not need a woman to fight my battles for me!" Nighthawk said hotly. "*I* will decide how to gain honor, and then *I* will do it myself."

"Then why haven't you?" Clara blurted. "All you do is talk."

"You anger me, woman."

"You complain constantly about your position in this village, about your lack of recognition among the other warriors and the council. It angers you when people laugh at us. But all you do is sulk. Nothing else. When I suggest something, you tell me that you want to do it all alone. They laugh at me as well as at you, and I don't like it either. But I intend to do something about it."

"*I* will tame the Thunder Horse," Nighthawk said quickly. "The honor shall be mine, not yours."

"Why haven't you tamed him before now?"

Nighthawk looked away. "I have been busy. I have had to make new weapons and hunt to keep meat in our lodge."

"I believe you have not tamed Firecloud because you cannot tame him. Nor can any other Kainah warrior. You do not understand him. You overpower your horses, work them into submission. You think of them as a tool to be broken for riding and packing loads and pulling a travois. Firecloud will never be broken in this manner. He is far too smart, and there is more strength of heart and body in that stallion than in any ten others. That is why he has never been caught. The only way to gain his trust is to be around him for a time without challenging him."

Nighthawk looked at her with doubt. "No one can control a

horse unless he makes the horse believe his rider is his master."

"Firecloud can never be owned that way," Clara argued. "He would choose death before loss of freedom."

"Then how do you intend to break him?" Nighthawk asked.

"I do not intend to break him," Clara answered. "I intend to gain his trust and make him understand that I want to live with him as a friend and companion. I will show him I can provide him with comforts that he cannot provide himself."

"What could you give the Thunder Horse that he does not already have?" Nighthawk asked.

"I can rub his neck and pat his nose, and I can dig wild carrots and find lush grass for him to eat. I can groom him with the quill comb I have made, curry his coat until it glistens. He will enjoy these things, and a bond of trust and love will form. In return he will carry me on his back."

Nighthawk shook his head. "I will not allow you to bring me the honor I must achieve for myself. That would be worse than never gaining honor at all. The laughter would be even louder. I would be weak to let a woman gain honor on my behalf."

"Why can't you share in the taming of Firecloud?" Clara asked. "We could be together, so that the stallion knows you to be his friend, also. You could ride him as well as me."

"The horse must be mine alone," Nighthawk said. "A warrior does not share ownership of his best horse with a woman."

"I believe you would have gone after the stallion before now if you thought you could tame him," Clara said. "Isn't that true?"

"I have gone after him, many times, but I have not tried to feed him and gain his trust. Many others have gone after him, but each time he leads his herd deep into the Burning Mountains where the land talks with the voices of evil spirits and their hot breath comes out of holes of hot mud and bubbling pools of colored water. It is a land of evil where no good

FIRECLOUD

things live. The horse is one of the evil spirits."

"That horse is not evil," Clara said. "He is noble and proud. He leads his herd into this land of hot pools and steam because he knows no one will follow him there. But evil is not a part of him. A horse becomes mean as a result of mistreatment, but this horse has been free his entire life. He is just smart."

"Maybe your words are true," Nighthawk said. "It will take much time and effort to conquer this—"

"Conquer?" Clara interrupted him. "You haven't been listening. No one will ever *conquer* him, but if we have enough patience, we can *tame* him."

"These are my final words," Nighthawk said angrily. "I will never accept honor that is gained for me by another, not even you."

After some thought, Clara said, "I don't intend to let Black Owl control my destiny. You don't want him to control your life either, but you do nothing to stop him. I am tired of listening to your complaints. The warm moons have arrived, and we are close to the Burning Mountains. Soon I will leave this village to find Firecloud. You can come with me."

"I will not go."

Clara stood her ground. "Then stay safely at home. I will come back with Firecloud. If you choose not to take me back as your wife, then that is your decision, not mine."

Nighthawk glared at her and stormed out of the lodge, knocking over some pots that were sitting just outside. She lay awake for a long time that night until Nighthawk finally returned. He snuggled in next to her. "Will you take back a husband who has acted like a small boy?" he asked.

"I did not realize I had ever let you go," she said with a smile and a kiss. "And don't ever think for even a moment that I would let you go. You are the most important thing in my life, and you always will be."

Nighthawk held her close. "I have finally come to understand that you are more important to me than anything else. As long as we are together, I will always be happy."

They let the fire die to embers, holding each other, cherishing the closeness. The time would come, they both knew, when their position in the village would be much higher than it now was. They would ignore Black Owl and his insults, waiting until the time was right to discredit him. They could not let the strain pull them apart. Their strength would grow together. In time, they would win.

16

EARLY THE NEXT DAY the horse tenders sounded the alarm, crying out from where they watered the herd in the river, some of them rushing into the village on their horses to spread the news.

Clara and Spring Bird had just returned from the river with skins of water. They stood near their lodge, following the eyes of others in the village to the crest of a hill above the river. Clara's eyes grew wide. "Firecloud!"

"It is he!" Spring Bird echoed. "It is the Thunder Horse!"

Nighthawk came out of the lodge where he had been making arrows and stood near Clara. "It is time!" he shouted, rushing back into the lodge. He came out with a long rawhide rope coiled in his hand and rushed for his horse, shouting, "He is mine! This time I will catch him!"

"Wait!" Clara yelled after him. "That is not the way to do it!"

Nighthawk never acknowledged that he had heard her. In a few moments he was urging his horse to a full gallop, trying to beat a number of other warriors to the hill where the stallion now pranced and tossed his head. Black Owl, riding his powerful black, rushed after him to meet Firecloud's challenge and keep the Thunder Horse from taking mares for his own.

E. P. Murray

Black Owl's stallion rushed ahead of the warriors who had gathered to try and catch Firecloud. The village had been expecting this, for the Thunder Horse was commonly seen early in the warm moons as he rampaged through the land taking mares. Because Firecloud had previously beaten Black Owl's horse, the black now ascended the hill to exact his revenge.

The two horses met at the crest of the hill, rearing with striking hooves and teeth that nipped and tore at shoulder and neck flesh. Firecloud, wanting a victory before the warriors arrived to chase him, administered a great deal of punishment to the black in a very short time. He struck with his forefeet, knocking the black off balance repeatedly, then turned and lashed out with pounding hind feet that slammed the breath from the stallion and sent Black Owl tumbling down the hill.

As Nighthawk approached the hill, Firecloud loped down the slope and out onto the open flats along the river with a snort and a shake of his head. Nighthawk and the other warriors formed a long, twisting line behind the stallion.

Firecloud would slow enough to let the warriors nearly catch up to him, then kick his heels and twist himself in sporting pleasure as he burst into greater speed, leaving his pursuers frustrated and angry. His speed and agility carried him with ease into rocky slopes above. Through stands of gnarled evergreens and patches of sage, over rocky ridges, and out into the sweeping breadth of the Three Forks Valley.

Behind the warriors Clara raced with Spring Bird, followed by almost the entire village, to a rise above the river. The rolling plain of the valley lay below as the majestic red and white stallion led the pursuing riders in a long line of flying manes and tails. Clara could see that Nighthawk remained at the head of the warriors, his horse keeping pace with Firecloud. Suddenly the wild stallion made an abrupt turn and circled around in a powerful surge of speed, rushing headlong into the middle of the column that had been behind him. The warriors began to shout, waving their ropes to ward off the charging stallion. Their horses, terrified and confused, broke formation and bolted. The big stallion rushed through the broken line, again kicking his heels, squealing mischievously as if enjoying the sport. A short distance away, he turned and watched as the warriors fought to control their horses. Firecloud pawed the ground, snorting and shaking his head, anxious for the chase to resume.

Most of the warriors shook their heads and turned their horses back toward the village. Again the powerful Thunder Horse had made fools of them. But Nighthawk and a few others kicked their horses into a run toward the stallion, who snorted and broke away from them with a wild toss of his head.

Clara shook her head and shouted, "No, Nighthawk! Come back! You can't hope to catch him!" She watched as the stallion again ran just fast enough to stay ahead of Nighthawk and the few remaining warriors, teasing them with zigs and zags and sudden surges of speed as they got close enough to throw a rope at him. He ran with ease, showing no sign of tiring, but only an urge to continue at a faster pace. One by one, the remaining warriors dropped out of the chase, climbing down from their exhausted horses to lead them to water and then back to the village, their heads hung in humiliation. In the end, only Nighthawk remained, his determination to catch the majestic wild stallion still strong.

Nighthawk rested his horse and let Firecloud come closer in his teasing manner. Finally the wild stallion advanced to just beyond the reach of the rope and began to prance back and forth, impatient to resume the chase. His dark red coat sparkled in the sunlight. He dazzled the eyes and set the mind to dreaming. To own such a stallion would bring more honor than a thousand ordinary horses. Now was the chance of his entire lifetime.

Slowly, with no quick movements, Nighthawk turned his horse sideways and tied one end of his rawhide rope to the wood frame underneath the hide covering on his saddle. He held the noose to the far side of his horse so that the stallion could not see it. He then raised his left hand in the air with a quick, jerky motion. Firecloud bolted, but then stopped when he saw that Nighthawk did nothing but lower his arm and hold his horse in place. Snorting, the wild stallion again moved to just out of rope reach from Nighthawk and resumed his prancing. Once again Nighthawk quickly raised his left arm, and Firecloud again bolted, but not so quickly as before. The big stallion saw this, too, as a game.

When Nighthawk raised his arm a third time, he kicked his horse into a gallop and held the noose up. Firecloud, no longer afraid of the arm movement, did not push himself into full stride until Nighthawk's noose had fallen neatly around his neck. Whooping loudly at his success, Nighthawk coiled the rope around his hand.

Angered by the trick, Firecloud tossed his head and broke into a run. The stallion surged into blinding speed, a pace that Nighthawk's mount could never match. Feeling itself being pulled forward off its feet, Nighthawk's horse squealed in terror. Holding tight to the rope, Nighthawk felt himself being pulled through the air over his horse's head.

"Let go!" Clara screamed from the rise, knowing Nighthawk could not possibly hear her. She rode down into the valley, Spring Bird and the other villagers following. Only Black Owl and some other members of the Brave Wolves stayed behind, laughing.

Nighthawk felt the rope burn like fire around his hand. The explosion of pain he had felt with the fall was growing worse, but he blocked it from his mind. This horse would be his! He continued to hold on, believing the stallion would slow and give in to the rope. He held fast, the burning in his hands growing unbearable, the ground pounding against his head and body like a continuous series of brutal clubs as he bounced along the valley floor behind the racing wild stallion. Suddenly Firecloud swerved for the hills, changing directions abruptly. Nighthawk found himself rolling over and over as the rope swung out behind in an arc with the turn. Over and over, in a dizzying tumble, over brush and rocks and cactus, Nighthawk's body was tortured to the limit. Then the searing pain in his hands and the pounding in his head and body grew

FIRECLOUD

to crescendo, and he swirled into blackness.

In one last act of defiance, Firecloud lowered his head and shook off the noose, which fell to the ground. With a snort and a shake of his head, he galloped along the valley floor while the villagers shook their fists in the air, yelling for the evil horse to leave their lands. They watched as the stallion took several mares from the herd and drove them high into the foothills.

Clara rushed to Nighthawk, lying still at the edge of the valley floor where the foothills rose into the mountains. She turned him over, bringing a moan from his lips.

He was covered with blood from head to foot, and his skin was already dark with bruises.

Clara looked high into the mountains far above the village where the stallion had lost himself and his herd in the distance. Now it would be that much harder for anyone in the village to believe her when she said the stallion was only powerful and not evil. She would not talk about the horse anymore. When the time came, she would prove that he was not an evil spirit.

The villagers crowded around Nighthawk's fallen form. He tried to rise, but Clara held him down, telling him not to move.

Nighthawk tried to push her hands from him. "I have to catch the Thunder Horse. My rope is still around his neck."

"Not anymore," Clara informed him. "He worked it off and is now on his way to the Burning Mountains with half the mares from the herd."

Nighthawk blew his breath out in frustration, wincing at the pain it caused. Again he pushed Clara's hands away from him and sat up, trying to struggle to his feet. Clara pleaded with him to lie back down. "I cannot fail," he said over and over again, slurring his words in pain. He got to his knees, but suddenly slumped back to the ground. Clara turned him over on his back, placing her hand under his head and wiping the blood from his face. Her beloved warrior, too determined for his own good, had again lost consciousness.

Aged One crowded through the staring villagers and knelt

beside Nighthawk. He moved his experienced hands over Nighthawk's body, searching for broken bones beneath the puffy, discolored skin. "Nighthawk has the good spirits with him this day," he said. "We must get him to the lodge of the shaman, Eagle Foot, to receive prayers and medicine."

A young warrior pushed through the crowd, leading a pony with a travois attached. It was Deer Chaser, a youth Nighthawk had once helped to find a lost colt. "I have come to help my friend," he said. "And to join in praying that he recovers."

Aged One nodded. "You have honor, young warrior. You are not afraid to do what you think is right. You are strong, and the strong are rewarded."

They put Nighthawk on the travois and took him to the village, where the shaman, Eagle Foot, awaited them. The throng of villagers followed closely, talking about the warrior who had come so close to catching the Thunder Horse. This warrior had shown great courage and power. He had refused to let this stallion mock him and make a fool of him. He was strong, this warrior named Nighthawk, and worthy of honor.

Deer Chaser stood next to Spring Bird in front of the shaman's lodge. "Nighthawk proved to everyone in the village that he is as brave as any warrior among our people. Black Owl can say all he wishes, but what your brother has just done will remain strong in everyone's mind."

"You are very kind," Spring Bird said shyly.

Deer Chaser looked at her a moment, shuffling his feet. Finally he said, "Many warriors will offer horses to Nighthawk for your hand. You are very beautiful." He smiled and quickly walked away.

Clara, who had overheard the exchange, smiled at Spring Bird. "You will see more of him, I believe."

Spring Bird watched as Deer Chaser rode out to the herd. She wondered why she had not noticed him before. Maybe it was because of the troubles Nighthawk was having with Black Owl. She had thought of little else lately.

Aged One came out of the shaman's lodge. "It is best if we

FIRECLOUD

all return to our lodges now," he told the throng of villagers. "There is nothing more we can do. He is in the hands of Eagle Foot and the One Above."

The villagers went about their business, discussing the event that had made them change their minds about Nighthawk. Black Owl, knowing he had taken a beating, stood apart from the others, his arms folded across his chest, his eyes filled with contempt. His black stallion had suffered yet another defeat at the hands of the evil Thunder Horse. How could the villagers think so highly of Nighthawk all of a sudden? Didn't they know that the evil spirits had given him the power to rope the Thunder Horse? He could not allow the people to believe that Nighthawk was brave and worthy of honor, for they would soon consider Nighthawk a better leader than he.

As the days went by and Nighthawk lay unconscious under the care of Eagle Foot, Black Owl began a new avenue of attack against his half brother. He told the people that Firecloud had disrupted the natural course of events in the valley. A herd of buffalo had traveled north along the river, he pointed out, instead of entering the Valley of the Three Forks. Even the buffalo-calling ceremony had failed. Black Owl told the village that the wild stallion had driven the buffalo herd away and had left the people with empty stomachs and no hides from which to make new lodges and clothes. The Thunder Horse was evil, he told them, and had brought the disfavor of the underground spirits upon the village. The spirits had followed the evil stallion from their home high in the Burning Mountains. Firecloud, the leader of these evil spirits, had led them to the Kainah people.

Black Owl continued to point out unfortunate events that were surely the result of the evil stallion. Rain had not yet come to the valley, and the grass was short. Buffalo would never come to a place where there was no food to graze. A lightning storm caused a fire in the mountains above the village. If the fire moved down into the valley, they would have to move their homes. The people wondered about all the strange things that were happening. Black Owl declared them to be Nighthawk's fault, for he had roped the stallion and thus angered him. The Thunder Horse was exacting revenge.

One afternoon Aged One talked with Clara alone in the lodge. "Black Owl can make people believe him. Since there is evil in his heart, evil spirits are on his tongue. I do not think everyone believes him, though. Deer Chaser does not, and he is respected among the younger warriors. The older warriors, especially the Brave Wolves, believe Black Owl, however, and it is they who have the power in this village."

"It is foolish to think that a horse is evil," Clara said. "Horses cannot call upon spirit helpers to give them power. Surely the warriors of this village must know that."

Aged One nodded. "True, but this stallion is different. We believe that the Thunder Horse has powers above all other living things, that he has strength not of this world and knowledge to use this strength. That is why people listen to Black Owl."

"If you gain power from this horse," Clara said, "then you cannot believe that he is evil."

"He is good," Aged One said without hesitation. "If he were evil he would surely destroy this village and drive our people into the hills. But the people no longer listen to me."

"The day will come," Clara said, "when the people of this village will stand in line to hear your stories of the old days."

"A difficult time will pass before this village changes," Aged One said, concern in his voice. "It will take deeds of great honor to change the minds of the people." He asked Clara to accompany him to the hill above the village where he said his nightly prayers and talked to the spirits. It was a sacred place, and Clara was proud that he had asked her.

In the sacred place Aged One built a fire of sage and juniper boughs. When the fire settled into an even blaze, Aged One began to sing, raising his hands to the west where the sky burned gold in late afternoon. When he finished, he turned to her, unashamed of the tears that now flowed from his eyes.

"You must know the truth about Nighthawk," he said.

Clara stiffened immediately. "What do you mean?"

"Nighthawk has not awakened from the head sickness. Eagle Foot listens to Black Owl's words, and this is not good. If Eagle Foot believes that the evil spirits are in our village, he will not be able to help Nighthawk."

"I will move him to our lodge," Clara said quickly.

"No!" Aged One said in a strong voice. "If you interfere, Nighthawk will surely die."

Clara felt despair at being unable to help her husband.

"You must find the strength within yourself to undergo a very severe test," Aged One said.

"I will do anything to save the life of my husband," Clara said earnestly.

"You must pray as you never have before," Aged One said. "You must fast and be cleansed in the purification lodge. Then you must pray again. If Nighthawk recovers, you will be worthy to face the hardest part of the test. You will become the medicine woman of the Sun Dance."

Clara held her breath. "But I have never even seen a Sun Dance ceremony."

"You will learn," Aged One told her. "Deer Chaser's mother was a medicine woman. She prayed that her husband would return from a revenge raid on the Assiniboin people. He had not come back with the others, much the same as Nighthawk, but he walked into the village two days after Deer Chaser's mother began her prayers to Sun."

"But I am not even of your people."

"It is true, a white woman has never performed the ceremony before, but the villagers believe Nighthawk will die. If your prayers are answered, there will be no question of your faith. Even Black Owl will not dare speak against you."

Clara, her spirits rising, looked into Aged One's eyes, seeing the hope that he now held.

"You will suffer much," he told her. "As a Long Knife you would not have done anything such as this."

"I am not afraid," Clara said with confidence.

"You are strong," Aged One said, "but you must not underestimate the hardship you will face."

"I am not afraid," Clara repeated.

Aged One nodded. "You must prepare for what is to come." He pointed to the edge of the river, where Deer Chaser's mother was cutting willow branches. "Do everything she tells you. When the time is right, I will see you again."

Clara began her walk down the hill toward the river. Nighthawk's life was now in her hands, and she must save him by showing her undying love through faith. The villagers began to gather near their lodges. The word had already been passed that she was to give sacrifice for Nighthawk. She looked at the western sky, where a crimson light shone on the horizon and marveled at the beauty of the sunset. She also thought of the many days that had passed in her life and how she had taken them for granted, without a thought of how important the gift of life was and how easy it was to lose. Now, as the day ended, she realized that her life had again been changed in a very special way.

17

Napi, Old Man who is all powerful and the maker of all things, the protector of all who walk the Earth, the womb of life, behold me here before you. Humbly I ask your help. You, who are the light of the world, the face of love and kindness, hear me as I cry in anguish, see me as I look to you for your strong hand. Bringer-of-Days, with unending adoration, I ask you to bring from sleep my beloved Nighthawk, one of your children, strong in his love of your name. Let it not be his time to leave this life, I beg. Let him rise up from his bed in the lodge of Eagle Foot to become as he once was so that I might again share with him the gifts of love and happiness.

Give me strength, O Great One, grandfather of all beings, to lead these people of my husband, who are now my people, in the ceremony of sacrifice. Make me worthy to lead them along the path of the Sun Dance. Hear me calling, O Great One, ruler of land, fire, water, and air. I am weak but you can make me strong. Hear me calling! Hear my words!

E. P. Murray

* * *

CLARA REMAINED IN THE HILLS above the village while the sun crossed the sky three times. On the fourth day a crier came to tell her Nighthawk had opened his eyes and asked for her. He had been told of her pledge and had smiled with pride. Aged One had nodded with satisfaction, his wrinkled features alive with joy at the news of Nighthawk's recovery. The young Long Knife woman was now more than a daughter to him: She was a gift bestowed upon him by the sun.

Nighthawk recovered rapidly. His cuts and bruises had healed completely while he lay unconscious. Now his head seemed clear and he suffered no loss of memory or eyesight, no change in speech or movement. He was alert and in good spirits, eager to hunt and return to his lodge.

Because of his recovery, Clara was chosen to be medicine woman for the Sun Dance, to be held soon with other bands of the Blackfoot confederacy. The village had come to see that she was gifted with uncommon strength and fortitude. Criers were sent throughout the Blackfoot lands to announce the event. The camp would be made at the foot of the Mountains of Big Snows, near the huge flow of spring water that poured out of the hillside, east of the Three Forks and a short distance north. It was the most solemn ceremony of the summer, the most important spiritual occasion of the year. For a woman, no honor was greater than being medicine woman for the Sun Dance.

The buffalo calves were being born, and deer and elk fawns lay hidden all along the rivers and streams when the Blackfoot people came together near the Mountains of Big Snows. Clara and Nighthawk immediately were looked upon with honor by all. There were those who refused to accept this. Black Owl, together with some of the Brave Wolves, chose not to attend the Sun Dance ceremony. Aged One told Clara that Black Owl's honor would suffer greatly because of absence; the Sun Dance ceremony held a deep meaning for all who watched. By turning his back on Clara and Nighthawk, Black Owl was telling the people he did not wish to offer sacrifice.

FIRECLOUD

Spring Bird helped Clara erect their lodge in the center of the camp, the appropriate location for the medicine woman's lodge.

When the ceremony began, Deer Chaser's mother offered a buffalo tongue to the sun, and other women repeated the offering. All the tongues, now sacred, were cut up and boiled. They were then placed in hide parfleches for later use.

Clara began a four-day fast, which would allow her to open her senses and receive wisdom. Her body was painted with white clay, a symbol of purity and virtue. Each day camp moved to a different place near the foot of the mountains, with her leading, and she would again follow the prescribed rituals for the ceremony. In her possession were the sacred buffalo bull tongues and the sacred Sun Dance bundle. It was a time of deep spiritual commitment. Clara began to feel closer to the the mysteries of life than she ever had before. The fast had opened her spirit to new understanding: The sky seemed closer, the colors of the land and the water more vivid, the drums and the chanting more compelling. She and Nighthawk grew closer, as if they had become one person. Clara again purified herself in the sweat bath, as she had the night before going to the hills to pray for Nighthawk. Now, as part of the ceremony, Nighthawk and Aged One joined her in a small lodge made of willows and covered with buffalo robes. They sat on blessed robes while red-hot stones were brought in on forked sticks and placed in a pit. Water was then poured over these stones until the interior of the small lodge became clouded with steam.

She rubbed her body with sage and sheaves of a soft, delicate sweetgrass with a pleasing fragrance. It was a special time for Clara, made more special by the presence of her beloved husband and the help of Aged One, who prayed with Nighthawk for her success.

On the fourth day, when camp was moved for the last time, the lodges were erected so that a special medicine lodge could be built near Clara's lodge. Special warriors selected a cottonwood tree trunk, upon which an attack was made by the warrior societies, simulating aggression against an enemy. Clara and all the village watched as they broke limbs from the trunk and counted coup, as if in battle, while everyone cheered. The drumming and singing grew louder, exciting the warriors to a fever pitch.

On the fifth day, Clara was to make her final and most important offering. Deer Chaser's mother and father transferred to her a very special object, the *natoas* bundle. Among the sacred objects in the bundle was a specially made elkskin dress, with a robe and a headdress. Ceremonial songs were then sung, and Nighthawk's body was painted with charcoal to symbolize devotion and love. An altar was then constructed, and the rituals moved to a ceremonial lodge. For Clara, it was the beginning of an experience beyond imagination.

Clara had now been without food for four full days. She did not feel fatigued or weak as she had while traveling during the extreme cold of the winter before. Her mind seemed to be rising out of her body and looking down at the world. As the ceremony of the fifth day began, Clara saw herself following Aged One and Nighthawk while behind her walked her attendants. She saw herself praying and moving around the medicine lodge, still an unfinished skeleton of poles leaning against the center cottonwood log. Here they prayed for a time, allowing the lodge to be completed before the Sun Dance began. Like a spectator, Clara saw herself in a special place receiving gifts from the villagers and watching them raise their wrists and their faces to be painted.

It was now time for the pieces of buffalo bull tongue to be distributed. The worshipers now faced the sun, which was descending in the western sky, and ate the tongue in communion. Clara felt the saliva rush into her mouth as the meat rested on her tongue. She chewed the tongue with relish. As she ate, the blood returned to her stomach, and the weightless feeling gradually began to diminish.

The drums continued their unearthly rhythms, and the chants of the worshipers filled the evening air. As the center of this sacred ritual, she was the honored one, who had been looked upon with great favor by the sun.

FIRECLOUD

Suddenly some of the villagers began to point. High on a ridge to the west the wild stallion, Firecloud, tossed its head and pranced. Disorder began to erupt.

"There is nothing to fear," Aged One assured the people. "He was drawn here by the power of the ceremony. He comes in respect. It is a good sign."

The majestic stallion stood on the ridge, looking down on the village. His coat of red and white caught the rays from the falling sun, and he appeared a dark, flaming red before them. Clara, as if drawn by a secret, powerful force, began to walk toward the powerful stallion. Again the villagers began to murmur, and again Aged One calmed them, telling them that the mighty horse had come to greet the Long Knife woman who had been looked upon with favor by the sun. Again Aged One emphasized that it was a good sign.

"The Thunder Horse wishes to know the power this woman possesses," Aged One said. "He wishes to make peace with her and to show that he is sorry for hurting her husband, Nighthawk."

Taking a large bundle of the sweetgrass from the ceremony with her, Clara began to make her way up the ridge with the utmost caution and patience. Firecloud stared at her, his ears forward, his nostrils inhaling her scent. Never had anyone approached the wild stallion this way. Usually, many horses ran toward him full speed, or a two-legged creature tried to sneak close to him. None of them had come forward with seemingly no intention of catching him.

Clara talked to him softly, slowly making her way closer, holding a handful of sweetgrass out for him to eat. Snorting and shaking his head, the stallion pranced in front of her, watching her, but not approaching. Continuing to talk softly, Clara left a portion of the grass on the ground near him, backing away so that he could approach it.

"It is yours," Clara told him in her softest voice. "A gift from me to you."

Cautiously, the big stallion made his way toward the grass, eyeing Clara constantly, his muscles taut, ready to bolt at the slightest movement. Clara continued to talk to him in low tones. But Firecloud would not take the grass. Instead, the stallion shook his head and squealed, telling her she was too close to the grass, ordering her to back away so that he could take it. Clara knew the horse wanted the sweetgrass but would not jeopardize his safety for it.

"You have nothing to fear from me, you beautiful horse," she said to him. "I am only a new friend who admires you a great deal."

Clara remained close enough to the sweetgrass to frustrate the stallion, yet far enough away to allow him access to it. The stallion had tasted this grass before and was unable to resist its smell. Finally, realizing she was not going to move from her position, he inched his way up to the offering and quickly reached down for it. He took a mouthful and jerked back quickly, bolting a short distance to eat it, his eyes ever on Clara.

Clara laughed softly and gathered up the remaining grass. She began to go back down the hill, slowly, looking back up at the stallion. Firecloud, disturbed at her leaving with the remains of the offering, squealed again and shook his head. Clara continued slowly down the hill, leaving a small amount of grass in a spot along the hillside. She continued to talk to him, making sure that he understood there was more for him to take if he would come down the hill for it.

Finally the stallion came down the slope, zigzagging his way, watching for any sign of movement from either Clara or the villagers who stared, unable to believe their eyes. He approached the sweetgrass with mistrust.

"You will learn that I will never try to catch you," Clara said to the stallion.

Clara did not entice Firecloud any farther down the slope. She could not afford to have any of the villagers cry out, or come up the hill, or otherwise ruin the impression she was making on the horse. The stallion was now finishing the last of the grass. The offering had accomplished its purpose. The memory of this occasion would linger in the stallion's mind, and the next time he saw her he could connect with her the good taste of the sweetgrass.

FIRECLOUD

As she rejoined the villagers, she turned to watch the stallion disappear into the hills. Clara knew that the stallion would remember this meeting with the two-legged creature who did not try to catch him. There would have to be many more of these meetings before the stallion would trust her enough to eat out of her hand. But that day would arrive and she would ride Firecloud before the cold moons returned to the land. The stallion had shown her he was a high-spirited horse with intelligence far superior to any other. It was easy to see why people called him a spirit, for his strength and spirit were unequaled. He had never been beaten. He could outrun or outfight any other stallion in the land. Even the bravest of warriors could never capture him. He reigned supreme.

Clara heard Aged One tell the villagers that the sun had guided her to speak to the Thunder Horse and that they should now realize the stallion was not evil.

"I have been greatly blessed by the sun, who has saved my husband from death," Clara told the people. "He has also blessed me with the power to greet and make friends with the Thunder Horse."

The ceremony continued, and the worshipers gained even greater confidence in the powers of their medicine woman. It seemed to be true: The Thunder Horse had traveled from his home in the Burning Mountains to pay homage to this woman and make peace with her. This stallion had injured her husband and now wished to make amends. To satisfy their medicine woman this powerful horse had come to offer himself for the medicine woman to own and have as her own.

As the moon turned full, warriors gathered at the cottonwood pole in the medicine lodge and had skewers placed through cuts in the skin on their chests and backs. They pulled hard against the thongs that held the skewers to the pole, inflicting upon themselves more pain and torture than they ever thought they could endure. When the skewers finally pulled through the muscle and skin, leaving loose flaps of injured tissue, they jumped with excitement, for they would now have scars to show during the Sun Dance of the Long Knife medicine woman.

When the time for feasting came, the people rejoiced as they never had before. Rain had fallen on their lands. The grass would again become green and bring the buffalo to feed. The sun, happy with their sacrifice, bestowed good fortune on them because of the efforts of their medicine woman, who had sacrificed so greatly for her husband.

When the camps finally broke and the various bands returned to their homes, the Black Horse band of Kainah Blackfeet decided to return to the Three Forks. Late one evening, Clara, Nighthawk, and Spring Bird sat in their lodge with Aged One.

"I have seen many unusual things in the winters I have counted," Aged One said to them, looking at Clara as he spoke. "But some of the most unusual sights have appeared since your coming."

"She is unusual," Nighthawk said, hugging her closely. "That is why I love her as I do." He showed the healing scars of his Sun Dance torture. "She has brought great honor to me, and I am proud of her. Much has changed in this village because of my wife. Honor has finally come to me."

"Your battle is not yet over," Aged One warned. "When Black Owl returns from scouting with the other Brave Wolves, there will be much trouble. Though he has lost honor by leaving during the Sun Dance ceremony, he still has power in this village and will surely use it to try to destroy you both. I fear that difficult times lie ahead."

"We will be prepared for him," Nighthawk said with confidence. "The people will see my wife ride proudly into this village on the Thunder Horse, Firecloud."

"You came very close to death at the hands of the Thunder Horse," Spring Bird told her brother. "You will have to be very careful."

Nighthawk shook his head, remembering his folly. "I now know there was no need to act as I did. I understand that the best horse and the strongest rope could never catch the Thunder Horse. Now I will listen to my wife, who knows how to tame him. She will ride the Thunder Horse, and then I will ride him."

FIRECLOUD

Aged One studied Clara for a short time. "I am now sure that it was you whom I saw in my visions of winters past, riding the stallion and speaking Nighthawk's name. Yes, the words Nighthawk speaks are true. I believe the Thunder Horse will be yours."

Clara beamed with happiness. In her mind was the big stallion, with her on his back, looking out across the spacious meadows and ridges from among the high peaks that were his home. She could barely contain her excitement. She would now be fulfilling a dream that had been with her since she heard the legend from John Huston, far, far back along the rolling Missouri River, a time that now seemed long ago. Her dream would soon become reality. She was going to tame and ride the most powerful stallion this wild land had ever known. And she would do it with the man she loved.

18

THE JOURNEY TO THE BURNING MOUNTAINS was a joyous one for Clara and Nighthawk. They followed the middle river of the Three Forks, the Madison, ascending the peaceful valley to where the stallion made his home in the high mountains of many wonders. They passed streams and lakes that shone crystal clear, while trout jumped and surfaced for flies, and eagles and hawks swooped down to make meals of them. On both sides were the high peaks of the wilderness, still capped with snow at the very tops and in the pockets and north slopes where the sun never gave warmth. The rocky peaks ran in a continuous line far into the deep wilderness where the wild stallion lived. Each day brought them closer and filled Clara with awe at the majesty of the land.

The days passed swiftly and they pushed higher and higher into this land of noble splendor. Herd upon herd of elk watched them pass, the bulls with their huge racks of antlers now trimmed in velvet. Mountain sheep crossed the rocky passes and fed on the lush growth near hidden springs and cascading waterfalls. The air grew cooler as they climbed, for here the warm moons came much later and lasted a shorter time than in the valleys far below. Flocks of migrating birds were returning to build their nests and raise their young amid the dense grasses and brilliant wildflowers. The snow on the flats and in the open meadows was gone; but under the trees and in the shadows patches would remain until the night breezes turned warmer.

They built their lodge at the edge of a small meadow near the river called Firehole. Nighthawk would remain at the lodge to hunt while Clara began the long process of gaining Firecloud's trust. Having found a good supply of sweetgrass near a small, secluded spring, she began her quest.

The home of the bad spirits was a broad, sweeping expanse of dense timber and open meadows filled with hot, bubbling springs of green and aqua waters that hissed out onto open, flat areas of white crystal salts. Beneath her feet, boiling water roiled through interconnected underground tunnels and was pushed to the surface by the heat of the earth. She understood why people feared this valley of unusual sights and sounds, uncommon smells and mixtures of color and texture.

And deep within this valley of the unexplained Clara saw a flash of red and white that vanished as quickly as it had appeared.

Like a ghost dashing among the geyser basins, the stallion emerged here and there, eerie amid the rising vapors. Clara made her way out into an open area bleached white by the spouting waters of now dormant geysers. She dragged a log out into the open and, leaving an offering of sweetgrass nearby, made herself comfortable.

Soon the stallion made his way into the open, his ears erect and his nose testing the air. He had received her scent, and his manner told Clara that he remembered her. He eyed Clara for some time before turning his interest to the sweetgrass.

Clara stared in wonder; the magnificent horse seemed to grow more beautiful each time she saw him. In sunlight that reflected off the white ground, the stallion was a majestic sight. Steam and vapor from the bubbling geysers trailed into the sky behind him and into the deep green of the pines beyond.

After a time, the stallion came forward slowly, as if recall-

FIRECLOUD

ing the evening of the Sun Dance ceremony when he had first received an offering from this two-legged creature who appeared not to be after his freedom. Again Clara talked softly to him, admiring his powerful frame and his shining coat. As he stepped closer to the grass, he again grew cautious. He watched her for a time before finally bending his head to take some of the sweet forage. Then he ran a few yards away to eat what he had taken. When he returned, he did not bolt, but remained standing near her as he ate. When Clara slowly rose and advanced a few steps forward, the stallion snorted and leaped back.

"Don't be afraid, Firecloud," Clara told him. "I have come to be your friend. You are the most beautiful horse in the world, Firecloud."

Clara repeated his name many times as she continued to speak to him, for she wanted him to hear it and know it when spoken. She continued to talk to him, for a soft, soothing voice could do much toward taming a horse. Force was out of the question; he had resisted every form of it with uncontrollable power.

When Firecloud finished the first offering, Clara placed more sweetgrass on the ground and moved the log closer, still speaking to the stallion. Firecloud squealed and tossed his head, telling her he did not approve of her being so close to the grass.

Clara laughed softly. "Don't be so ornery, Firecloud. The least you could do is thank me."

The stallion pranced back and forth, tossing his head and laying his ears back, continuing to display his disapproval. He continued his antics most of the morning, refusing to approach her, yet not willing to forgo her offering. Clara continued to sit with her elbows on her knees, watching him continuously.

"I have all the time in the world," she told him. "You might as well come and eat this grass, for I won't leave until you do."

Each time Clara added more grass to the pile in front of her,

Firecloud would stop prancing and watch her closely. The stallion did not understand this two-legged creature who seemed only to want to please him. She was alone and she had no ropes or snares. Her smile and her soft voice made him feel more and more at ease.

Finally, late in the day, the big stallion seemed to abandon all caution and come forward. With slight hesitation at first, the wild horse lowered his head and began to eat the sweetgrass.

"Oh, isn't that good!" Clara beamed, so pleased she could hardly sit still. "Eat all you want."

Thrilled, Clara watched the beautiful stallion eating contentedly just an arm's length away. She dared not move, for fear of scaring him and breaking down the trust she had established. He had come far closer than she had dared to hope he would on the first day. But she must not rush things. She had plenty of time to win the stallion's trust. One day soon they would be the best of friends for all time.

WATER FROM THE SPRING bubbled fresh and cool. Clara filled a bag and returned to the small bark lodge. The snowbanks had vanished from beneath the pines, and the cool air had given way to the whisper of warm rains. The meadow was now filled with tall, lush grass that waved in the breeze. The entire mountain wilderness was bursting with color, alive with the joys of summer.

Clara prepared a meal of plant bulbs and greens, with fresh elk steak, and placed it before Nighthawk. He was looking into the fire, toying with an arrowhead. He said nothing to Clara as she sat down beside him.

"Firecloud no longer eats off the ground," Clara said. "I feed him out of my hand all the time. And he lets me pet him and hang on to his neck. I'll be riding him very soon."

Clara had noticed a growing tension over the last few days. As usual, Nighthawk was keeping it to himself. Clara did not want things to go too far.

FIRECLOUD

"Nighthawk," she said, "I know what's bothering you. I don't know why you can't talk about it. Until a short time ago you were willing to let me work with Firecloud as slowly as I needed to. Now all you do is sulk. Why?"

"We've been up here a long time," Nighthawk said. "Too long. We should be back in the village participating in the hunts and the summer ceremonies, hunting with the other warriors in the village, and maybe leading a war party against an enemy. I need to strengthen my honor among the people."

"Yes, but you agreed that taming Firecloud would bring us more glory and honor than any ten successful war parties."

"It will bring *you* honor, not me."

Clara blew her breath out in frustration. "Are we back to this? I thought that you understood we were taming him together."

"*You* are taming him," Nighthawk said. "Nearly one whole moon has passed, and I have yet to even *see* the stallion. I have not gone with you because you did not want me to."

"The time has to be right," Clara said. "You told me you realized that Firecloud would remember you as the one who threw the rope around his neck and tried to take his freedom. We have talked many times about the fact that he must trust me totally before he can accept that you are with me and trust you also. That time will come after I have begun to ride him. Not before. If he becomes scared before this time, I may never be able to ride him. It could destroy all the work I have already done."

"Listen to how you speak," Nighthawk said. "You have come to tame the horse only for your own honor. We are not together in this." He threw his bowl of food aside and left the lodge.

Outside the moon had grown nearly full again, and the night air carried the cries of loons from a lake. Crickets and other night creatures made their sounds in the grass and trees, while the Firehole River murmured nearby.

"You are wrong, my husband," Clara told Nighthawk when she found him leaning against a large pine, gazing out into the meadow. "You told me you would trust me. Now, please trust me."

Nighthawk talked to her, but he kept his eyes on a small herd of elk foraging in the meadow. "You make me less than a man. You tell me when I may do things and make me feel that I am not worthy to be here while you tame the stallion. I have hunted enough for our fires, and there is meat enough to last through nearly another full moon for one person. I will return to the Valley of the Three Forks."

Clara put her arms around him, resting her head against his strong back and shoulders. "In my eyes you are more a man than any woman deserves," she said. "You are gentle, yet strong and brave. You love me, and you mean more to me than anything else in the world."

Nighthawk turned and looked into her eyes. "More than the stallion?"

"Of course. If you go back to the village, I will go with you. I will go with you wherever you choose."

"You would leave the stallion and go back with me?"

"It would break my heart to leave Firecloud now, but he is not the most important thing in my life. You are."

Nighthawk took her in his arms and held her close. "I feel weak at times because you are so strong. Forgive me."

"There is nothing to forgive," Clara assured him.

"From this day forward," he continued. "I will do my best to make you happy. I am in no hurry to go back to the village. I want to see your eyes the day you ride to me on the Thunder Horse. Soon."

"Nighthawk," Clara said, "I love you so very much. I never knew life could be so beautiful."

Clara held him tightly, feeling his strong, muscular frame against her and his lips filling her with warmth. He lifted her from her feet and took her inside the lodge, to their bed. The warm breeze whispered through the tall pines, bringing the summer to the high wilderness. And the far off cries of the loons echoed through the painted rock canyons and over the valley where the geysers' steam rose into the moonlight. The small fire within the lodge flickered merrily, bringing an orange-red glow to the inside. Under the buffalo robes Clara and Nighthawk were warm, sharing a love as strong and wild as the land itself.

THE DAYS MOVED BY QUICKLY, with Clara enjoying each one to the fullest. She had found inner peace in the mountains, spending most of her time with Firecloud. She rode him over the high ridges and across the broad valleys of the spectacular wilderness that had grown to be a part of her. She never tired of flying through this paradise of mountain splendor, her hair blowing in the gusty winds that rustled the leaves of the quaking aspen and carried the wings of soaring eagles that screamed from high above, their cries echoing through the rocky peaks that towered into the clouds.

The stallion had grown to trust her completely, and now willingly carried her on his back. With patience, she had broken him to lead. Then she used the braided horsehair bit to control him. The stallion was so intelligent that he quickly learned to turn and stop at only the slightest signal from Clara. He seemed to enjoy having her atop him, racing over the meadows like a bird in flight, carrying her to the tops of high ridges and into alpine meadows with effortless bounds and leaps.

An added joy came to Clara the day the stallion invested his trust in Nighthawk, allowing him to ride just as Clara did. After a few hours Nighthawk returned on the stallion's back, his eyes filled with admiration.

"I have ridden him, as I have always dreamed," he told Clara, "but he is yours and yours alone. You will become a legend among all the peoples of this land, and I am very proud of you."

In token of his love, Nighthawk devised for Clara a sturdy saddle of cottonwood, covered with a beautifully tanned antelope hide. He made for her, from the white mane and tail of the stallion, a striking bridle.

With Nighthawk on his own horse, they traveled through the land. Nighthawk showed her landmarks and told her of places that lay just beyond the mountains to the south, the land of the Snake People, the Shoshone. He thought it strange they had not seen sign of these people, their bitter enemies, long before this; he told Clara that the spirits had been with them while she tamed the Thunder Horse. They could not stay much longer, Nighthawk said, for the spirits could not always protect them.

As they passed the deep canyon where the Yellowstone River spilled down over two giant waterfalls, they encountered a Shoshone war party headed across the mountains into Blackfoot lands. It was the first day of their journey back to the village, a beautiful morning just beginning. The deep canyon with the foaming river far below presented a striking sight. After such a long time of peace and happiness, death was now so near.

"They have seen us surely," Nighthawk said as he and Clara took cover in a grove of pines along the edge of the canyon. "They seemed confused to see you on the Thunder Horse. But they will come to find us, and we will die if we cannot outrun them."

"I do not think that is a good idea," Clara said, thinking of the unsure footing of the rocky ground all around them. "If your horse fell, I would come back, and we would both die. It would be better if we fought them."

"There are no more of them than the fingers on two hands," Nighthawk said. "But that is still too many."

"I will take your extra bow with arrows and leave while you take the trail down into the canyon," Clara said. "They will come after you, thinking you have tried to sneak away and have become trapped. Then I will ride Firecloud down the trail behind them. We will have them between us. They will be afraid of Firecloud."

Nighthawk rode down the trail toward the falls while Clara took Firecloud deeper into the cover of the pines. As the sun rose higher, the pale yellows and tans of the canyon changed to flaming orange and gold. The lower falls roared, the tumbling water crashing over the high dropoff into the jagged rock bed far below. The Shoshone warriors appeared at the edge of the canyon, whooping and yelling. They would take a Kainah scalp this day.

Nine warriors wearing brightly painted war shirts and carrying feathered weapons urged their horses down the steep canyon trail toward Nighthawk, raising their bows and lances into the air above them. Nighthawk dismounted and faced them, fitting an arrow to his bow. The Shoshone warriors mocked him, making sign to him that he would die in a very short time, crying like a small child before they killed him. Nighthawk only smiled, for he could see Clara riding Firecloud down onto the trail above them.

Clara notched an arrow into her bow, her hands trembling. The terrible cries of the Sioux warrior Cut Face again echoed in her head, and it took all her courage to ride down the trail toward the screaming Shoshones.

She was nearly upon them when they turned to see her behind them on the trail. The awesome stallion towered above them, and their faces turned to masks of fear. A Long Knife woman had ridden toward them on the Thunder Horse to send them from this world. Trapped on the trail high above the pounding river below with no escape, they began to sing their death songs.

One of Nighthawk's arrows struck a warrior high in the chest, and he tumbled off the trail into the depths below. Clara loosed an arrow that took a warrior in the shoulder. Another warrior climbed along the rocks above the trail. Nighthawk sent an arrow deep into the Shoshone's ribs. The warrior gripped the rocks in one last effort to live before sliding off onto the trail.

The remainder of the warriors turned their horses toward Clara, screaming in frenzy, begging their spirit helpers to guide them past the Long Knife spirit woman who was master of the most powerful stallion in the mountains. But her arrows and Firecloud's front hooves, striking and thrashing in powerful arcs, sent them over the edge, screaming and bouncing off the steep, jagged rocks. Now only three horses remained and the warrior who had died on the trail with Nighthawk's arrow deep in his side.

Nighthawk raised his bow high in the air and sent out a war cry. Clara answered, her bow also raised. Nighthawk took the scalp of the fallen warrior, and together he and Clara herded the three horses out of the canyon. With Firecloud and his herd, these three Shoshone horses would bear witness to their accomplishments since leaving the village.

At the top of the canyon Clara pointed to two Shoshone warriors on horseback staring at Clara and Nighthawk from the edge of a deep gorge. It was plain that they feared greatly for their lives, because of the Thunder Horse, for they fled at a full gallop. Nighthawk had foretold these events: Clara and her stallion were already a legend throughout the land. Little time would pass before she would be at the center of many stories told around campfires.

For Clara, happiness meant being with her husband and the stallion. She knew that her appearance in the village riding Firecloud would cause as great a stir as there had ever been among the people, but it would be no great shock. They had seen her approach the stallion during the Sun Dance ceremonies, and they knew full well that she intended to bring him and his herd back to the village. It would be easy for them to accept the presence of the powerful horse among them. They would see that Nighthawk was worthy of honor.

All this would certainly happen. But there would be trouble, too, for Black Owl was surely waiting for them.

19

CLARA FOLLOWED NIGHTHAWK's pointing finger to a column of riders making their way along the elk trails adjoining the river. A party of trappers, new to the country and no doubt new to the trade as well.

Clara remembered her first look at this wild land and watched the intruding traders with apprehension. She knew now that riches would come not from the beaver pelts she had hoped to gather here, but from the land itself.

As they rode closer, Clara could make out facial features. The leader appeared to be a seasoned trapper who knew the country, leading his party into the hills to scout for trapping and trading grounds. He seemed amused by a man riding behind him, out of place in his English tophat, his white hair curling out from underneath. The man in the tophat seemed unsure of himself in this strange, wild land. In the line behind him, other trappers laughed as the leader yelled something about Indians coming out of the trees at them. With Nighthawk following, Clara rode out into the valley to face the men, and raised her hand in the sign of peace.

The laughing and talking stopped as the column approached Clara and Nighthawk. They halted and raised their rifles.

"Peace," Clara yelled to them in English. "We wish to talk."

The riders looked astonished at the sight of a white woman who spoke English.

The rider in the tophat with the white hair rose up in his stirrups. "Clara? Clara Melton, is that you?"

Clara stared, unable to believe her eyes. It was George Whittingham, her father's dearest friend and her partner in the fur trade business.

"George," she answered, "it is Clara."

One of the others pointed at Nighthawk and yelled, "That one's a Blackfoot or I don't know Indians!"

"We come in peace!" Clara said quickly. "George Whittingham is my friend."

"Blackfeet ain't friends to no one but skunks," the trapper yelled.

"Hold your water, Sturns!" the leader bellowed. "There's only two of 'em."

The trapper lowered his rifle, grumbling. "I kin see your hair is set to decorate a coup stick afore long, Immell," he shouted. "Just kiss your ass and trust them trees behind 'em ain't crawlin' with a war party."

"Well, I'll be a gut-shot buffalo!" another trapper exclaimed. "I ain't never seen the likes of it. White women out here?"

"Just one, I'd venture to say." George Whittingham rode up next to Clara and dismounted.

Clara got down from Firecloud and gave him a warm hug. "This is a surprise."

"To say the least," Whittingham added. "I cannot believe all this."

"It really is me," she laughed. "And this is my husband, Nighthawk, a Kainah Blackfoot."

Trying not to appear shocked, Whittingham bowed graciously to Nighthawk. After another moment, he said, "Finding you is a great relief, Clara. I heard in St. Louis that everyone on the expedition was massacred by Sioux late last fall near the Mandan villages."

"We were attacked by Sioux," Clara said. "And John, along with half the crew, was killed and the *Rosebud* was destroyed. But LaCroix and the others escaped."

Whittingham looked confused. "You were not aboard the *Rosebud*?"

"No. I swam to safety. LaCroix took his boat to the Hidatsa villages and traded for horses. He believes he is now sole owner of our possessions."

"I see." Whittingham nodded. "This past winter I got word that LaCroix had established a post on the upper Yellowstone, in Crow country. Patch-Eye LaCroix, people call him now. I found the report confusing. There was no mention of you, and I could not recollect LaCroix being blind in one eye."

"It is a long story," Clara said.

"Well, no matter," Whittingham said with a reassuring smile. "You are alive and well, and I am grateful for that."

"Did you travel out here to find LaCroix?" Clara asked.

"Partly," Whittingham said. "I also wanted to find you and explore the business possibilities out here."

"What have you learned?" Clara asked.

"The attitudes of investment seekers in the East have changed," he said. "Many are now able to see that the returns far outweigh the risks of investment out here. Manuel Lisa died recently. He jointly owned a trading company with a Joshua Pilcher, whom I met recently. Pilcher has proposed that we join his venture and call it the Missouri Fur Company. With added capital and you here to oversee the operations, I don't see why we shouldn't consider the proposition seriously. What do you think?"

Clara quickly understood the logic behind the proposal. Any business venture worth investing in was worth getting into in a big way. Companies that hoped to do well in the fur business had to get in with many men and supplies. The more men a company could employ in the mountains, the more furs would reach St. Louis at the end of the trapping season. In a short time the entire territory purchased from France would be the scene of fierce business competition. Aged One had spoken to her many times about his fear that one day the Blackfoot hunting grounds would be a battleground where Long Knives and Indians fought one another. Clara could see that if she stayed in the business, she would stand in the middle between her fur company and the Kainah people. It would then be very easy for Black Owl to tell people that she lived with the Kainah, but remained a Long Knife in her heart and took the beaver from Kainah lands. Her love for Nighthawk and the life she now shared with him was too great to risk. She could still keep in touch with the forts and learn how things were changing in the East. George Whittingham could continue to oversee her business affairs at the reasonable salary she had been paying him. What she now owned in the East could remain as she had left it. She would not bring her past into this land.

"Well, what do you say?" George Whittingham asked. "We could control the entire trade."

"I think not, George," Clara answered. "Before the end of the first season I would have the entire Blackfoot nation and the Missouri Fur Company both shouting for my demise. I would be putting those I love in great jeopardy. I now have what is important to me, and I couldn't bear to lose any part of it."

George Whittingham nodded in understanding. "I couldn't have expected you to say anything different under those circumstances."

"I could have secured a great many furs for us at the onset," Clara said. "But things would soon have become very complicated. I have a husband now, and I do not want to leave this country, even with a fortune."

"Yes, I understand," Whittingham said. "I must say that this does not come as a surprise to me. When you boarded the *Rosebud* in St. Louis over a year ago, I could have sworn there was someone else inside that Indian dress John Huston bought you. I suspected that you had put New England far behind you. Your Aunt Katherine will be shocked."

Clara laughed. "If she were here now, she would faint and never arise."

George laughed with her. "No doubt. But your father would have appreciated all this."

"Yes," Clara agreed. "I wish he could have seen this land.

FIRECLOUD

He would have loved it. There is no place like this on earth. It's home to me now."

"It is good to see you so happy," George said. "That's most important."

"Have any loads of furs gone down the river?" Clara asked. Her mind had gone back to LaCroix, and she knew the time was at hand when she would need to act if she was to succeed in getting their investment back.

George Whittingham guessed what had brought her to that subject. "A few loads have gone out," he said, "but there have been no shipments from the upper Yellowstone."

"We can't afford to let LaCroix get the shipment to St. Louis," Clara said. "By then it would be too late to prove who owned what. Besides, LaCroix is unscrupulous. I would rather take care of it out here. Some incidents during our journey upriver showed me that LaCroix was dishonest. I blame myself for not dismissing him at that time. It would have surely saved us all these problems now."

Whittingham took a deep breath. "Maybe we should forget the whole thing. I wouldn't want you to risk your life for the sake of our investment. I am not encumbered by the loss, and I'm sure Martin Folmon isn't either. I know the man and—"

"George," Clara cut in, "you are very kind, but I am responsible for our present condition, and I intend to make good. I cannot stand by and see LaCroix become wealthy at our expense."

Whittingham looked concerned. "How do you propose to take our property from LaCroix without risking your life?"

"I will not be alone," Clara said, motioning toward Nighthawk. "LaCroix is likely to make mistakes we can benefit from. With the right plan, I can regain all that we have invested and make some profit as well."

"I hope your father isn't rolling in his grave," Whittingham commented. "I was a dear friend of his for a long time, and I watched you grow up. I would feel responsible if things went wrong with LaCroix."

"They won't go wrong," Clara said with confidence. "Besides, my father would not just roll over, but sit up in his grave if I turned my back on all this."

"Perhaps." Whittingham spent a moment studying her. "We must be off," he said at length. "I am to meet Joshua Pilcher on the Big Horn River in a few days. Then I'll be off to St. Louis."

"Do you plan to return to this country?" Clara asked him. "I want to take you to the village where Nighthawk and I live. It would be an experience I'm sure you would remember for the rest of your life."

Whittingham nodded. "This trip has been a revelation."

Clara gave him a last, long hug and a kiss on the cheek as they prepared to go their separate ways again. The trappers whistled and laughed, making ribald comments.

"Common ruffians," George told Clara in disgust.

Clara laughed. "Don't ever take them too seriously. If you do, you'll be grumbling all the while you are out here."

Whittingham mounted his horse, chuckling with Clara. "They do make a laughingstock of me, don't they," he said. "I suppose I appear out of my element, but I'll show the lot of them. Maybe I shall eat a bit of raw liver from a buffalo one of these days. Do you suppose that would quiet them?"

"No."

"Well, I suppose not." He laughed again and turned to rejoin the trappers.

"I want you to come back," Clara insisted. "I'll be waiting." She waved until the column had lost itself in the distance. Knowing that man, Clara thought, there was a very good possibility she would indeed see him again. It was reassuring to know that LaCroix had not yet left the fort with the many furs he no doubt now had from the winter's season of trapping and trading. She hoped, with the influence Nighthawk now had among the people and the increased honor returning with Firecloud would bring, that they could take a war party to the fort and settle the problem of LaCroix. They would have to act quickly, for LaCroix would not wait much longer to take the furs downriver to market.

* * *

FIRECLOUD

CLARA AND NIGHTHAWK came into the village in early morning, the best time to receive honor for glorious deeds. Clara rode Firecloud, who pranced magnificently, and Nighthawk rode beside her, while the stallion's immense herd trailed behind. With the herd stretching far back up the valley, it was an impressive sight to the Black Horse band of Kainah Blackfeet. But there was no yelling, nor did a great crowd of villagers gather to welcome them. They seemed instead to be struck with fear and uncertainty, herding their children into the lodges and closing the flaps, some of them peering out timidly. Many of the warriors paid little attention and resumed making weapons or decorating personal belongings. Only Deer Chaser and Aged One stood with Spring Bird and some of the young warriors at the edge of the village, waving and shouting in welcome.

"This is very strange," Nighthawk said, shaking his head. "I do not understand."

Clara looked closely into the village. Most of the warriors present were horse tenders and older warriors. Black Owl, whose presence was always conspicuous, was nowhere to be seen. Clara did notice that a few of his followers were staring. Black Owl had certainly returned and made his presence felt among the people. There was no doubt he was responsible for this change of attitude.

"Much has happened since you have been gone," Aged One told them. "Black Owl's return has again cast evil over our people. He is sent by the bad spirits, I am sure. When he is here, there is little to laugh about. Yet the council and the villagers all listen to him. He has again told everyone that the Thunder Horse is evil. Since the buffalo have not yet come in large herds, people believe him. Black Owl says the Thunder Horse has driven them away from our lands."

"There is no limit to the evil in that man," Clara said through clenched teeth as the villagers stared at them and at the big stallion and his immense herd.

"They do not even notice the Shoshone scalp we have brought," Nighthawk added in disbelief. "What is happening to our people? They grow confused from seeing that my wife and the horse are not evil, then allowing themselves to believe Black Owl's words. We must make them understand that Black Owl speaks only lies."

"There is other news which is not good," Aged One added, looking directly at Clara. "Black Owl has formed an alliance with the Long Knife trader who is your enemy and who stole your possessions. Black Owl has smoked the pipe of peace with the one called Patch-Eye LaCroix."

Stunned, Clara could only shake her head in disbelief. Nighthawk asked Aged One how such a thing could be possible.

"Patch-Eye LaCroix has taken a Piegan Blackfoot woman as his wife," Aged One explained. "This Long Knife enemy of yours took her as his wife while trading with her people during the past cold moons. This Piegan woman is a cousin to Black Owl, a daughter of his mother's sister who married a Piegan warrior and went from our band to live with her husband."

"How did Black Owl know of this union and then smoke with LaCroix?" Nighthawk asked.

"LaCroix came to our village with this woman as his wife not long ago, while you were in the Burning Mountains taming the Thunder Horse. He met Black Owl, and they smoked the pipe of peace. LaCroix gave Black Owl many presents and told him he would bring more if Black Owl would deliver the Long Knife woman to him. This Long Knife was very evil, as evil as Black Owl himself. He said he wanted you for his slave. This made Black Owl very happy. He told LaCroix he would do his best to bring the Long Knife woman across the mountains to the Yellowstone."

Clara looked at Nighthawk, whose eyes were ablaze with anger.

"I will leave this day," Nighthawk said. "I should have killed LaCroix, long ago."

"No," Clara said quickly. "LaCroix has too many men with him. We must have a good plan before we go after him."

"Her words are wise," Aged One said to Nighthawk. "Besides, if you kill LaCroix now, you will give Black Owl a reason to approach the council and have you banished or even

FIRECLOUD

killed. By killing the husband of his cousin, you would be killing a member of his family. This would give him the right to seek tribal action against you."

"I will not stand by and let Black Owl take my wife to the evil LaCroix!" Nighthawk said hotly.

"You must conceive a plan," Aged One said, trying to calm him. "First you must regain the loyalty of the people. The best way to do that is to make them happy."

"Buffalo," Nighthawk said quickly. "The people will surely be happy if the buffalo come."

"You are now speaking with wisdom, my young warrior friend," Aged One said.

"Where is Black Owl now?" Clara asked.

"Scouting for buffalo," Aged One answered. "He left at the beginning of the new moon."

"We shall bring the buffalo to our village," Nighthawk said to Aged One with a nod. "Near the eastern branch of the Three Forks, Clara found a sacred buffalo hair ball. We will hold the buffalo-calling ceremony. Then we will have a good hunt, and the people will again be happy."

Clara took the ball of buffalo hair from her pouch and showed it to Aged One.

A broad smile appeared on his face. "This is a good sign," he said. "The buffalo are coming. We will again be a happy people with food to eat and hides to make new lodges. Once again the feasting will go on through the night, and there will be much joy. The buffalo are coming!"

Nighthawk and Clara prayed while Aged One and Spring Bird joined in the buffalo-calling ceremony. Deer Chaser, his parents, and many other young warriors and their families also attended.

At the end of the second day of the ceremony, a crier arrived in the village, having come from a Piegan camp. The Piegans had completed a successful hunt, the crier announced, and the herd was now on its way into this valley. Black Owl could not take credit for finding the herd. The people recognized that Nighthawk and Clara had brought the buffalo.

As the sun rose the next day, the herd appeared on the hills above the village. It was a large herd, and the hunt would be very productive. The people lit a ceremonial fire and offered prayers for a successful hunt, thanking the sun for having sent buffalo into their lands. Clara and Nighthawk received presents from the villagers, tokens of appreciation for having conducted a successful buffalo-calling ceremony. Deer Chaser and some of the other young warriors in the village told everyone who would listen that the sun would not have sent the herd to the Kainah people if the Thunder Horse were evil. The Thunder Horse had brought good things, and its rider, the Thunder Horse Woman, was also good.

When Black Owl returned, he could not make anyone in the village listen to what he said. He resolved to restore his influence by excelling during the hunt. Through brilliant manipulation of the council, he saw to it that the Brave Wolves were appointed to police the hunt. Again he had full power to discipline and even to execute those who defied him. The hunt was carefully planned, for it could fail if the buffalo became excited and stampeded. Black Owl enjoyed being in command of an important event in the village. Once again he had an opportunity to convince the people that he was truly worthy of leadership and that his half brother and the Long Knife woman with her Thunder Horse were bad omens who should be cast out from the village.

20

THE HUNT BEGAN when the herd had finished drinking at the river and had made its way atop the flat where Nighthawk had chased Firecloud early in the spring. Black Owl and the Brave Wolves had taken their positions to oversee the hunt. After an extended argument with Black Owl over being allowed to kill for his lodge only when all the other warriors had finished their kills, Nighthawk was sent back to camp, forbidden to participate under penalty of death. His anger was excessive and it took all of Clara's persuasive powers to keep him from returning to the hunt and putting his life in danger. There would be other hunts, Clara told him, when Black Owl and the Brave Wolves had no authority.

The hunt progressed with Nighthawk, Clara, and Aged One watching from a hill above the village. It was hard to see what was happening for the dust rose in great clouds. They caught only fleeting glimpses of warriors shooting arrows or driving lances into running buffalo. The warriors ran the herd in circles, causing confusion and often pileups, making it easier to get closer and shoot accurately. Usually, they broke the herd into smaller groups; teams of hunters would run these groups until enough kills had been made. As this hunt progressed, however, there seemed to be a lack of order. Aged One expressed his growing concern to Clara and Nighthawk.

"There will be trouble," he said, pointing to the edge of the herd nearest the river. "The buffalo will soon stampede past the few who are hunting there." He set his jaw firmly against the anger that was welling up within him. "If he is not stopped soon, Black Owl will destroy this village. He cares for only himself."

As Aged One finished speaking, the herd broke out from their poor containment and began a frantic rush down off the flat and toward the river bottom. Though a crier was leaving the hunt to warn the village, Nighthawk and Clara left Aged One on the hillside and hurried down into camp to move the villagers to safety. They rushed about the village warning the people that the herd would soon be upon them. Women gathered their children frantically, crying out for those who were away from their lodges. Already the heavy pounding of hooves along the river sent tremors through the village. Nighthawk helped the horse tenders drive the herd across the river while Clara and Spring Bird brought crying children to the arms of their tearful mothers and gathered valuables for delivery up the slopes above the village. The pounding of the advancing herd had now grown to a steady thunder. Amid shouts, Clara, Nighthawk, and Spring Bird hurried to rejoin Aged One on the hill overlooking the village.

The herd poured into the village like a brown sea, crashing over lodges as if they were but driftwood before the onrushing waves. A wailing and crying went up from the villagers as they watched helplessly from the hillsides while their homes became trampled hides and lengths of broken wood beneath the onslaught. Wives and mothers envisioned their husbands and sons having fallen beneath the herd as it broke free from containment. But soon the warriors began to return, riding their horses among the last segments of the herd, calling to the people on the hill for loved ones, hugging one another, and praising the spirits for keeping death from their doors. Clara and Nighthawk watched Black Owl find his own family and gather many of the villagers around him, pointing to Clara and Nighthawk, and then to Firecloud.

"Now is the time to make him pay for his evil actions,"

FIRECLOUD

Nighthawk said. "I have heard enough of his lies."

"It is best," Aged One told Clara and Spring Bird, discouraging them from stopping him. "Nighthawk can no longer stand by and watch. He must face Black Owl man to man in front of the people. If Black Owl refuses, he will lose honor."

The two men were already shouting at each other, face to face. Nighthawk was persistent and would not allow Black Owl to gain the upper hand.

"Your time has come," he told his half brother. "Now the village will know how evil you really are. There are those of us who watched the hunt from the hills. We saw how you failed to keep order among the hunters and your Brave Wolves so that you could kill many buffalo and declare yourself a great hunter. Look what you have done!"

Black Owl glared back in anger. "You only try to cover up for yourself. You bring to our village a Long Knife woman who is an evil spirit and can tame the devil horse from the Burning Mountains. You have invoked the power of the evil spirits. And now you try to tell the people I have caused this thing to happen."

"You did not allow me or my wife to hunt," Nighthawk retorted. "Firecloud was here with us, not out with the herd. You were responsible for containing the herd, but you were so greedy for the largest kill that you destroyed our village. *You* are the evil spirit, Black Owl."

Black Owl swung his fist, but Nighthawk blocked the blow and struck savagely at his half brother. Black Owl moved quickly, but Nighthawk's fist opened a gash below his right eye. Screaming, Black Owl lunged, and the two men went down in a tangle of arms and legs.

One of the scouts who had been watching the village rode to the large group of villagers watching Nighthawk and Black Owl fight. He reported that a large group of Shoshone warriors was advancing on the village.

"So you have brought our enemies, your mother's people, back with you from the Burning Mountains," Black Owl said spitefully. "Tell our people now that you do not mean to bring harm upon our village. Our enemies come just after our lodges have been destroyed, and we must defend our families when we are not prepared for war. They have come to avenge the loss of their brothers at your hands in the deep canyons where the Yellowstone flows over waterfalls. Surely you have caused this, not I."

A second scout arrived, confirming that the advancing column they had spotted was indeed a Shoshone war party. Immediate alarm broke out among the people as the warriors rushed to find what weapons they could from among the ruins of the village.

"Many will die this day," Clara told Nighthawk, "unless we use special medicine against the Shoshone."

"There is no time to do anything but defend the village," Nighthawk said as he searched for his war paint among the articles they had saved from their lodge before the buffalo had destroyed it.

Clara seized the Shoshone scalp Nighthawk had taken after the battle in the Yellowstone canyon. Quickly she tied it to a bow and dipped her fingers into the bowl of war paint he was preparing.

"The warriors we saw after the battle in the canyon, the ones who saw us and ran, will be on this revenge raid," she said. "If they see me on Firecloud, it may again fill them with fear."

"You will meet your death," Nighthawk told her. "You must not do this."

"It is the only way. If something is not done to break their medicine, we will all die anyway. Please, do not try to stop me." With Nighthawk's war paint, Clara made red stripes across her cheeks and forehead. "This will be the day of the Thunder Horse Woman," she said with conviction.

With a quiver of arrows on her back and bow raised high, the scalp dangling from the lower tip, Clara urged Firecloud out of the wrecked village toward the advancing column of Shoshones.

"That is a woman of incredible medicine," Aged One told Nighthawk. "She is afraid of nothing. Not even death."

"I must go with her," Nighthawk said, mounting his horse.

"I will not let her fight alone."

"She will not be alone," Aged One said, pointing to the warriors in the village. When they saw Clara dash out to fight on the big stallion, they, too, rode out of the village, screaming war cries. Black Owl, his fist in the air, shouted for them to wait so he could lead the charge.

The Shoshones, confident after finding the village in confusion, had dismounted in a clearing below the camp and were making their final preparations before advancing against their enemy. Clara, with Firecloud now at full speed, a vision of power and grace, bore down upon them with her bow raised high in the air and her black hair streaming out behind her, shouting triumphantly. The warriors stopped dancing and stared in disbelief. Their eyes grew wide with fright as one warrior pointed.

"The Thunder Horse Woman!" he shouted.

The Shoshones scattered in all directions, running for their horses or trying to escape to the cover of the timber. They had been told about this woman who had killed their warriors in the land of the Burning Mountains, the spirit woman who had captured the mighty stallion and rode him as her own. Her medicine was too powerful to stop this day. Clara continued toward a small group of warriors who seemed willing to stay and fight.

Clara fitted an arrow to her bow as one of the remaining warriors, who was afoot, braced himself to throw his lance. As his arm came forward, Clara turned Firecloud, and the big stallion veered slightly as the lance sang past her left shoulder. Now upon the warrior, who was struggling to arm his bow, Clara loosed an arrow, which pierced his chest and tore out through his back, leaving him doubled over in the grass.

Two other warriors mounted their horses and rushed her. Clara turned Firecloud to meet one of the horses head on. The Shoshone warrior's gelding twisted away in terror, bumping into the other horse and sending both warriors sprawling. One of the warriors lay still, while the other limped toward the cover of the cottonwoods.

Seeing the Shoshone warriors scatter during Clara's first

charge, Nighthawk and the men of the village began to chase down their fleeing enemy. A large war party of Shoshone had come to fight, but they seemed few in number now that they were running their horses into the hills in all directions to avoid the power of the Thunder Horse Woman and the Kainah warriors who had gained favor with the spirits. Some of the Shoshone were ridden down and killed, but most of them escaped. All the villagers would rejoice this night, for they had been saved from death.

Nighthawk took Clara in his arms as she stood near one of the fallen Shoshone warriors.

"What is this trembling I feel in you?" he asked. "You have almost single-handedly defeated our enemy this day. What could you possibly fear now?"

"I don't know," Clara answered. "Do you think the Shoshone will leave?"

"There are many of them, and they might decide to attack again," Nighthawk answered. "But I think they have had enough of you and the Thunder Horse. You showed the people of this village much power this day."

"I worry about Black Owl," Clara said.

Nighthawk's half brother stood talking to members of the council, pointing to where the Shoshone had retreated and then to Clara and Nighthawk.

Clara spoke softly to her husband, "When you fought with him, I could see in his eyes that he meant death for you. Now he is trying even harder to convince the council that you and I are enemies of the people. He will stop at nothing."

"It will be settled soon," Nighthawk said. "There are more and more who do not believe Black Owl. He is losing honor."

"He is afraid of that," Clara said. "That is why he intends to harm us."

"Aged One has said that the good will win in the end and that those who are evil will be punished," Nighthawk said. "Black Owl has seen the end of his days of lying to these people."

"Maybe so," Clara said. "But I fear there will be a terrible struggle first."

FIRECLOUD

* * *

BLACK OWL stood before the council, his jaw clenched in anger and determination. He had argued long and emphatically that the Long Knife woman and her evil horse had caused bad spirits to turn the buffalo herd against the village. Since Nighthawk had brought this woman to the Kainah people, Nighthawk should be forced to leave with her, never again to return to this band.

Nighthawk had told the council about seeing Black Owl and his Brave Wolves running buffalo toward the river, not away from it as had been planned. Nighthawk's testimony was given little weight, as he had not even been allowed to hunt. Black Owl had convinced the council that Nighthawk would surely blame him for the stampede.

Deer Chaser had come forward in Nighthawk's behalf, charging Black Owl with violating tribal law in his blatant disregard for hunting procedures. He told of seeing Black Owl break the structure of the hunt in an effort to make more kills himself and thereby gain more personal honor. Again Black Owl succeeded in getting the council to disregard this testimony, contending that Deer Chaser was courting Nighthawk's sister and would gain more favor in Nighthawk's eyes if he stood up for him before the council.

Black Owl was using the Shoshone raid to get Nighthawk banished from the Black Horse band. Black Owl accused Clara and Nighthawk of going into the land of Nighthawk's birth and conspiring with the Shoshone to send a war party to destroy the Kainah people as vengeance against Black Owl and the people of the village for not giving him honor and authority.

"Why should my wife, the Thunder Horse Woman, help me set up a Shoshone raid and then risk her life to turn it back?" Nighthawk countered.

Discussion began among the members of the council. It was up to Black Owl, they decided, to prove that Nighthawk had arranged the Shoshone raid. Most of the Brave Wolves sided with Black Owl. As long as Black Owl retained the power he now had, they would continue to rule the village.

"Since your mother was Shoshone," one Brave Wolf said to Nighthawk, "you could gain favor with their people, especially if you had little favor among our people."

Black Owl grinned with satisfaction. His friends among the Brave Wolves seemed to have influenced the council in his behalf. Nighthawk would have a difficult time proving himself now.

"Did the Shoshone offer you favors if you would help them destroy our village?" the warrior asked Nighthawk.

Nighthawk stiffened with anger. "I wear the clothes and the paint of a Kainah warrior," Nighthawk said. "My weapons and my war honors bear the markings of the Blackfoot tribe. I am a Kainah Blackfoot, and my heart is Kainah Blackfoot. You have seen the Shoshone scalp my wife and I brought back from the Burning Mountains. You have heard the story of our fight with the Snake People, the Shoshone, in the canyon of the Yellowstone, where the water falls far down over the rocks in two places. My mother was Shoshone, but she became the property of my father, who was a proud Kainah warrior. I was born a Kainah, and I will die a proud death as a Kainah warrior."

"Well spoken," one of the warriors in the council commented. "Your words are strong."

Then one of the Brave Wolves spoke up. "Nighthawk's words may be strong, but how strong is he? We need to know if he can live as he has spoken."

Another Brave Wolf added, "We hear only words from Nighthawk. Now he must show us some action."

Black Owl grinned again. Things were again going his way.

Nighthawk spoke proudly. "I will lead a war party on the Shoshone who came to our lands. I will bring back scalps to dance and feast over."

Black Owl, still grinning, said, "You speak strong words so that you can lead us into a trap and help our enemy destroy us. You would receive many honors from them if this happened."

"Are you afraid I will return victorious?" Nighthawk asked

FIRECLOUD

Black Owl. "If you are afraid to fight our enemies, you can stay in the village and gather berries with the women."

Black Owl's eyes flashed hate. "We will see who the woman is," he said through clenched teeth.

One of the council members spoke up. "You can both show your anger against the Shoshone. We will fight our enemy, not each other. Nighthawk must lead our warriors against the Snake People. Soon."

"What if we find that Nighthawk wishes harm to our people?" Black Owl asked.

"That is something we must decide as council," the warrior answered. "You two must now leave and allow us to discuss the matter. Nighthawk, when you have prepared yourself to lead our warriors against our enemy, the drums of war will begin and you will show us how strong your words truly are."

Nighthawk and Black Owl left the council to decide the matter. Black Owl seemed pleased. He knew the Brave Wolves on the council would put Nighthawk to a strenuous test. Perhaps Black Owl could rid himself of his half brother and the testy Long Knife woman, finally and forever.

"I am finally going to lead the warriors of this village against our enemies, the Shoshone," Nighthawk told Clara a short time later in their lodge. "This is the time I have waited for. It will now be possible for me to show that I am truly of honor. I can already hear the victory drums."

"I will go with you," Clara said. "The Shoshone are afraid of Firecloud."

"No," Nighthawk said quickly. "This is for me to do. Even if I wanted you to come, the council would not permit it. They are testing me, and me alone. They want to know that I am Kainah in my heart, not a Shoshone like my mother."

"Many villagers want you to fail," Clara warned. "Will you be able to choose the warriors who will follow you?"

"The council will choose. I will be victorious, no matter who goes with me. They all want to gain a victory over our enemy."

"But how many of them will want it to be *your* victory? If

Black Owl goes, they will want it to be *his* victory, and they will say that you did not lead them and that Black Owl should rightfully gain the honor. This is not good."

"No one will be able to take this victory from me," Nighthawk said emphatically. "Now I must prepare for battle."

Clara watched him gather his best weapons and his war shirt. He had suddenly drawn himself apart from her into a world of his own. Clara saw that he had crossed into a realm of no reasoning, an absence of clear thinking. The council would no doubt choose Black Owl and the other Brave Wolves to go with Nighthawk on the raid. If this happened, Nighthawk could be the finest warrior the Kainah Blackfeet had ever seen and still gain no credit for his courage. What worried her most of all was the possibility that he would not even come back alive.

21

NIGHTHAWK BEGAN HIS PREPARATION for leading the war party against the Shoshone. He told Clara he wished to be alone while he prepared himself. He decided to purify himself and deny himself all pleasures of life in this world. He would speak with his helper spirit, the hawk who hunts in the light of the moon, to gain strength and guidance. He would fast to clear his senses and thereby gain the wisdom to make the right decisions and lead his warriors to victory. He would cover himself with white clay and spend many hours in the sweat lodge. Then he would take his weapons and go by himself into the high rocky ridges above the village. There he would remain until he was ready to lead a war party into the lands of the Snake People.

Confused and unhappy, Clara sought out Aged One, who was saying his evening prayers before a special fire, asking the sun's guidance in Nighthawk's journey to war.

"I am afraid for Nighthawk," Clara told Aged One. "He does not want me to speak to him or come near him. I cannot bear to see him this way."

"It is the custom," Aged One told her. "It is the way of gaining strength and wisdom for battle. The mind must think of nothing else, and the body must know only the things the strain of war will bring. The power to endure must come and live within, or there can be no victory."

Aged One then raised his head to the sky above the fire of sage and juniper and prayed that Nighthawk might know this earth for many winters to come. He prayed that his young friend would have the wisdom to make the right decisions, that he might walk the path to honor and glory among the Kainah people, that he might remain strong and steadfast in his faith, no matter how hard his life would become, and uphold the values so long cherished by the Blackfoot people. When Aged One finished praying, he lowered his arms and bowed his head.

"You did not speak of victory over the Shoshone," Clara said.

Aged One addressed her with a small measure of impatience in his voice. "Those who are young ask for things they sometimes cannot have. Those who have seen many winters are content to accept things as they are meant to be. It is not for us to know if Nighthawk will be victorious against the Shoshone. It is not for us to know when or how the battle will be fought. It is only important that his life not be taken from us. I pray that he may return to your arms and that these old eyes of mine may see him so that my heart can be happy again. I will not be saddened or angered if he does not return with great honors. It is important only that he return."

Clara sat for a time while he resumed his prayers, having gained from him a greater understanding of the importance of life itself. She now realized that her husband could have no greater friend than this old warrior who cared so deeply for his well-being. His love for Nighthawk was as great as her own, she realized; as great as any man could have for a son who pleased him greatly. Merely having Nighthawk in his life gave Aged One reason for thanksgiving. In Aged One's eyes, Nighthawk had already proven his honor many times over, but he understood that Nighthawk needed respect from those in the village as well. Aged One spoke to her again.

"You have been born with great strength of body and mind," he told her. "I do not believe there are many women like you in any land. I now understand why Nighthawk has given you his love. And because you love him as deeply as he loves you, the bond between you is like the fiber that builds the trunk of a great tree. But you are Long Knife and he is Kainah Blackfoot; you are different. You must try to understand the ways of our people. He must do what is set before him. It will be hard, but you must accept that. As a Long Knife, you do not think as we do about some things. Our minds travel different paths. But this is not a bad thing. Remember to show your love for him as he did for you when he journeyed with you to the Burning Mountains to tame the Thunder Horse. Many of the warriors in the village laughed at him. He did not hear them. This was hard for him. Now it will be hard for you. Accept it, and your love will grow stronger."

Clara left Aged One on the hill, overwhelmed by his words. She felt as though she were entering a time of trial even more difficult than the long, cold journey to the Kainah village or the days of her preparation for the Sun Dance ceremony. Those times had required physical strength. Now she would be tested mentally.

The sun crossed the sky three times, and the fear within Clara grew, the heaviness pressing into her more and more. Gaunt and pale, Nighthawk had come down from the hills above the village and was now preparing for the dancing that would begin when the sun fell from the sky. The war drums would sound throughout the night until the sun again rose; then his journey to war would begin.

Clara knew that Nighthawk was totally separated from all those around him now. Clara had maintained her distance from him, observing but not going near him or letting him see her. She watched him every moment she could, her mind reaching toward his to try to understand. She grew more and more anxious as the village prepared for the evening's activities. The other women, knowing what to expect, walked about in silence, saving their talk for a less serious time.

The afternoon passed. A tremendous fire was built in the center of the village, and final preparations were made for the war dance. The warriors were preparing themselves for the ceremony. They brought out articles that were kept in special places to be used only during these ceremonies. Among these objects were scalps and weapons seized during earlier raids. The warriors would dance over them and stab them with arrows and knives in mock fighting. There were a number of fingerbone necklaces as well, and even a skull. Clara retreated to the lodge, trying to erase the scene from her mind. But she could not keep visions of Nighthawk from appearing before her. As the sun disappeared and darkness fell completely, the entire village gathered around the fire, chanting and keeping rhythm as the drums began their monotonous pounding that would go on until dawn again broke.

Before long, Aged One appeared and Clara invited him in to sit down and eat, glad to have someone with her in this strange world that now engulfed her.

"Have you prayed?" Aged One asked her.

"I have tried. I cannot say if I was heard."

"That is good," Aged One nodded. "You were heard. But you must not stop."

Suddenly Spring Bird burst through the door, looking angry. She could hardly control herself as she spoke. "If I were a warrior, I would kill Black Owl and care little what happened after that," she said in a slur of words.

"Sit down and tell us what you have heard," Aged One said.

"My heart is filled with hate for Black Owl and fear for the safety of my brother," Spring Bird said. Tears began streaming down her face.

"Spring Bird," Clara asked, "what is it?"

"Deer Chaser has told me that he and many of the other young warriors will not be allowed to go on the raid that Nighthawk is leading. He was told by members of the council that they are not yet old enough for such a journey and that they must remain in the village to defend the people against other enemies who might attack while the war party is gone. Most of the warriors going on the raid are Brave Wolves. Some of the other warriors also think the way they do. Black Owl has succeeded in getting his evil way again. Only the warriors who follow him are going."

FIRECLOUD

Clara herself was overcome with both anger and fear. As she had feared, Black Owl had again gained full control of events in the village and appeared well on his way to ridding himself of Nighthawk forever. This would give him a clear path to undisputed power within the band. Nighthawk's earnest preparations to lead the Kainah warriors into battle had distorted his ability to think clearly, and he seemed not even to care who was going with him. His sole aim was to prove his honor as a warrior and gain respect for his actions. Clara knew that Black Owl intended to prevent Nighthawk from ever gaining glory for himself.

"I must stop Nighthawk from going," Clara said.

"No!" Aged One said quickly and with force. "It would be very bad to interfere."

"I cannot stand by and let him leave, knowing I will likely never see him alive again," Clara protested.

"You must have faith and let the good spirits, under direction of the sun, take care of Nighthawk," Aged One reminded her. "If you stop him now, you will destroy him."

Clara shook her head, frightened and confused. "I do not understand."

"You *must* understand," Aged One emphasized. "It will be very hard to stand by and do nothing, but you *must*! Nighthawk has prepared himself for this day. The drums are in his head; the strength of a warrior is in his heart. If you tell him he must not go, it will destroy his medicine. It will cause him anguish and terrible torment, for he will then fear that his powers have left him and he will wonder if his death is not at hand. A warrior often sees a bad omen before a raid. When this happens, he will sometimes call off the raid, for he feels his medicine is not good. But Nighthawk cannot call the raid off, for if he does, Black Owl will have proven that Nighthawk does not deserve to have honor in this village. No, you cannot interfere now. You must have faith."

Clara felt like screaming. Outside, the drums continued to pound, a throbbing, rhythmic beat that grew more intense as time passed. The drums were talking, telling the events that were happening in the ceremony: The drums said that the power of the warriors was increasing, their hearts beating ever stronger for the battle in which they would face their enemy, the Shoshone. It only made Clara's head throb more and her fingers squeeze together tighter. Suddenly she could sit no longer. She rushed outside the lodge, Spring Bird and Aged One behind her. Trembling, Clara watched the huge fire blaze high into the night sky. Around it a circle of painted warriors danced like crazed men, as if they no longer knew where they were or what a normal state of mind was. Nighthawk shouted the loudest, smashing a war club against a cottonwood log that had been erected near the fire. It had been painted and decorated with the scalps and war items taken out earlier from their storage places for this purpose. Clara shook her head. She did not know him now, this warrior she loved so dearly. This could easily be the last time she would see him alive, and there was nothing she could do about it. She watched him take a human arm bone between his teeth and dance frantically among the other warriors, his eyes round and wild.

As Clara watched the dancing, the night seemed to drag on and on without end, but the sun was now climbing toward the eastern horizon, spreading the light of dawn into the valley. It would not be long until the warriors made ready to leave for the Shoshone lands. The warriors were all making final preparations. Nighthawk, in his final act to make himself ready, gashed his legs in front and back with his knife, deep gashes that flowed heavily with blood. Clara turned and saw Aged One making his way up into the hills above the village. He would pray almost continuously until the war party had returned. Spring Bird, her eyes blurred with tears, chanted a good-bye song of hope and courage.

Unable to stand the torment any longer, Clara turned and untied Firecloud from the post in front of their lodge.

"Where are you going?" Spring Bird asked Clara quickly, her voice wavering, tears still flowing from her eyes.

"I don't know," Clara said, her own tears now filling her eyes. "I am so frightened for Nighthawk. I cannot watch him leave."

"Do not fear, my sister," said Spring Bird, holding Clara in her arms and taking a deep breath to control her own emotions. "Nighthawk has prepared himself well. His helper spirits are very pleased. He is strong, my brother. Very strong. We must now also be strong and wait for his return."

"Do you think he will return?" Clara sked.

Spring Bird nodded. "His heart is good. He will not die."

Clara took Firecloud to the river and let him drink deeply of the cool water. She composed herself and talked with Spring Bird, trying to understand how the women of the village could watch their men leave for war so often and accept it so readily. War was a way of life with them. They had grown accustomed to it from early childhood when they saw their fathers leaving, riding painted horses and waving lances and bows as they disappeared from view, some of them never to return.

Clara and Spring Bird came back from the river and stopped at the edge of the village. Clara stroked Firecloud's neck while she stared through the empty lodges to the ceremonies in the center of the village. The drums and the dancing, the screaming and barbaric displays of strength seemed distant now. The entire village was still gathered in an outer circle around the inner circle of drummers and dancing warriors. The light in the eastern sky was now pink-scarlet, and the silence around the place where she and Spring Bird stood began to creep into Clara. The air was still and the lodges stood motionless, like tall, cone-shaped skin markers in a graveyard. The paintings on each lodge seemed to glare at her in a threatening way; the circles of bright red, the jagged lightning bolts, the eyes of the running bison, spears and arrows sticking from their bodies, and stick warriors on horseback close behind. Nothing moved, but a roar again rose inside her head.

"I have to be by myself for a while," she told Spring Bird.

Spring Bird nodded. "I understand. Return when you are ready."

Clara rode Firecloud through the hills and far away, pushing the dancers and the drummers and the knives and the lodge paintings from her mind. She looked ahead, unmindful of time, urging her big stallion ever higher while the sun climbed across the sky. She traveled on and on, through stands of pine that broke into sprawling meadows, across flowing brooks and streams, not looking back but knowing that a column of warriors traveled somewhere far below her, led by her beloved husband. Try as she could, the visions would not leave her alone.

She reached a small meadow sheltered by trees where a spring bubbled from rocks on a hillside. She wished Nighthawk were with her to see it. Again she fought tears. She tried not to see the beauty of the trees and the sun and the peaks just above her. If Nighthawk could not be with her, she did not want them. She did not care about life itself. But the tears won, and she bent forward, sobbing, on Firecloud's neck. She slumped from his back and struggled forward through the grass and flowers of the meadow, not knowing where she was going nor why. Her tears blinded her, and she stumbled, collapsing in the green and gold and scarlet and blue of the lush meadow, burying her face in the softness while Firecloud nudged her back with his nose.

When she had released all her anguish, she arose and wrapped her arms tightly around the stallion's neck. She felt the tears come again, wetting his sleek, beautiful coat. Never in her entire life had she felt so helpless. Firecloud kept turning his head while she held his neck, rubbing her with his nose, nickering to her softly, his eyes sad and filled with worry for her. She kissed his muzzle and petted him, leading him to the spring, whose voice was like a song over the rocks. The smell of the flowers was refreshing, and the soft rush of alpine air through the trees comforted her.

"I will calm myself," she told the big stallion, rubbing his nose with the palm of her hand. "Don't worry about me."

Clara let Firecloud wander off to graze and made herself comfortable near the spring on a sand flat that had been washed down from the rocks with the melting of the spring snows. She leaned back against the trunk of an old dead pine that had been blown over by the wind. She closed her eyes and listened to the sounds around her. The peace of the meadow

FIRECLOUD

was like a gift. High above, the pines rustled in the wind while the thick shrubs and quaking aspen around and below the spring were alive with birdsong. Flowers of every size and shape grew in thick masses where the water seeped in slow trickles and filled the rocky soil with its freshness.

Hearing a slight rush of movement near her ear, Clara opened her eyes to see a chickadee sitting on a branch of the fallen tree an arm's length away. He looked inquisitively at her from wee black eyes. Searching among the new grass, Clara found some dried remains of last year's growth. She rolled the brittle heads of the old grass between her palms, allowing the chaff and seeds to float out into the sand in front of her.

The chickadee, not wasting a moment, hopped to the sand, his tiny bill poking for the seeds. Clara's hands moved to gather more old grass and the little bird, fearing she intended to catch him, quickly flitted to the safety of the branches in the old fallen tree, scolding her in a hoarse, gruff little call. Clara smiled, remembering Firecloud's actions when she had first offered him the sweetgrass. When she shelled more seeds, the chickadee hopped back down and went back to searching for a meal among the grains of sand.

From the forest two bluejays appeared and perched on the branches of the fallen pine. They sent sharp caws of warning to the chickadee, making it known that they intended to have the seeds for themselves. Instead of retreating in fright, the much smaller chickadee continued to poke his beak into the sand, keeping his quick little head turned up at them while he ate. Clara noticed that the feathers on his head and neck had risen. After another series of warnings that went unheeded by the chickadee, the two jays hopped from their perches and down into the sand to claim the seeds.

Enraged, the chickadee attacked the nearest jay, ramming the larger bird and knocking him off balance. He then went directly to the other jay, who had risen to attack him. The chickadee darted in behind, scolding loudly all the while, his tiny beak hammering on the jay's back and head. As quickly as it had begun, the battle was over. The jays disappeared

E. P. Murray

back into the forest, and the chickadee settled back down to his meal, changing his song to one of satisfaction, as if nothing had disturbed him.

Clara sat staring at the tiny bird, her eyes wide with revelation. The strength and determination of the little chickadee had been too much for the two larger jays, though either of them alone would have been more than a match for him under different circumstances. The words of Aged One again came back to her: There is no limit to what one can accomplish if one has faith and hope present. If one then adds strength of mind and heart, nothing is impossible.

Clara watched the chickadee for a while longer, threshing the last of the seeds out of the old grass for him. When he had finished his meal, the little bird darted to the branches of the fallen pine, his eyes on Clara. He had decided that she was a food source, in much the same way as the brown buffalo birds clung to the backs of the animals in the great herds, eating ticks and other insects from their hair and hides and searching for seeds among the droppings. Finally, realizing his meal had only been happenstance, the chickadee lost himself among the boughs and needles of the forest, finding a limb somewhere from which to sing his dee-dee-dee song, telling all those who heard him that he was content and happy.

The sun was now low in the west and the day would soon be gone, a day that had started for Clara with much torment and unhappiness. The night would now find her asleep among the flowers of the meadow, for she knew Nighthawk would survive what lay ahead for him. With the new light, she would return to the village and tell Spring Bird and Aged One that she would show more strength and faith from now on. She had no way of knowing if the raid would be successful or if Nighthawk would lead a victorious war party home. Black Owl would cause as many problems as he could. But she now knew her husband had more strength of mind and body than Black Owl. No matter what Black Owl did, Nighthawk would win in the end.

22

CLARA AWOKE to the noise of the villagers. Dawn was just breaking, and shouts of joy and admiration could be heard as the people gathered together and ran to the edge of the village.

"The war party has returned!" Spring Bird told Clara.

Clara and Spring Bird ran to join the others as they yelled and pointed to a group of riders standing motionless a distance from the village, singing victory songs and waiting for the sun to climb into the sky before coming in. Spring Bird tried to find Aged One in his lodge but came back shrugging, speculating that the old warrior was in the hills praying.

"Aged One will come down when he sees that the war party has returned," Spring Bird said. "He will not want to miss Nighthawk's time of honor."

As they waited for the light to get better and the warriors to come into the village, Clara rubbed her hands together nervously. She could not bring herself to feel the excitement of the others. Something was twisting her stomach into knots. As the ball of light began to appear in the east, the villagers grew more excited and waved blankets and articles of clothing in the air to signal the war party that they were ready for them to come, and that they awaited them with great pride. Spring Bird began to sense Clara's anxiety.

"Where is your happiness?" she asked. "This will be a great day for Nighthawk."

"Can you see him?" Clara asked.

"They are too far away," Spring Bird answered, staring at Clara. "He is with them, isn't he?"

Clara took a deep breath. "I hope so."

With whoops and yells the warriors began to ride toward the village at full speed, waving lances and bows in the air as their paint-covered horses stretched their necks and snorted in the run. Slowing their horses only a little, they rode into the village, darting among the lodges, waving scalps and Shoshone war items above their heads. Some of the warriors were driving stolen horses, and all of them yelled, raising their blackened faces to the sky.

Clara strained her eyes in the dust, and Spring Bird now had a look of concern on her face. Searching among the parading warriors, Spring Bird finally shook her head in disbelief.

"Nighthawk should have been first into the village," she said to Clara. "Instead, Black Owl leads. And I see neither Nighthawk nor his horse.

What if he was killled? Clara dared not ask aloud, but she saw the same question in Spring Bird's eyes.

Spring Bird continued to talk, as if to herself or in a trance. "It is hard to tell how many have been wounded or how badly. They ride with great courage and act as if nothing is wrong with them. I see no ponies with bodies draped over them. I do not believe anyone was killed. There is too much celebration among them."

"But where is Nighthawk?" Clara asked, almost frantic.

"Maybe he stayed behind for some reason," Spring Bird answered, not believing herself. "Maybe he wanted to steal more horses by himself. I do not know. But surely he would have led the victorious war party and not have left it to Black Owl. No, something is wrong. Black Owl has done something."

Clara became suddenly angry as she watched Black Owl prance his horse through the village and let other warriors ride up to him and praise him. He rode past with his lance pointed

FIRECLOUD

to the sky and his black face held high in triumph, telling the village that his power had brought glory to the Black Horse band of Kainah Blackfeet this day. Fires had sprung up all around, and singers and drummers were assembling to begin the celebration. Warriors were giving their ponies to the horse tenders for care while they exhibited their battle trophies to the people. All of them were pointing to Black Owl, speaking loudly of his great leadership.

From the excited crowd, Aged One slowly made his way over to where Clara and Spring Bird stood in stunned silence. His face showed not the slightest hint of joy or pride, but was cast with a look of deep disgust.

"I have been watching the war party since they first came to the edge of the village," he said to them. "When I did not see Nighthawk among them, I walked down from the hills. I want you both to follow me to my lodge."

Clara and Spring Bird followed Aged One silently into his lodge and sat down to hear him.

"I have just spoken to some of the warriors," Aged One began. "Black Owl would not let me approach him, so I made some of the Brave Wolves tell me what they knew." He took a deep breath to compose himself. "I learned that Nighthawk has been banished from this band."

Spring Bird drew her breath in sharply and uttered a faint cry of alarm.

"What do you mean?" Clara asked. She tried to remain as calm as possible, but she began to tremble.

"Nighthawk led the war party into the Shoshone lands," Aged One went on. "But Nighthawk and the others could not find the Shoshone. After a time, Black Owl told the others that they had traveled far and should return to this village. He said Nighthawk had taken them far and had not kept his promises. He convinced the others that Nighthawk had made fools of all of them and that they had gone on a long journey for no real purpose."

"That was no reason to banish him," Spring Bird said.

"There is more," said Aged One. "No one knew this, but the council decided before the raid that Nighthawk would be banished if he did not lead a successful war party against the Shoshone. The village was told only that he would lead a war party to show that his heart was Kainah Blackfoot and not Shoshone. When they could not find our enemy, Black Owl convinced the war party that the decision to banish him must be upheld. The warriors drove Nighthawk away from them and told him never to return to the Black Horse band, under penalty of death. Black Owl is now very happy."

Spring Bird was sobbing, her face buried in her hands. Clara could hardly stay seated, and her fists were clenched so tightly that she felt she would squeeze the joints apart. She could not believe that Black Owl had again turned the people against them.

"Then Black Owl and the war party found the Shoshone on their way back to the village," Aged One explained, his lips pursed in anger. "The Shoshone were camping one valley over from where Nighthawk had led the war party. Black Owl was probably scouting when he came upon the enemy by chance, but he told the warriors that the spirits had chosen him instead of Nighthawk to bring victory to the Kainah people."

"What will become of Nighthawk?" Clara asked Aged One.

Aged One spoke with confidence. "You know your husband as well as I do. He may be back already, watching from the hills above the village. Black Owl knows only evil, and such a person often makes mistakes. Black Owl's first mistake was to lie about speaking to the spirits. He no doubt made the spirits very angry. It is a very bad thing to lie about the spirits. He will be very sorry for doing this. He will pay for his evil. Soon."

Suddenly the flap of the lodge was pulled open and held back by a warrior. Black Owl entered, followed by two other warriors, and stood with his arms crossed.

"You have no respect!" Aged One said angrily, standing up. "Do you forget how to announce yourself before entering a lodge that is not your own?"

Black Owl pushed Aged One to the ground. "Be silent, old one," he said gruffly. "This is business of the Brave Wolves.

FIRECLOUD

You are not to interfere." He took Clara by the arm and yanked her to her feet. "You are to leave this lodge. Now!"

Clara pulled away from him, her eyes narrowed. Black Owl quickly grabbed her again and flung her out the door, where several warriors dragged her to her feet and surrounded her. Black Owl then stood in front of her, his jaw set and hard.

"You are not to enter the lodge of Aged One again," he said. "You are to remain with Spring Bird in your lodge and do only as you are told from this day forward."

"You have no right to rule me," Clara said. "I am free to do as I choose. And I now choose to ride my horse from this village." She tried to make her way through the warriors, but they would not let her pass.

"Do as I say," Black Owl said. "You cannot leave this village, for you now belong to me. You and the stallion."

"I will never belong to you!" Clara shouted. Taking one of the warriors by surprise, she pushed him backwards and sent him sprawling into the dirt. She then rushed past him and ran toward Firecloud.

"Bring her back to me!" Black Owl ordered the warriors. "Do not let her get away!"

Three of the warriors ran Clara down, seizing her by the arms and feet, struggling to hold her while Black Owl approached.

"They have the authority to kill you if you cause trouble," Black Owl warned. "It is not wise to fight the Brave Wolves."

The warriors released Clara and she stood glaring at Black Owl. "You have no right to treat me like this," she spat.

"You are mine, Long Knife woman." He gave her an evil grin. "It is a custom among our people. When a warrior dies in battle, his belongings, including his wives, become the property of his brother. Since Nighthawk is now gone, you and the horse belong to me."

"But Nighthawk is not dead," Clara argued. "Only banished. I shall leave this village and find him."

"I do not think so," Black Owl said through narrowed eyes. "Nighthawk brought the Shoshone to our village, and you were with him. You both should have been killed, but the council decided to allow you to remain alive. Nighthawk was banished, but you will remain here to gather wood and prepare skins for my lodge. From this day forward you are mine!"

"You will have to kill me!" Clara spat.

Black Owl shook his head, still grinning. "No, I will not. If you do not obey me, I will kill the horse instead. And you will watch."

"You would never do that," Clara said.

"You would be wise not to force me to make my words come true," he said. "What I do will depend on your actions. I will not tie you up. I will leave you free to do as you wish when you have finished each day's work for me. You may go where you want. You may even leave if you desire. But I do not think you will leave. And I will be sure that you cannot ride the Thunder Horse away from this village."

Black Owl motioned for a group of warriors standing ready with rawhide ropes to begin their work. They went to where Firecloud was tied near Clara's lodge and quickly threw their ropes over his neck and legs, pulling them tight and wrapping them around the pole. There were many warriors, and they pulled as hard as they could, choking the big stallion and tying his legs together tightly. Firecloud fought with all his might, but they had taken him by surprise, and there were too many ropes and men to overcome. Other warriors seized and held Clara, who screamed when she saw what they were doing to her horse.

When the warriors had finished, Firecloud lay on his side unable to move, so tightly hobbled were his feet and legs. The big stallion snorted in rage and frustration, trying time and again to free himself, meeting with failure each time, squealing as he fought a hopeless struggle against the ropes. Patches of hair pulled loose from his legs and fetlocks; his powerful muscles bulged and strained. Finally, totally exhausted, he lay on the ground, his beautiful coat covered with dirt and lather.

"You can't leave him that way," Clara sobbed. "He'll die."

"We shall see how you obey me," Black Owl told her

coldly. "If you do as you are told, we will loosen the hobbles. We will never take them off so that he can run, but we will loosen them. He will be able to walk. But first you must show that you can do as you are told, and do it well. Then we will loosen the hobbles so that the horse can rise."

With Firecloud down and breathless, and Clara reduced to tears, Black Owl let the Brave Wolves go back to their business in the village. Black Owl had not allowed the people to gather and watch, and the village seemed strangely quiet. Clara knelt over Firecloud, soothing and calming him as best she could. At seeing her, the big stallion again tried to rise.

"No, my stallion," Clara sobbed. "You must stay down. I cannot free you."

Black Owl came over and jerked her to her feet, shoving a skin waterbag in to her hands. "You need to work now," he said. "We will move camp soon. We need water. I will take you to where you are to fill these bags."

Clara followed him toward the river, knowing full well why he was taking her away from camp. She had been to the river many times to get water and knew the way very well. She knew it would do her no good to struggle. Black Owl would use any excuse to destroy the beautiful stallion. This horse was the one thing he knew he could never control, and he hated anything that he did not have absolute power over.

As she followed Black Owl far from the village and deep into the cover of the trees along the river, she suddenly realized that she would not need anger and defiance to win this segment of her battle against Black Owl. His situation within his own lodge was all she needed to keep him from thinking he had absolute control over her. Since first realizing that his sits-beside-him-wife, Eyes-Like-Black-Stones, was a very demanding woman with a violent temper, Clara had realized further that his woman was insanely jealous of Black Owl. Clara had felt her penetrating stare often. Black Owl could not afford to let people know he was having serious trouble with his most important wife.

Black Owl moved off the trail and led Clara to a secluded grassy spot under the trees. He turned and took the skin water-bags from Clara, throwing them aside.

"The water can wait," he said to her. "First you will know the powers of a true warrior."

Clara pushed him back and glared into his startled eyes. "I do not intend to allow you access to me or to Spring Bird. You had best understand this. It could mean your life!"

"What is this silly talk?" Black Owl hissed. "You would not dare to try to take my life!"

"I would not take your life, you demented fool," Clara said, her voice sharp and clear. "I speak of Eyes-Like-Black-Stones, your sits-beside-him-wife. She is very jealous of me, and I know that you are afraid of her anger. If she hears that you tried to lie with me, she would sharpen her knife. It would be easy for her to sneak up on you in the night."

"Your words are crazy," Black Owl said, backing away a step. "You have lost your senses."

"No, Black Owl, I have not," Clara said, a confident smile crossing her face. "If this were not true, you would have ordered me to move into your lodge, as is the custom. But you did not, because Eyes-Like-Black-Stones will not allow it." She watched Black Owl draw his mouth up tight and flush in embarrassment, as if a deep hidden secret had just been exposed. "Maybe I will go now and tell her that you were out here with me. Maybe she is looking for you."

Black Owl quickly grabbed her arm. "No!" he barked.

Clara immediately pulled away from him. "Black Owl, understand this: If you ever go near my stallion again, I will tell your wife about this meeting. I will tell her that you intend to meet me here every day."

Black Owl's eyes flashed, a mixture of intense anger and fear.

"Neither I nor Spring Bird will carry even one drop of water for you, now or ever," Clara went on. "We will leave here whenever we wish, and you will not stop us. I will pretend to be content with my situation. If you kill me, you will bring dishonor to yourself. If you want peace in your lodge, you will bother me no more." Clara pointed to the waterskins on the

FIRECLOUD

ground. "Now, if you want those filled with water, you can get it yourself. I am going back to the village and release Firecloud. If any of your warriors try to stop me, I will go straight to your lodge. You can explain things to Eyes-Like-Black-Stones when you bring the water in."

"Wait!" Black Owl said as she turned. He rushed past her and made his way back to the village.

When Clara arrived, Firecloud had already been untied and the warriors were standing in groups. She took her stallion to the river, bathed the rope burns on his legs, and covered them with bear grease. As she calmed her big stallion, she thought back to what Aged One had said concerning evil and how it eventually destroys itself. Black Owl was headed toward destruction, and it was happening very rapidly. He would have been wiser to have left Clara alone. Showing his power by having Firecloud tied up and then releasing him with no explanation only made him look like a fool. Now even his own warriors who had followed him with such devotion could not help wondering what was happening.

Clara found Spring Bird and Aged One together in the lodge. Upon hearing Clara's story, Spring Bird immediately began to feel better, and Aged One smiled for the first time since Nighthawk had left.

"Faith, with strength behind it, can be more powerful than even the bear that owns the mountains," the old warrior said. "Nighthawk will come soon, when the time is right."

"Black Owl will think of a way to make things difficult again," Clara said. "I hope Nighthawk has a good plan."

"You must do all you can to help Nighthawk," Aged One said.

Clara knew there was little time to decide what they would do. Spring Bird had learned from Deer Chaser that many warriors felt the Brave Wolves had too much power. Many of them thought Nighthawk should not have been banished. But Black Owl was very treacherous and would think of something soon. Clara knew it was imperative that she discredit Black Owl in the eyes of the warriors who still followed him.

Through Spring Bird and Deer Chaser, she could organize Nighthawk's supporters into a force of opposition against Black Owl. With the present state of unrest growing, it would become ever easier to bring the trouble before the council. Soon the council members would find that a good many warriors questioned the decisions that were being made for the supposed good of the band. Questions would be asked of the council, questions they would have a difficult time answering. A change was coming. It was coming soon.

23

THE RIVER LAY IN SHADOW, and the hills above the village were bathed in scarlet as the day ended. Having hidden himself for several days, Nighthawk arose and melted into the shadows, determined to get closer to the village. The time had come, and he would again see his wife under the cover of night. He had studied the movements of the village each day: where the women bathed and gathered wood; where the horse tenders watered the herd; and where the warriors who watched the village each night, mainly the Brave Wolves, took their places. He had watched all that the village had done until he was sure he knew where everyone would be all the time.

The hardest thing had been to watch his wife, the Thunder Horse Woman, without rushing from his hiding place to be with her. She had often looked into the hills, knowing he was there and understanding why he had not come for her. Knowing he wished to communicate with her, she had found a shady place away from where the women usually filled their bags with water, and she had gone to this place every day. He had then begun to draw sign for her, and she had found it. From this sign she would now know that tonight he would again be with her and discuss what they would do.

With the darkness came a breeze and the clouds that Nighthawk knew would fill the sky. The rain finally came, a gentle drizzle that would mix the smells of the valley and the hills with his own, masking his scent. The falling water would produce a sound of its own and deaden the sound of his footsteps. With no light from the moon, the warriors would not see him.

As the village slept and the fires dwindled to wisps of smoke, Clara finally heard the call of the hawk that hunts in the darkness. Her heart jumped, and she rose to her feet. Nighthawk was at the meeting place.

"Be careful," Spring Bird whispered in the darkness. "And give my love to my brother."

Quietly, on feet now accustomed to moving without sound, Clara made her way through the village to the river. The rain was steady, making a dull, continuous thud against the lodges. A breeze rustled the tops of the cottonwoods, adding to the sounds of the rainstorm. No one would hear them this night.

Finally she went into his arms, the warmth of his caress driving the chill of the rain from her body. She could not hold him tight enough; she wished to hear his soft voice in her ears forever and feel the strength of his embrace for all eternity. The night was theirs to do with as they pleased. No one suspected that they were here, or that Nighthawk was anywhere close. The night watchers continued to make their periodic calls back and forth to each other, to indicate that all was well.

Clara raised her arms, and Nighthawk pulled her dress off as she knelt together in the wet grass beneath the trees. His kisses were hot, and his hands firm as they found her breasts and worked their magic on her. He moaned, and his mouth found hers as she pulled his breechclout from around his waist and stroked him gently at first, and then more rapidly. His lips went to her nipples and soon the sounds of the rain were blocked completely from her mind.

Though the rain was cool, the air was pleasant and the feel of her back against the matted grass was comforting. Nighthawk gently pushed himself into her, and their bodies locked in a feast of sensitivity and fulfillment. They rolled in the carpet of wet green unmindful of the drizzle that soaked their hair and sent rivulets of water trailing over their bodies. Nighthawk surged ever deeper into her, and Clara arched ever

FIRECLOUD

higher until their gasps and cries of ecstasy were lost in the patter of water against leaves and grass.

Much later, as he helped Clara with her dress, Nighthawk said, "I have spoken with Deer Chaser. He tells me that many in the village are angry that I was banished."

"Black Owl continues to lose more favor each day," Clara nodded. "Deer Chaser is trying to get the council to meet and discuss the actions of Black Owl. This time the entire village would be present, not just those of Black Owl's choosing."

"Do you think the warriors who feel as Deer Chaser does would stand behind me?" he asked.

"I am sure of it," Clara said. "I believe there are enough of them that Black Owl would not dare to have you killed if you appear in the village. Not until the council had met and much discussion had taken place. If you come into the village, that would force the council to meet. Aged One believes the time is right, also."

"Can it be done tomorrow?" Nighthawk asked.

"I will tell Deer Chaser that you plan to come into the village," Clara said. "He will then alert those who are closest to him of your plans. If he believes the time is right, I will leave sign for you at our secret place along the river."

The rain began to let up, and Clara realized she must get back to the lodge before long. Her time with Nighthawk had been like a breath of new life, and the thought of him coming back to the village for good gave her a measure of hope as she silently made her way back. Happiness again seemed possible.

She had barely fallen asleep when a group of warriors pushed their way through the doorflap and into the lodge, talking loudly. Black Owl was with them.

"We are going on a journey, Long Knife woman," he said haughtily. "Bid farewell to Spring Bird, for you will never see her again."

"What do you mean?" Clara demanded.

"The Long Knife trader, Patch-Eye LaCroix," Black Owl told her, "has sent a messenger to our village. He has many presents for me."

Into the lodge came one of the *voyageurs* with whom she

had journeyed up the river. When John Huston and Nighthawk had fought LaCroix, this man had been at LaCroix's side on both occasions. He was undoubtedly now one of LaCroix's right-hand men. He looked at Clara with surprise.

"Ah, it is you," he said. "I thought it was all just so many stories. LaCroix will be pleased."

"I'm not going anywhere with you," Clara told Black Owl. "Remember what I said about telling your wife?"

Black Owl laughed. "That is not possible now. She and her sisters, my other wives, left early to visit her relatives among the Piegans. They are not here." He laughed even louder.

Clara sank back. Spring Bird was angry and frustrated, but said nothing.

"That one," the *voyageur* said to Black Owl, pointing to Spring Bird. "I like her."

"She is my present to you," Black Owl said joyfully. "To warm you during the night when the cold moons again come."

The warriors herded Clara and Spring Bird outside. Firecloud's ears were flat against his head, and he was turning around to kick Black Owl when the *voyageur* shouted a warning.

"Can you see how he also hates you?" Clara said to Black Owl, petting the stallion to calm him.

"He would be dead already if not for the fact that LaCroix is willing to pay much for him," Black Owl said with hate. "Keep him away from me."

Clara and Spring Bird looked around the village. It was unusually quiet, and no other warriors were in sight.

"Deer Chaser and the younger warriors have gone to scout for buffalo," Black Owl said. "The Brave Wolves will journey with me to take you to the fort of LaCroix. We will get many presents and then return to this village with honor."

"Nighthawk watches you now from the hills above the village," Clara told him. "Along with Deer Chaser and the other warriors, he will find us, and you will die."

Black Owl laughed. "Do not tell me things that are not true," he said. "Nighthawk would not dare return. Besides, my warriors have searched for him each day and have found

FIRECLOUD

no one. Do not tell me Nighthawk is here. He has run back to his mother's people, the Shoshone dogs."

"Think what you wish," Cara told him. "You will soon learn different."

"Enough of this foolish talk," Black Owl said. "We have a long journey ahead, and we must be on our way."

Throughout the journey, Clara and Spring Bird stayed together. Firecloud was ever close to Clara, protecting her from any harm that might come at the hands of Black Owl or his warriors. For this reason, Black Owl and the *voyageur* could not abuse Clara and Spring Bird as they had hoped they would be able to do. This infuriated Black Owl, but he could do nothing about it. He wanted to kill the stallion in the worst way, but he had promised the horse to LaCroix along with the Long Knife woman. LaCroix wished to give Firecloud to his wife, the Piegan woman who was Black Owl's cousin. It would do little good to go back on that promise, Black Owl thought, for it would no doubt anger both LaCroix and his cousin. He wished this to be a friendly visit, and he hoped to receive many presents in return for Clara, Firecloud, and the many furs he was bringing.

Finally they reached the pass that took them out of the valley of the Gallatin and into that of the Yellowstone. When Clara had last seen this place, the snow had been very deep and her breath had frozen to her face. It had been a trying time then, and it was equally hard now. There was no way they could escape, for they rode in the middle of the column, where the warriors could watch them closely. Firecloud had not allowed anyone near them to tie them up, so they both rode free of bonds. Clara knew she could easily have escaped on the big stallion if Spring Bird had not been present. It would never work now, however, for Black Owl had placed Spring Bird on a slow and very old mare to prevent her from running away. He knew very well that Clara would never leave her sister-in-law.

Soon they reached a hill that overlooked the fort. Additional buildings and fence had been added since she had torn out LaCroix's eye the winter before. Clara could see

LaCroix's men lining up along the tops of the walls and pointing to the column. Spring Bird was silent as they approached the fort, her eyes downcast and her spirits low at not having seen either Nighthawk or Deer Chaser during their journey to the fort. She had expected them to appear within a short time after Black Owl's party left the village, and she could not understand where they could be. It was too late now for anyone to help them.

"Now is not the time to become discouraged," Clara told her as the column descended the hill and came to a halt in front of the fort. "Maybe Nighthawk had to go far to find Deer Chaser and the other warriors before he could lead them after us. No matter. They will come for us."

"But we are almost inside the fort," Spring Bird said. "Once we are there, they cannot help us."

"Be alert and watch me closely," Clara said. "As soon as the gates open, jump from your horse to Firecloud's back. Then my stallion will carry us both away from here."

LaCroix appeared at the top of the wall, pushing his way through his men to where he could look directly down on Clara. "Ha, ha!" he laughed out loud. "It is good to see my she-cat has not forgotten her man." He held up a jug of whiskey. "This is a special day, worthy of celebration."

Black Owl then began to speak to him, telling him that he had also brought fine furs that were worth many presents. The *voyageur* who had been sent to the village to see if Clara was there and lead Black Owl back to the fort came over on his horse to where Spring Bird sat waiting to jump on Firecloud's back.

"You do not need to stay with her now," he said to Spring Bird. "You belong to me." He gestured to the fort. "This is your new home. You will like it here."

"You will have time for her," Clara told him. "Leave her with me for a while, until they open the gates."

"Yes," the *voyageur* said, turning to LaCroix and the others atop the wall. "Open the gates and we will all celebrate," he yelled. "Bring the medicine water."

"There is medicine water for all," LaCroix yelled down.

"We will celebrate with all our Kainah brothers. But first I must see the furs you have brought. Stand by the gate."

Black Owl ordered the column of horses forward and the furs unloaded. A chest-high door swung open, and one of LaCroix's men began to take the furs in, passing jugs of whiskey out in return. Clara, expecting the main gate to open, was ready to signal Spring Bird to jump behind her onto Firecloud's back. But only the small door, barely large enough to push the furs through, remained open.

"This is strange," Clara said to Spring Bird. "Why don't they open the main gate?"

Black Owl was drinking from a jug while trying to maintain order among warriors, who had already begun to fight over other jugs coming from inside the fort. LaCroix's men standing along the wall of the fort held rifles out ready to aim and fire.

Clara looked up at LaCroix, who was pacing back and forth along the wall impatiently, staring down at her often.

"Why don't you open the gates?" she called up to him.

"Soon," he answered. "I know you have missed your man, as I have missed my she-cat. We will be together again. Soon."

Clara turned to Spring Bird and spoke in low tones, "They are watching us very closely. If we make a break for it now, they will shoot us."

"What are we going to do?" Spring Bird asked.

Clara shook her head. "I don't know yet. It is strange that LaCroix hasn't opened the gates and herded us all inside. Something is wrong."

"He is filling Black Owl and all the warriors full of the evil medicine water," Spring Bird said.

Suddenly she sat up in the saddle. "I just realized something," she said. She looked at LaCroix, "Where is your wife, the Piegan woman who is Black Owl's cousin?" she asked. "Surely she wants to see her cousin and talk with him."

"She is alseep," LaCroix shot back.

"Asleep?" Clara asked. "Does she sleep when the sun is high?"

"She is tired."

"She is too tired to see her cousin?"

"What is this English talk?" Black Owl asked. "Speak in Blackfoot." The whiskey was already affecting his speech.

Clara shouted to him in Blackfoot, "LaCroix says your cousin, the Piegan woman, is sleeping. He does not want to wake her up, not even to see you."

"Silence!" LaCroix roared from the top of the fort. "There will be no more talk of my wife!"

"What were his words?" Black Owl demanded. "He angers me by speaking the Long Knife tongue."

"He called you a fool, Black Owl," Clara said. "He says you cannot see your cousin because he has killed her."

Black Owl asked LaCroix in Blackfoot if he had killed the Piegan woman. LaCroix began to scream insults down from the top of the wall, directing them toward Clara. He said she was lying to cause the heart of his brother, Black Owl, to become bad for Patch-Eye LaCroix, who only wanted to trade in peace. Black Owl ordered five of his warriors to surround Clara and Spring Bird, their lances leveled.

"Do not kill them," LaCroix shouted in Blackfoot. "You will not receive your presents if they are killed."

Clara turned to Black Owl. "Why don't you ask LaCroix why he doesn't invite you inside the fort? If he wishes to be your brother, he will smoke with you, and he will wake up your cousin so that you may speak with her. Ask him if he *can* wake your cousin up, or if he has killed her with his knife while he lay with her."

Black Owl raised the jug again and glared at LaCroix.

"Ask him," Clara repeated. "Ask him before you and all of your warriors are so full of the medicine water that you cannot stand. Ask him before he kills you all."

"No Long Knife would dare to kill me," Black Owl said haughtily. "No one dares to challenge the power of Black Owl!"

Clara pointed to the top of the wall where LaCroix's men stood in a line, rifles aimed. Then she pointed to the warriors

FIRECLOUD

near the gate, the majority of whom were now drunk and stumbling aimlessly, unaware of what was going on. "Do you think you can overcome all those Long Knives by yourself?" she asked Black Owl. "Your great warriors cannot even stand up straight. Soon your Brave Wolves will all be dead."

"The Long Knife woman is right," one of the warriors told Black Owl. "Patch-Eye LaCroix intends to kill us. He already has taken our furs inside the fort. He has not yet given you the presents he promised. And your cousin, the Piegan woman, has not yet appeared."

As if a sudden realization had struck him, Black Owl frantically waved his warriors away from the fort. Clara and Spring Bird galloped their horses out of rifle range, but the five warriors kept guarding them. Clara clenched her fists in frustration. If only she could get Spring Bird behind her on Firecloud, the warriors would never catch them. Instead, the warriors had separated her from Spring Bird. They watched the younger woman carefully, knowing Clara would not break loose and leave her sister behind.

LaCroix ordered his men to fire. Within seconds, most of the Brave Wolves had been slaughtered. Only a few managed to ride to safety.

"Are you proud?" Clara said to Black Owl, who had remained near her and Spring Bird. "Look at your warriors. It is too bad you can't be closer so you can see their blood staining the dirt for you."

"Enough!" Black Owl shouted. He fitted an arrow to his bow and rode still closer to Clara. Firecloud's ears went back, and Black Owl retreated on his stallion. "I can hit you from here, Long Knife woman," he yelled. "But I will keep my arrows for now. With you I am certain to get my revenge on the dog, Patch-Eye LaCroix."

LaCroix was becoming increasingly angry, and at seeing Black Owl point his bow at Clara, he lost control. He disappeared from the wall and appeared again on a horse as the gate was opened partway for him. He rode out and unleashed a string of Blackfoot oaths and curses at Black Owl.

"Do not point your weapon at my woman!" he yelled to Black Owl. "Release her and let her come to me, along with the other woman."

"You are a coward dog!" Black Owl yelled back. "You tried to kill me and all my warriors, but you have failed. Now it is my turn to kill!" Again he aimed his bow at Clara.

LaCroix urged his horse toward Black Owl, disregarding the shouts from his men to come back and allow Black Owl to approach the fort. Startled, Black Owl saw LaCroix fire his Hawken from the hip and jerked to one side as the ball sang past his head, nipping his ear. Enraged, Black Owl urged his stallion into a run toward LaCroix, who was trying with difficulty to reload atop his jittery horse. The whiskey and the pain in his ear had driven Black Owl to madness, and he released an arrow at LaCroix, who lurched forward onto his horse's neck and shoulder as the arrow whizzed over his back. Black Owl then quickly pulled a war club from its sling on his saddle and pressed in against LaCroix, whose horse was rearing in terror. LaCroix blocked Black Owl's initial blow with his rifle, cracking the stock. Unable to control the horse any longer, LaCroix jumped from its back, and Black Owl made ready to charge, screaming a war song.

Laughing, LaCroix pulled a pistol from his belt and fired as Black Owl bore down on him. The ball took Black Owl high on the arm, and he slipped sideways on his horse, finally falling to the ground as the black wheeled around when LaCroix charged forward, swinging his rifle. "She is *my* woman!" he was screaming as he approached Black Owl, who was still dazed from the arm wound. LaCroix held the gun high over his head ready to strike.

Black Owl moved in time to avoid being struck on the head with the stock of the rifle, but took a glancing blow off his lower back. He twisted in pain, rolling twice before coming to his hands and knees. "Your Piegan cousin was a dog!" LaCroix yelled as he came forward to strike again with the rifle. "And you are a dog!" Black Owl had pulled his knife and had struggled to his knees, preparing to lunge as LaCroix again hoisted the Hawken. With LaCroix rearing back to put all his strength into the blow, Black Owl shot forward.

Black Owl's slashing blade caught LaCroix above his right knee, cutting through muscle and tendon before scraping against bone. LaCroix screamed and dropped the rifle. Blood pumped from the wound in a pulsating stream, and LaCroix hopped forward on his good leg, holding his wound with spread fingers that now glistened red. Black Owl came to his feet and darted behind LaCroix, his knife making a dull, rasping sound as it sank into the French trader's back, just below the neck. LaCroix's knees buckled, and he tried to scream again through lungs that held no air. He slumped to his hands and knees as Black Owl took his knife in both hands and repeatedly drove the blade deep into LaCroix's back.

Rifle shots came from the fort in an endless barrage, but the balls only made harmless puffs in the dirt far from where LaCroix's blood was now puddling under him as he coughed and groaned. Still on his hands and knees, he looked like a mortally wounded bear who was fighting to keep his feet. Black Owl then put one foot on each side of LaCroix's back and grabbed his hair, cutting a wide circle in the scalp with his knife. Screaming a war cry, Black Owl then ripped the circle of hair free and raised it in the air for those in the fort to see. LaCroix, his eyes dazed and his face without expression, let his chin fall, exposing the red blotch on the top of his head. Then his arms gave out, and he flopped forward into the dirt.

Black Owl, riding back to his warriors with his dripping trophy, stopped his war cries when he saw what he was facing. Nighthawk and Deer Chaser, along with many warriors from the village, were sitting their horses around Clara and Spring Bird.

"You are lucky, Black Owl," Nighthawk said. "If we had not come, the Long Knives in the fort would surely have killed you. Instead they could only try to hit you with their thunder sticks, whose fire would not reach you."

"The Long Knives are lying dogs!" Black Owl said. "We should now kill them all and burn the fort."

Nighthawk pointed to the dead warriors strewn in front of the fort. "Will you tell their women that they died an honorable death in battle?"

"The Long Knives killed them!" Black Owl shouted.

"*You* killed them!" Nighthawk shouted back. "You led them to this place, and you let them die so that you could receive presents in return for my wife and her stallion."

"That is not true!" Black Owl shouted. His frown showed more worry than anger as the warriors glared at him.

"You deserve to die here and now, Black Owl," Nighthawk said, "but you will return with us to answer questions before the council."

Black Owl and the five Brave Wolves who had been guarding Clara and Spring Bird were tied and placed under guard. Nighthawk's men gathered the horses and made ready for the journey back. The men placed over the horses' backs the bodies of their owners, who had died as a result of Black Owl's greed. Nighthawk ordered the remainder of his men to circle the fort. Clara rode forward with him to address the men standing along the walls.

"I'm coming in to claim what's mine," Clara yelled to them.

One *voyageur* acted as spokesman. "We will not let you in," he said.

Nighthawk fitted an arrow to his bow and tied to it a strip of cloth dipped in bear grease. Clara lit the grease with powder and flint. Aiming high in the air, Nighthawk released the flaming arrow and watched it carry up and over the walls of the fort to land on the roof of one of the buildings within. This was followed by a lot of shouting from within before the smoke died down.

The *voyageur* appeared at the wall again. "If we come out, you will kill us."

"We will allow you to journey downriver to the Crow villages," Clara promised them, "if you come out and choose not to fight. Otherwise we will burn the fort and kill all of you."

"You will not burn the fort," the *voyageur* yelled. "You

would destroy the furs, and you want them worse than we do."

"They are no good to me if you have them," Clara yelled back. "I would rather burn them than let you take them to St. Louis."

The *voyaguer* began talking to the others. After a time he turned back to her and shouted, "Leave now while you can. The Crows will come soon, and there are many of them."

Clara nodded to Nighthawk, and another flaming arrow flew the walls. Two more followed despite the *voyageur*'s pleas for them to stop.

"We do not intend to wait for the Crows," Clara said.

"We want to talk," the *voyageur* said.

Clara shook her head. "No talk. If you don't come out now, you will never have another chance."

"We'll come out," the *voyageur* said quickly. "No more arrows."

The gates swung open and the men rode out in single file, leaving their weapons behind. The *voyageurs* picked up LaCroix's body and rode into the trees along the river where they were quickly lost from view.

"Now we can bring the other Long Knives to take your furs to St. Louis," Nighthawk told Clara.

"What do you mean?" Clara asked.

"Some of the Long Knives who were with George Whittingham are trapping along the middle fork of the three rivers that form the Big Muddy," Nighthawk explained. "Deer Chaser found them while scouting for buffalo. When I saw Black Owl take you and Spring Bird away, I sent Deer Chaser to find the Long Knife trappers and bring them here. That is why we did not catch up to you before now."

"Why didn't they come with you?" Clara asked.

"The big one, Immell, did not want any of his men hurt or killed. He said we had more than enough warriors to win any fight. He will take your furs to the fort at the Big Horn along with his own."

Clara went inside the fort while Nighthawk sent a delegation of warriors to tell the Long Knives led by Immell that the trouble was over. Clara remembered Immell, the big trapper who had been leading the party she had met with George Whittingham. Inside the fort she was relieved to find a great many fine beaver pelts that had been readied for transport to St. Louis. There would be more than enough to satisfy her debts, with a good share of profit in addition. She had been very lucky: A few days later the furs likely would have been gone. LaCroix had only been waiting for Black Owl to bring her and the additional furs to the fort.

When Immell arrived, the men loaded the furs and took everything of value out of the fort. There was no sign of LaCroix's Piegan wife, Black Owl's cousin, but Clara felt sure she had met her death at his hands. It would be good to leave all of this behind her, Clara thought, as she rode toward Blackfoot country again, looking over her shoulder at the flames that rose into the evening sky from the fires she had set herself among the buildings and log walls of the fort. As she turned back toward the trail, leaving the nightmare she had lived for so long behind her, she felt joy. She was riding at the head of the warriors with Nighthawk. Behind them were Deer Chaser and Spring Bird. They were leading the new warriors from the Black Horse band of Kainah Blackfeet. Black Owl, by his own doing, had lost all of his honor. Nighthawk had sent three warriors ahead to carry the news to the village. The first thing she and Nighthawk would see upon entering the village again, Clara guessed, would be the flames of a council fire.

24

BLACK OWL WAS KEPT in a specially guarded lodge to await his appearance before the council. Many in the village wished to kill Black Owl outright, such was their anger. He had cost the lives of many good warriors. The hills outside of camp resounded with the cries of those who had lost sons and husbands. Many of those who had been council members would never again sit in the circle of honor to decide issues affecting the Black Horse band of Kainah Blackfeet. A great many of them had been Brave Wolves, and it was resolved within the village that this group of warriors would from this day forward have no more power than any of the other warrior societies.

When the cries of mourning had subsided and sufficient time had gone by to allow the remaining members of the council to make decisions with open minds, a fire was built and one of the most important gatherings to ever come to pass within the Black Horse band began. The entire village would be present.

New members would be inducted into the council to replace those who had lost their lives at the fort. Suggestions would be considered on how better to distribute authority and ensure that young warriors were better tested for character.

Tragedies such as the one that had just occurred had to be

avoided in the future, and so it was resolved that all family disputes be regarded as potentially dangerous to others and therefore subject to intervention by outside parties designated by the council. Enough lives were lost to enemy war parties and hunting accidents without adding to the toll by fighting one another.

When Black Owl was brought before the council, he seemed unafraid and insolent. He was asked why he took so many warriors with him, leaving the village almost defenseless against attack. He had not announced that he wished to lead a war party against the Long Knives, but had taken the men away in darkness and secrecy. The Brave Wolves who had not been killed by LaCroix's men told the council that Black Owl led many warriors to death only because he wished to show LaCroix that he was important among the Kainah people.

"I was among evil spirits!" Black Owl shouted in his own defense. "I have felt the power of evil since the day Nighthawk brought the Long Knife woman to our village. It is she who is to blame for all of this, for she brought the Thunder Horse down from the Burning Mountains, the land of evil, and the horse has brought evil with him. It is here, all around us, at this very time."

Black Owl made the same accusations he had hurled at them before. He again blamed the stallion for everything. And as he continued to describe the evil things that lived in the Burning Mountains, where the stallion had for so long lived with his herd, he again succeeded in bringing gasps from many of the villagers and instilling doubt in their minds as to whether or not the stallion had brought evil spirits with him.

When Black Owl had finished, Clara walked to her stallion and petted him affectionately, rubbing his neck as she talked to the council and the villagers. She was careful not to bring the horse too close, for she did not want to jeopardize her plan. After explaining how she had tamed the horse, she asked Spring Bird to come forward.

"Black Owl has said that this horse is evil and all those who ride him are evil spirits," she began. "I will show you that

FIRECLOUD

Black Owl has his words mixed up. What he means is that all those who *can't* ride this stallion are evil."

The people began to talk excitedly among themselves.

"I will show you that my words are true and Black Owl is again lying," Clara went on. "This stallion has no evil in him."

While Clara continued to rub Firecloud's neck and nose, Spring Bird jumped upon his back. The people in the village gasped in surprise. They had never seen anyone but Clara and Nighthawk on the horse. When Spring Bird dismounted, Deer Chaser jumped upon Firecloud's back. Deer Chaser's mother and father followed in turn. Then the small son of a council member sat on the stallion's back. The boy showed no fear, and Clara led the stallion in a circle for all to see while the boy laughed with glee.

"I was your medicine woman during the Sun Dance ceremonies after praying to the sun for my husband's life," Clara told them. "I have gathered berries beside you and gathered wood with you. Not one of you has been injured or fallen sick. Still Black Owl insists that I am evil and that the village suffers because of this beautiful stallion. None of the people you just saw ride Firecloud is evil. Even a small child who does not yet know what evil is sat on my horse's back and did not want to get down." The people nodded at the truth of her words.

"You have shown us that the Thunder Horse is not evil," a spokesman for the council told Clara. "I listened to Black Owl before, and now I bow my head in shame. We of this village have treated you unjustly."

Other members of the council added their own apologies, and the people began to crowd around Firecloud, looking at him in wonder. After a time, Clara asked them all to take their places, for she had yet another lesson to give them.

"Now it is time to see who is truly evil in this village," she said, looking directly at Black Owl. "If you are not evil, you will be able to ride this horse, as others have."

Black Owl drew his breath in sharply. To decline would be to admit defeat. He had no choice but to accept the challenge.

E. P. Murray

The villagers watched him step forward, hesitantly at first, then with great determination. Firecloud's nostrils flared, and his ears went back flat against his head. Clara did her best to soothe him, but the stallion did not want Black Owl near him.

Black Owl pointed an accusing finger at Clara. "She makes the horse angry! She is saying evil things to him!"

Nighthawk came forward with a piece of trade cloth, which Clara draped over Firecloud's eyes. She then crushed some wild mint and rubbed it around Firecloud's nostrils to mask all other odors. The stallion immediately settled down, and Clara again turned to Black Owl.

"Firecloud can now neither see nor smell you," she said to him. "You no longer have to be afraid."

There were a few muffled laughs among the villagers. Angered, Black Owl rushed forward and mounted quickly. Black Owl started to shout in triumph, but the stallion squealed in rage, arching his neck and shaking his head. He shook the cloth from his eyes and twisted his body into a powerful turn, arching his back in midair and kicking out violently with his back feet. The full force of the surge snapped Black Owl's head back violently and jolted his body with tremendous force. Black Owl landed on his neck and shoulders, then bounced over onto his face and stomach and skidded to a stop, groaning in agony.

There was a chorus of clapping and cheers from the villagers. Aged One nodded, his face beaming. Clara again soothed Firecloud, and the people surrounded her and her stallion. This woman, who had come into their land and tamed the powerful wild stallion, had not been sent by evil ones; she was a gift of the guardian spirits to the Black Horse band of Kainah Blackfeet. Now they could see that she had brought them only good fortune. Because of her, Nighthawk had become a warrior of great honor, while Black Owl had been shown for the evil one he truly was. Though her skin was not like theirs, she had become one of them, a child of the earth, and had taken the land as her own.

The council ruled to banish Black Owl from the Kainah Blackfoot tribe for all time. As was the custom, his wives were told of this decision and forced out of their lodge. It was then torn down and all his possessions laid out for distribution among the people. But no one wanted them; no one cared to claim any of the many things he and his wives had possessed, for no one wished to be reminded of the evil one who nearly destroyed their band with his lust for power. Instead, all that he owned was heaped upon a fire, to be remembered no more. Except for the black stallion, which he was allowed to keep, his horses were distributed among the poor of the band, who traded them to other bands for different horses. No one cared to even hear the name Black Owl.

Eyes-Like-Black-Stones and her sisters chose to leave their dishonored husband and start new lives among members of their mother's family in another band.

No one would look at Black Owl or come near him. He stood alone and watched his lodge and all his possessions turn into flames and smoke. His neck and shoulders ached from the fall, and the wound in his arm from LaCroix's pistol had broken open. His face was swollen from bruises and cuts, and his mind still echoed with the shrill scream of the powerful stallion that had thrown him from his back with such force. This day would stay with him forever, and it would make his hatred that much more intense. In the fire, his war shield was eaten by flames, his lance now only a burning shaft of wood. Everything was now gone except a bow and some arrows that he had hidden in a tree. Now he needed them to ease his anger.

The villagers continued to ignore him, knowing the warriors would kill him if he had not left the camp by day's end. No one noticed as he made his way into the hills behind the village and returned cautiously, keeping to the trees for cover. They did not see him eyeing the stallion called Firecloud and the Thunder Horse Woman, who rode him at the edge of the village. Black Owl smiled as he mounted his own black stallion, Firecloud's old enemy. He would ride quickly up to her, draw his bow, and end her life, as he should have done long ago.

Aged One had spotted Black Owl as he made his way into the hills, and the old warrior had seen him returning stealthily. He had told Deer Chaser to alert Clara and Nighthawk, for he was sure Black Owl would make one last desperate try for revenge.

It was Nighthawk, sitting at the edge of the village, admiring his wife and her stallion, who gave the loud whistle of alarm as Black Owl charged toward Clara from the cover of the trees. Clara turned, seeing the stallion, and Black Owl on his back with bow drawn. She quickly leaned far over Firecloud, gripping his mane and locking her knee against his sides. The arrow whizzed past her shoulder, the steel trade point singing death as it clipped her doeskin dress. Black Owl swore and reached for another arrow.

In a rage, Firecloud turned and lunged in pursuit. Clara, thrown off balance, jumped to her feet, calling her horse. But the big stallion had one purpose in mind and a determination so great that not even Clara could have stopped him.

Black Owl had turned the stallion for another charge, but Firecloud, like a bolt of lightning, took him completely by surprise. In a display of unequaled force, Firecloud rammed Black Owl and his stallion broadside, knocking them over and leaving them in a cloud of dust. A short distance away, Firecloud turned for another charge while Black Owl screamed in pain.

Firecloud rushed again, his ears back and his teeth showing, as Black Owl, dragging one leg, struggled to the shelter of the trees. The black reared, intent on avenging the defeats he had suffered at the hands of this most powerful ruler of wild stallions. The villagers had gathered around Clara and Nighthawk to watch, holding their breath as the two stallions met with the sun crossing behind them.

All watched the awesome display of wild power. Firecloud, his mane and tail flowing free, his rage at its peak, rose like a tower of red and white over the black, striking downward with powerful hooves, crushing skin and bone beneath his force. The black forced himself to stay to the attack. He lashed out at Firecloud with his forefeet and grabbed for the neck with his teeth. But the wild ruler of the mountain herds was far too quick and agile to suffer any serious blows. Then, with a

FIRECLOUD

powerful surge of force, Firecloud crashed forward and drove himself up and over the black.

The black rose and met the striking forefeet. Then, wheezing for air, the black fell back and lay motionless.

Clara screamed and ran toward Black Owl, who had emerged from the trees and was fitting an arrow to his bow. She slammed into him as he drew the bowstring, sending the arrow astray. Enraged, Black Owl pushed her to the ground and reached into his belt for his knife, but Firecloud was already upon him, his eyes alive with hate. His injured leg useless, Black Owl fell backward and shielded himself with his arms as Firecloud's hooves rose to strike.

Black Owl's left forearm caught the first blow from the stallion, shattering the bone and bringing an intense scream of pain and terror from him. Fearing Black Owl would cut Firecloud's legs with his knife, Clara grabbed the reins and tried to calm him. Black Owl managed to struggle back into the trees while Clara, with difficulty, prevented the stallion from running after his hated enemy. Nighthawk, Deer Chaser, and a group of warriors rushed into the trees and hauled Black Owl out. They stripped him completely naked and drove him from the village. It would be dark soon, and Black Owl knew the men would kill him if he stayed any longer.

Amid jeers and catcalls from the villagers, Black Owl left the Black Horse band of Kainah Blackfeet, the people he had once hoped to rule over as lord and master. Now reduced to the level of a camp dog, he left with his head high. Night would fall upon him as he wandered along through the vast land he could no longer call his own.

ABOVE THE VILLAGE, in a meadow surrounded by pines, Firecloud grazed contentedly with his herd. Aged One, his face lifted to the sky, prayed over a fire layered with sage. Nearby, amid aspen adorned in their golden fall color, Clara sat in Nighthawk's arms watching her stallion feed as his coat glowed in the crimson light of sundown. Forgotten was the memory of Black Owl, for they had moved their village into the valley of the Gallatin, where they had just completed a successful buffalo hunt. Food for the upcoming cold moons was now plentiful. Things were changing for the good within the Black Horse band of Kainah Blackfeet.

Clara pointed to where Deer Chaser and Spring Bird walked along the river, talking of their approaching marriage. Nighthawk, now a member of the council, had made Deer Chaser a member of the Brave Wolves society, a highly respected warrior society now that Nighthawk was its valued leader. Deer Chaser, in time, would also become an honored warrior. Clara, in Nighthawk's arms forever, had found a deep, satisfying happiness. She now rejoiced in her contentment as her stallion came toward her to take her offering of sweetgrass. She would ride him less often now, for a new life stirred within her, giving herself and Nighthawk added joy.

The big stallion finished Clara's offering, and his white mane and tail streamed behind him as he galloped across the meadow and to the top of a ridge to survey the land. The sun was setting behind him and the bank of clouds above the horizon was shot with scarlet. He shook his proud head and pranced along the ridge, his beautiful coat absorbing the last rays of light. He had brought happiness and honor to many Indian people. He was the Thunder Horse, the ruler of the mountains. He was Firecloud.

The story of an era...
The story of a woman...

ON WINGS OF DREAMS

by Patricia Gallagher

The eagerly awaited sequel to the
million-copy-bestseller *CASTLES IN THE AIR*

Rejoin Devon Marshall Curtis, fiery Rebel beauty, in her struggle to survive the war-ravaged South. Industry and technology are booming, wealth is boundless, and Devon's passion is as tumultuous as the era she lives in. Three men love her—but only one can win her heart.

____ ON WINGS OF DREAMS
0-425-07446-3/$3.95

Prices may be slightly higher in Canada.

Available at your local bookstore or return this form to:

BERKLEY
Book Mailing Service
P.O. Box 690, Rockville Centre, NY 11571

Please send me the titles checked above. I enclose ____. Include 75¢ for postage and handling if one book is ordered; 25¢ per book for two or more not to exceed $1.75. California, Illinois, New York and Tennessee residents please add sales tax.

NAME_____
ADDRESS_____
CITY_____ STATE/ZIP_____
(Allow six weeks for delivery.)

**Turn back the pages of history...
and discover**

Romance

as it once was!

__07622-8	**TWICE LOVED** LaVyrle Spencer	$3.50
__07910-3	**MASQUERADE** Susanna Howe	$3.50
__07743-7	**THE LAWLESS HEART** Kathryn Atwood	$3.50
__07100-5	**THE WAYWARD HEART** Jill Gregory	$3.50
__06045-3	**RENEGADE LADY** Kathryn Atwood	$3.25
__04756-2	**A SHARE OF EARTH AND GLORY** Katherine Giles	$3.50

Prices may be slightly higher in Canada.

Available at your local bookstore or return this form to:

JOVE
Book Mailing Service
P.O. Box 690, Rockville Centre, NY 11571

Please send me the titles checked above. I enclose _____. Include 75¢ for postage and handling if one book is ordered; 25¢ per book for two or more not to exceed $1.75. California, Illinois, New York and Tennessee residents please add sales tax.

NAME_____

ADDRESS_____

CITY_____STATE/ZIP_____

(allow six weeks for delivery.)

SK-35